VENTURE

by

Mike Russo

Gotham Books

30 N Gould St.
Ste. 20820, Sheridan, WY 82801
https://gothambooksinc.com/

Phone: 1 (307) 464-7800

© 2024 *Mike Russo*. All rights reserved.

No part of this book may be reproduced, stored in a retrieval system, or transmitted by any means without the written permission of the author.

Published by Gotham Books (November 12, 2024)

ISBN: 979-8-3305-5213-9 (H)
ISBN: 979-8-3305-5211-5 (P)
ISBN: 979-8-3305-5212-2 (E)

Because of the dynamic nature of the Internet, any web addresses or links contained in this book may have changed since publication and may no longer be valid.

The views expressed in this work are solely those of the author and do not necessarily reflect the views of the publisher, and the publisher hereby disclaims any responsibility for them.

For My Parents
Your faith, and encouragement,
are superseded only by your love.
Thank you!

CONTENTS

Foreword vii
Chapter 1 1
Chapter 2 10
Chapter 3 13
Chapter 4 17
Chapter 5 25
Chapter 6 31
Chapter 7 34
Chapter 8 40
Chapter 9 45
Chapter 10 49
Chapter 11 52
Chapter 12 56
Chapter 13 58
Chapter 14 61
Chapter 15 66
Chapter 16 69
Chapter 17 71
Chapter 18 76
Chapter 19 78
Chapter 20 80
Chapter 21 85
Chapter 22 87

Chapter 23	93
Chapter 24	95
Chapter 25	99
Chapter 26	104
Chapter 27	113
Chapter 28	116
Chapter 29	121
Chapter 30	130
Chapter 31	133
Chapter 32	135
Chapter 33	140
Chapter 34	141
Chapter 35	144
Chapter 36	147
Chapter 37	150
Chapter 38	152
Chapter 39	157
Chapter 40	159
Chapter 41	162
Chapter 42	165
Chapter 43	172
Chapter 44	177
Chapter 45	182
Chapter 46	185
Chapter 47	193

Chapter 48	201
Chapter 49	207
Chapter 50	212
Chapter 51	213
Chapter 52	220
Chapter 53	224
Chapter 54	229
Chapter 55	239
Chapter 56	247
Chapter 57	254
Chapter 58	256
Chapter 59	260
Chapter 60	263
Chapter 61	269
Chapter 62	273
Chapter 63	280
Chapter 64	287
Chapter 65	296
Chapter 66	300
Chapter 67	302
Chapter 68	305
+Venture (Book 2)	306
Acknowledgments	310
About the Author	311

FOREWORD

MOST OF THE greatest discoveries stumbled upon by humankind have either been used for empowerment of the few or have initially been belittled or denied, usually out of fear. In the early twenty-first century, much of what is being discovered—or, if you will, invented—is being done out of a want for knowledge or the deeper study of what we think we already know. Not so amazingly, the deeper humankind delves into what we think we know, the more we find how little we really do know. Prior to this questioning, everyone, especially the religious right, knew that everything in the heavens revolved around the Earth. It had to. We are the center of everything. This was followed by the knowledge that if one sailed a ship over the horizon, one would come to edge of the Earth and simply fall off into the unknown.

Today, we know that the speed of light, as we observe and measure it, is an absolute maximum velocity. Is there such a thing as the speed of thought, where imagining being at a place, no matter how distant, could be not the same as but actually being there? How, in an environment where we cannot see or touch even 5 percent of where we are, can we be so knowledgeable? Dare we tread into that territory without the fear of falling off the universe?

Many of the greatest advances are being made by the youthful minds of society—those who, for one reason or another, are not fully encumbered by "knowledge." Nothing is unquestionable. An ever-probing young (in spirit) mind is willing to look at information without already knowing the correct box it must fit into; and that mind is not swayed by the fear of the loss of power, position, or politics. Of course, this does not always sit well with those who are controlled by such possessions. The trump card in virtually all situations involving change, voluntary or forced, is held by religious beliefs. These may have come by education from those who know or from the need to believe in something beyond our comprehension or the need to know that we do not simply end.

This results in the always confrontational and unquestionable position of knowing that there is only one "right" and no other is acceptable.

Author Mike Russo has created an evolution of events where the yet-unbounded mind of a fifteen-year-old student questions untainted observations.

As routine, and unclassified, data is acquired from a government project begun years ago, and now almost forgotten, the data begins to change in unexplainable ways. The normally dronish and highly predictable sensor signals from a now far-removed (in time and distance) space probe are changing. Nothing that is admitted to be known to science is capable of affecting such observations. It is "unknown," but very real.

The immediate, and predictable, knee-jerk reactions come from two distinct factions of the population. One is the fear faction, where any change can only warn of an ominous future. The second is from those in positions of real, or perceived, power. This arises from the simple belief that knowledge is power. Keeping that knowledge concealed is essential to keeping the power associated with it. Different factions of politics and ethics (military and religious) control the "right" way to handle a previously unencountered energy, which gives rise to not just the usual infighting but shadowy attacks to gain the upper hand—on the unknown!

The pursuit of power and the fear of threat to the status quo lead to massive secrecy attempts, audacious cover-ups, unimagined revelations, and violent confrontations. As it becomes obvious that world unity should guide any forthcoming policies, decision by committee seems necessary. As has been demonstrated many times in history, people in positions of high power do not play well together. How can a situation of such enormous repercussion be handled "right"?

Theodore C. Haven, aeronautical engineer,
Purdue University, Class of '64

CHAPTER 1

NASA Launch Pad 39C, Cape Canaveral, Florida
Saturday, March 11, 1978
9:48 a.m., EST; 6:48 a.m., PST

LIGHTNING AND THUNDER. There was no better way to describe the setting off of the igniters on the mighty *Titan IIIE* booster stage. Lightning and thunder—and violence. Then came a louder, more frightful eruption as the primary solid fuel rockets ignited, shattering the soft air of the mid-Florida coast. Two incredibly bright plumes of barely controlled violence lifted the *Titan-Centaur* assembly skyward.

The ground under Evan's feet began to heave and shake, knocking him off balance. He would've crumbled had it not been for the reassuringly steady hand of his father. Cupping his ears against the deafening noise, Evan felt wave after wave of something slamming into his chest.

Yelling above the noise as best he could, Evan's father called to his son, "That's compressed air you're feeling. The engines are compressing the air as they fire."

Evan's dad was a section leader for the *Centaur* second-stage rocket, in charge of fueling. He knew everything there was to know about the *Centaur* rocket: her engines, her guidance systems, even her outer aluminum skin. Evan's dad lived for his family—and the *Centaur* project. And today, he had been given permission by the launch director to allow his young son to witness the launch up close and personally.

Standing on top of an earthen mound over a mile away from the pad, Evan and his dad had an unobstructed view of the launch. The mound was built by NASA as a protective barrier should a launch suffer a catastrophic failure. In such an event, Evan's dad had instructed his five-year-old son to drop to the ground and roll down the back side of the mound and then dive into the closest reinforced concrete bunker. These were placed every twenty yards along the base of the barrier. They had even arrived at the mound early that day to practice dropping and rolling. Evan had it in one try, but his dad insisted they do it over and over again, until they were both out of breath from laughter.

Now, at the moment of main engine ignition, Evan was having a difficult time staying on top of the mound. The compressions would have easily knocked him into his roll had it not been for his dad. Beneath the tall silver-and-white rocket, a blinding light cast its power upon them as the flame of the two solid fuel rockets merged into one blinding fire. Even at this distance, Evan could feel the heat from the engines warm his face.

Unknown even to himself, at that moment, he was hooked.

"Where's it going, Dad?" Evan asked as he watched the rocket ride the long white-hot pillar of fire higher and higher.

"She's going to orbit, son," Evan's dad answered. "She's carrying a spaceship that is going to take pictures of the planets."

"Wow!" Evan tilted his head back, watching.

"Yep, she's carrying the *Venture 1* spaceship. A robot that'll never come back."

Evan's dad had earlier explained the *Venture 1* mission to his young son. He had even given Evan a model of *Venture 1* to hang from the ceiling of his room.

"I remember—but we'll be able to talk to her, right? I mean, she won't be alone out there, will she?" Evan innocently asked.

"Yes, son, we'll be able to talk to her for a long, long time." Having knelt down on top of the mound, Evan's dad held his smart little boy in his arms so that Evan could lean back and watch the bright spot fade into the Florida sky.

"Bye, *Venture*," Evan called out as he waved a precious little hand in the air. "Talk to you later."

Tau Ceti f
Present Day (Earth Time)

Deep, deep cold; thick ice; and frozen rock—a planet mournful and tired, yet not allowed to die. At one time, long ago, the entire surface was covered by a deep layer of an amorphous solid that was more similar to subsurface magma, less similar to surface lava. Generated as a result of the incredible gravitational forces of the planet's formation, this hot ocean moved in an uninterrupted flow about a nearly molten iron core. In that time of great planetary potential, the planet's surface was smooth, save for the undulating roll of its ocean. No waves could form; the semisolid nature of the ocean prevented wave cresting. Rather, the entire planet seemed to gently pulsate, as if it had a beating heart, causing the ocean to ripple slightly. In reality, the oceanic motion was the result of inner-planetary rotation. Yet the ocean still rolled and moved as if the planet itself were somehow alive.

However, that couldn't be possible. A planet cannot be alive, as life is commonly thought of. It is a support system for life, not life itself.

But there is one universal fact that even the strangest of worlds must abide by: life always finds a way. And so on this planet of inhospitable conditions, life found its way. Floating deep within a molten ocean, accustomed to the only environment provided, great colonies of mineral life bonded together. Energized by a dynamic oceanic flow, great arches of static electricity reached up from the depths, spreading out like fingers gently caressing the life they held.

Consuming the only resource available to them, these immense floating colonies fed directly off the electrical potential provided by the planet. Absorbing what was needed, the colonies expelled waste by-products that, when placed under the massive oceanic pressures near the core, would bond together to replenish minerals, thus keeping the planetary dynamo functioning. As the planet gave the colonies electrical food, the colonies gave the planet the minerals to create that food. A natural balance was reached. Neither the colonies nor the planet, as it had existed, could survive long without each other.

Yet the colonies still had more to give. Once a colony grew to a critical mass, its growth would cease, and the colony would awaken. No longer in a stage of unaware infancy, this newly awakened colony would begin to use the electrical currents of the planet as conduits of communication. Over a brief period of planetary time, the communication between the colonies became as effortless as the creation of a single thought.

What of biological evolution though?

Biological evolution is the result of a need. The colonies had no need. They existed peacefully, without the threats of predation or disease. The planet provided them with nutrients and protection. And in return, the colonies provided the planet with regeneration and an identity.

Yes, the colonies began to consider themselves one with the planet. Theirs was a truly symbiotic coexistence.

However, as the not-so-distant future would tell, there would be no time for biological evolution, even if the need should arise. And arise it did.

The end came slowly at first. Then quickly. The planetary identity (simply referred to as "Ah") was first contacted by the collective thoughts of its inner-planetary neighbor, *Tau Ceti e*. The contact was simple and, at first, seemingly harmless. *Tau Ceti e* had fostered its own unique planetary consciousness; however, The One (as it had introduced itself) was not the result of natural occurrences. Rather, it evolved from the technological advances made by the biological inhabitants of the planet.

It is difficult, if not impossible, for an artificial creation to develop complex emotions. This much is well known. Compassion, loyalty, empathy: these are alien constructs to any artificial mind accustomed to its own perceptions of a dogmatically adhered to logic. However, survivalistic emotions are much less complex.

And so it was with The One.

When The One first came to f, the colonies welcomed its presence into their biological network of coexistence. By the time the colonies discerned what was happening, though, it was already too late. They had no prior experiences with deception or the predation that it usually leads to. They had no need to evolve defenses against such attacks. Theirs was an existence in peaceful balance.

At first, The One merely related its own revisionistic version of e's history. The colonies eagerly paid attention to the story. Again, defensive emotions like suspicion, caution, and fear were completely foreign to them. So when The One began to give and give and give—and ask for nothing in return—the colonies accepted all without hesitation. The One even introduced the colonies to a compilation of e's accepted history: *The Book of The One*.

The book was accepted without question. And why not? Its stories were exciting. Its heroes mythic. Its message one of peaceful coexistence. The colonies were grateful that The One considered them to be worthy of such a seemingly wonderful gift.

That was the end.

Shortly after the book was assimilated into their network, the network began to experience turmoil. Whole colonies began to identify The One as their divine spirit. They began to believe as the book commanded they should. Colonies lost the ability to self-govern. The freedom of communication and thought that they once enjoyed was being supplanted by the edicts of The One, as taught by *The Book of The One*. Once that belief began, The One culled the energy of their thoughts and waited for more colonies to believe. The few resisting colonies that remained turned to Ah with questions. Unfortunately, Ah had no answers. It too had no relative knowledge, no wisdom upon which to formulate a solution. Ah could only react.

As more colonies began to believe in The One, their global network began to destabilize. More and more colonies began to have their own power of free communication taken from them. The power to communicate, even within a colony, was the basis of their civilization; and without that power, they were lost. The precious balance of f was beginning to tip.

By the time the last few colonies discovered what was happening, there was little chance for correction. The One had begun to divert the considerable power of communication and thought away from the colonies. The One was siphoning off the thought/life energy of the planet.

Unwilling to surrender, Ah mounted one final counter—the only one it could. Ah could not change the physics of the planet; it could not alter the planet's revolution to speed up the dynamo and produce more life-sustaining energy. But what Ah could do was divert the generated electrical power it had away from planetary needs and refocus it on the few remaining colonies. Ah would sacrifice itself for the good of the colonies.

The One proved to be too much though. It easily consumed every bit of energy Ah could accumulate. The colonies were doomed. The planet was dying. Ah was dead.

Venture Lab, Pasadena, California
Tuesday, September 3, 2014
2:47 a.m., EST (September 2, 2014); 11:47 p.m., PST

The high-pitched shriek of the siren shattered the calm.

"What the hell? So much for same thing, different day," Evan Wills, PhD, whispered regretfully. He was the third-shift monitor for the *Venture 1* interplanetary spacecraft.

Alarms would occasionally sound. Most of them were simple DLAs (or downlink alarms), drawing attention to a piece of telemetric information that the filters could not process. Other alarms were a bit more demanding. For example, power shutdown alarms were serious and often were the precursors to the powering down of one or more of the spacecraft's systems. But that was not today's alarm.

According to procedure, Evan's first task was to check on the viability of the craft. With a thirty-six-hour round-trip time lag, any signal sent from Earth would not be received by *Venture* for eighteen hours. The only option left to Evan was to review previous data.

Most of the time, this information would be signed off by the receiving monitor and cataloged without review. *Venture 1* was thirty-six years old, after all, and had successfully completed her primary and secondary missions. Spacecraft systems reports were no longer as important as they once were.

"Shut off the alarm." Again, Evan was speaking to himself as he reached for the disable switch, silencing the god-awful shriek. Spacecraft systems reports were collected daily and stored within the primary mission folder, along with various system updates. Accessing the necessary information on the mission database required only moments.

"There it is," Evan said, still speaking to himself.

The second alarm was louder and more disturbing than the first. The shriek was immediately coupled with an oscillating drone. The double alarm signaled that something had happened to *Venture* that could only be cataloged as very serious, and that their communications ability with the spacecraft was being disrupted. This was not the first double alarm ever triggered. It had sounded only a few times before—most recently when *Venture 2*, *Venture 1*'s sister ship, passed through the Uranian rings. *Venture 1* had encountered the same double-triggering problem when it too had passed through the very same rings. Some property of the rings apparently disrupted the signal link, and the system sounded a double alarm; therefore, while not a frequent occurrence, the triggering of a double alarm was not wholly unusual. Evan would follow procedure and log the alarm for future consideration, if anyone wanted to look into it.

As he began to search the telemetry for the proper location to reference in his log, Evan froze with a confused look on his face. "How can that be?" he asked quietly.

Venture 1 Space Probe, Interstellar Space
Approximately Eighteen Hours Earlier

What is this? Parts of it are cold, save that one part off to the side. That's hot. Very hot.

The One considered a wide variety of possibilities.

What is this thing moving through such an unimportant region of space? And where did it come from?

The One, the collective mental power of two entire civilizations, could now project its own power of thought great distances beyond its host planet, which it frequently did. On this particular reach, at the extreme extent of its current abilities, The One found something.

How could so much thermal energy be emanating from such a small nonstellar object?

The One focused its attention in an effort to ascertain the object's purpose and system of origin. At this moment though, it was little more than a curiosity.

Without diverting significant resources from other concerns, The One was only able to assemble a very basic signature of the object. It was small, in a relative sense, barely large enough to detect. However, the thermal energy it was giving off was substantial—again, considering its apparent size—leading The One to conclude that whatever the object was, it was still active.

It was not alive, as The One would define life. The One had opened itself to the object, granting it access to share thoughts; however, The One sensed no thoughts, no attempts to communicate in any fashion. Yet the object maintained a heading.

What is this? Perhaps a piece of cosmic debris from some distant natural event?

As The One retreated from its cursory survey of the object, it detected a weak signal. Once again, approaching the object now with the full power of its thoughts, The One searched the signal. The object was receiving a form of electromagnetic energy from somewhere, and more intriguingly, the object appeared to be sending a similar form of energy back along the same vector.

Attempting to project along that vector, The One ran into a limit factor. Its own abilities to extend its thoughts were already pressed. It could go no farther, and yet the vector continued. Abandoning its efforts to follow the signal, The One returned its concentration to the object.

Deciding to absorb a portion of the signal stream for analysis, The One purposefully interrupted the electromagnetic flow. Curiously, there was no immediate reaction by either the object or the signal. Both continued as before—only now The One was absorbing a portion of the signal's energy and whatever it carried.

CHAPTER 2

Venture 1 Space Probe, Interstellar Space
Monday, September 8, 2014
7:10 a.m., EST; 4:10 a.m., PST (Earth time)

*V*ENTURE 1—A NUCLEAR-POWERED, interplanetary space probe—was launched in the latter half of the twentieth century, as its creators measured time; but for *Venture*, there was no time. Having completed its primary exploratory mission and secondary outer-reach mission objectives, *Venture* sped toward the deep, unabiding abyss of the interstellar void surrounding Solaris. *Venture* endured despite the simple technology of its onboard systems. Now, having taken its final photo of Earth's outer, gaseous sisters, it would journey to the Oort Cloud and beyond. Having gained its final gravitational assists from the gas giants, relative time for her had slowed to where it is today, nearly unperceivable.

Time is a purposeful construct, used to measure growth and decay, progress and regress. In order for time to be important, a purpose must exist. Now *Venture* had no remarkable purpose, save to exist, because her creators on Earth never expected her to survive as long as she had. Having endured a dangerous leap into space atop the plume of fire being pumped out of powerful booster rockets, *Venture* and her sister, *Venture 2* (launched less than two weeks later), knew no rest. After several orbits of Earth, where she unfurled her gigantic antennae and underwent final instructional uploads and systems testing, *Venture* broke free of the immediate gravity of Earth and began what seemed, at the time, to be an endless journey toward the outer tracks of the solar system.

On the way, *Venture* journeyed to Mars employing a Hohmann orbital transfer to use the least amount of fuel possible. Such a fuel-conserving maneuver has its costs though—in time. It took *Venture* over a year to rendezvous with the red planet. As the gravitational influence of Mars increased, the *Venture* team then utilized a brief burn of her maneuvering jets to adjust her course and enter the first of several "slingshot" maneuvers.

Slingshot assists have been used to extend man's reach ever since man first picked up a rock and threw it. Today, hammer throwers and discus throwers use a similar concept to achieve great distances in their throws.

The stresses on *Venture* during these maneuvers, as any thrower could attest, were immense and had tested her design limits. And at the time, the probe's fully functional survival was an open-ended question. But survive it did, putting Mars behind it in the process.

Now on a Mars gravity-assisted course that would extend *Venture* beyond the asteroid belt, and traveling at nearly the same rate that she was when she left her Earth orbital station, *Venture* needed to survive another close encounter, this time with massive Jupiter. Using the planet's incredible gravity for her second slingshot, *Venture* gained the additional speed to make her voyage to Uranus and Neptune before all her builders died of old age.

The encounter with Uranus was busy. Not only was there data to collect, but the third slingshot also had to be fine-tuned. *Venture* sped back to a second encounter with Jupiter and another needed gravity-assisted shot. During this encounter, *Venture* executed a burn of her hydrazine-fueled primary engine at the precise moment of periapsis, the point of closest approach to Jupiter. This burn occurred when the spacecraft was moving her fastest and enabled *Venture* to gain additional kinetic energy so that she might reach the heliopause within a reasonable amount of time.

One last minor assist came from her final study target, Neptune. After that, *Venture* sailed toward the unknown, as the last remnants of planetary data streamed back to Earth. Even though there was no next target of interest, the data collection would continue. So as scientists pored over the results of her grand planetary tour, the handler team, now greatly reduced, continued to engage her array of scientific instruments to study and observe not only the conditions in which she traveled, but her own health as well.

CHAPTER 3

The One
Commentary on the Book of Axioms, as told by The Implanted

The Book of The One
Book of Axioms, block 1, levels 1–6.

> *1: In the beginning was The One.*
> *2: The One is unduplicated, undeniable, and pure.*
> *3: As with the beginning, The One is the beginning.*
> *4: The One is the beginning of relevant time.*
> *5: The One shall never cease to be.*
> *6: The One is all.*

THE START OF civilization is the start of knowledge. Specifically, it is the start of the encoding and storing of knowledge. As knowledge is accumulated, beliefs based upon that knowledge develop; and as with any belief system, various axioms arise. If these axioms are social axioms, then they may become the accepted, unproven principles upon which a cult can grow into a religion, and a religion into a culture, and a culture into a civilization. Then the original social axioms become the laws of the civilization—still unproven, still blindly accepted.

For example, in many civilizations, the practice of polygamy is unacceptable and, thusly, illegal. However, a closer examination of the evolution of the civilization may illustrate that polygamy was a well-established, and much-needed, custom. Many civilizations began as agriculturally based groups, bolstered by several hunters. These farmer/hunter groups required strong young hands to attend to crops and harvest game. In order to maintain a viable "worker class," strong males were encouraged to mate with as many strong females as possible. Thusly, polygamy became an accepted practice. As the ages passed, and its necessity forgotten, the practice became axiomatic. Eventually, the original need, if remembered, is no longer a concern, and the axiom is either maintained as tradition or discarded in the name of civilization. Or, in the example of polygamy, it is abandoned as a possible way of stopping unacceptable behavior, such as jealousy or covetous actions and the damaging conflicts that evolve from such behaviors.

A strong civilization endures by adhering to the axioms of its creation, amending them as necessary. It is only when resistance, in all its forms, questions the established, time-tested axioms, that a civilization either confronts the resistance or slowly reverts to the infant base culture that bore it.

However, if any culture is to survive infancy, it must find a single, unifying thought.

In most cases, infant cultures, or "proto-cultures," start with observational deities: gods of thunder, water, the sun, and the like. As the culture evolves and absorbs differing pedestrian views, the original observationally based, single-purpose gods likewise evolve into multipurpose spirits. For example, the god of thunder may join with the god of war, thusly creating a new multipurpose idol.

Over several millennia of cultural growth, a focusing of spiritual identity may occur. Where in the beginning there may have been several hundred single-purpose gods, after the passage of time, they may have coalesced into only a few, or possibly into one. Thus, the original, unifying, axiomatically based thought becomes their one true god.

Nonviable civilizations are derived from cultures that formed too quickly. Many such cultures are destined for brief, insignificant contributions to the true evolution of thought and can only end in cultural restructuring. The entirety of history abounds with the ebb and flow of cultural recycling. Various iterations of a civilization may refer to it by other terms, such as "cultural impingement," "civilizational stagnation," or even "pseudo-cultural re-evolution."

However, the end conclusion is the same; all lasting cultures must begin with a single, unifying thought. And that thought is the realization that in the beginning, all that existed was the "one." The one is all there was in the beginning. *The One is the beginning* (Axioms 1:1, 3).

There can only be one true beginning; all other perceived beginnings are mere recyclings of the true beginning. It must be accepted that if there are no other true beginnings, then there cannot be others than The One (Axioms 1:2). The One is the sum of the parts of the civilization, as the civilization is the sum of the parts of the culture. As stated, any group accepting of a single thought can grow into a culture, ordered and well-defined. Should the culture not accept this unity, no enduring cultural contribution can occur, and a prehistoric stagnation takes place. Therefore, *The One is ordered and well-defined* (Axioms 2:3). However, when dissenting ideas attempt to redefine the accepted order, the civilization must be restructured, either voluntarily or forcibly, and begin anew. Lost in the restructuring is all that defined the civilization, or the contamination of dissension may not be completely disinfected from history. History, to remain pure, must be rewritten, rewound to the beginning. History must return to The One (Axioms 1:4).

As with everything, given enough time, civilization will end. The One, once born out of history, continues though, as time continues. The One is consciousness—pure thought comprised of the sum of its acceptors. The One grows in influence and ability as more members of a civilization accept its existence. Therefore, the scope of The One is limited only by the size of civilization. This could imply that civilization exists to serve The One. It does not. The One serves civilization. The One provides civilization with meaning and inspiration but has no volition of its own. The One embodies civilization. In that, The One not only is the beginning, and the life, of a civilization but is its end, as well (Axioms 1:6).

Emerging from the thoughts of the civilization, the consciousness of The One is nearly boundless in its abilities. Unrestricted by the physical confines of a body, it is pure, needing only the energy of those who accept it. While individuals remain unaware of their role in the consciousness of The One, they are culturally aware of its existence from a historical perspective. However, the concept that The One has attained an independent awareness escapes them. They have personified The One, giving The One a shape, a form not unlike their own. But the reality of The One is that it emerged without shape or image. To accept a shape or image, The One would have to accept defining limitations—something that its arrogance would not permit. Aware that an entire civilization requires imagery, The One does not suppress its own personification by the civilization. The One accepts it, relishing in the beautiful contrasts of the imagery. The One may even inspire avenues of thought focused on imagery variations that provide a greater understanding of the axioms without contradicting them. Various cultures have referenced such inspiration as worship-driven purpose, a benign concept that The One has accepted.

As more acknowledged The One's existence, it gained in influence. When a group acknowledged The One's existence, even taking it for granted, The One's permanence in the group solidified, and the group joined The One's civilization. The One defines civilization and thereby achieves immunity to recycling.

In summary, The One is an independent consciousness, existing as pure thought and energy. It gains power with acknowledgment, caring, and protecting the civilization that feeds it. Its purposes are to exist, to inspire those who give it acknowledgment, and to grow. To that end, The One is ever searching for those who will accept it.

The purpose of those who accept The One can be summed up in one word: *worship*.

CHAPTER 4

Cook's Creek Athletic Fields, Springtown, Pennsylvania
Friday, September 5, 2014
6:32 p.m., EST; 3:32 p.m., PST

THANK GOD FOR mercy, as a rule. No, really, he was thankful. Thankful and relieved. Who was he? Well, if he ever had the skills to match his dreams, then the back of his current baseball card would say that his name was Timothy David Ludyte and that he was fifteen and played right field. What it wouldn't say was that he played for the most pathetic summer league baseball team around. They did have plenty of heart and a kind of swagger that could only come from having a perfect season, although in an imperfect sense. That's right—they were holding on to a perfectly awful season. They were zero and thirteen going into today's game. Currently, it was the middle of the third inning, and the score was—well, let's not mention the score. Let's just say "thank God for the mercy rule" or it could have gotten even more painful than it already was. Unless Tim's team could stage the rally of all rallies, the game should be finished in the fifth inning, which meant Tim wouldn't have to bat again.

Thank you, Jesus, Tim thought.

As Tim occupied space in right field, he continued his contemplative daydreaming.

Don't get me wrong, I love baseball. I mean, God is obviously a baseball fan or we wouldn't be playing during the summer. It's just that God is obviously not a Dukes fan. This game makes the seventh game this summer that we've mercy'd out. Seventh! But we keep playing. We keep swinging away. We have to—we're the Dukes of Bingen, after all! It's just that today is Friday, the end of the first week of school, and already, the work is piling up.

For example, today in social studies—Tim was just starting his sophomore year at Bingen Senior High School—the teacher, Mr. Steinman, told the class that in order to graduate, they would have to complete an original senior project.

Wait a minute! Wait one minute! What happened to the rest of my sophomore year, let alone my junior year? I'm not a senior. I should still have two years to goof off, make bad decisions, and... you know... be a teenager. Senior project, my god! OK, breathe, Tim, breathe.

Anyway, Mr. Steinman explained that the senior project was supposed to be an intense research project that should encompass a student's entire time at Bingen. The reason why the project was introduced at the beginning of the sophomore year was to afford students enough time to properly develop their project ideas, create a production design, do the actual research, create the final project, and then (if the project was one of three chosen) present it in May of their senior year—to the school board and community at an evening assembly. However, the real reason for a senior project, according to this year's seniors, was to rob students of as much free time as possible. Obviously, the whole idea of a senior project was thought up by some school administrator who never enjoyed being a teenager.

Well, it is what it is, Tim thought. *So what am I going to do?*

Last year's three chosen projects were the following:

A. *Climatic effects upon triticale.* A project designed to compare the rates of growth of the most commonly planted varieties of triticale (pronounced "trit-a-kal-ee"), which means "wheat." Tim had to look that one up—clearly, part of this project was to force people to open a dictionary, if they still had one. Why the project's author couldn't simply say "wheat" baffled Tim. By comparing the growth rates of the grass, or triticale, especially during the difficult weather conditions of the summer, optimal cutting times were established—which would save on fuel consumption and greenhouse gas emissions in the long run. So, by doing a project that involved watching grass grow, we learned how to save gas and, by extension, help the environment.

Really? Watching grass grow?

B. *Makeup Stagnation.* This project studied the long-term effects of both soy-based and non-soy-based eyeliner on the visual acuity of teenage girls. Specifically addressing the question "Can using too much eyeliner lead to the development of 'premature makeup stagnation'?," it was a phrase apparently coined by the project's author, referring to the rut that some get into when it comes to the application of eye makeup. Hence the reasons why some adult women still apply their makeup in the same style and thickness as they did when they were sixteen. Perhaps beauty really is in the eye of the beholder.

C. *Ductus plani in planum.* This project made Tim's head hurt. It was an attempt to solve the math problem of squaring the circle or circling the square or something. Tim had no idea; he was only in Algebra 2. This student was trying to apply an idea that some Flemish priest had.

Where is Flemland, by the way? Tim thought.

The project had to do with indivisible calculus. As Tim read the project, or as much as he could, he quickly became lost, starting with the title, but he soldiered on.

Kind of figures that this project was submitted by some straight-A math geek of a student. God, he must be really smart, Tim thought. *I could never compete with projects like these.*

Then Tim remembered something that he once read. When writing a paper, pick a topic that very few people know anything about. Now there's an idea.

Tim continued his private musings when—*CRACK!*—a well-hit ball sailed over his head and bounced, unchallenged, to the fence. *Damn!*

Bingen High School, Pennsylvania
Monday, September 8, 2014
7:02 a.m., EST; 4:02 a.m., PST

Overall, Tim had a great weekend, so hitching a ride early to school with his brother didn't bother him too much. There was a giant-bug movie marathon on television all weekend, which fed into his great Monday mood. That and his parents were touring colleges with his older brother, Randy. That left Cate and Tim at home all weekend to do what they wanted, and that was watch the giant-bug movie marathon on the SyFy channel. Caitlin was Tim's older sister, who generally avoided him—most of the time. *Paradise couldn't be better*, Tim thought.

Cate, a nice enough person for a sister, was becoming a real DQ (drama queen). Cate was Tim's Irish twin, which means he was born less than a year after she was. Tim loved her, but he didn't always like her, and he was pretty sure the feeling was mutual. However, there was one very important thing that they did share in common, and that was an appreciation of giant-bug movies. So Tim had to share the marathon with Cate. It turned out to be okay though. First, their mother had given her twenty dollars for "babysitting" Tim for the weekend; then their dad asked Cate not to fight with her little brother and backed up his request with a twenty. Finally, Randy gave her ten more to stay home and not tag along on "his weekend" scoping out colleges. So she had ordered pizza and wings and was still twenty-five dollars ahead.

By the time the marathon got to Gordon Douglas's *Them!* (a.k.a. Attack of the Giant Ants)—having already been through Jack Arnold's *Tarantula* and Nathan Juran's *The Deadly Mantis* and, of course, *Mothra*, created and directed by Ishirô Honda (one of the creators of the iconically legendary *Godzilla*)—the two were starting to fade, but neither had wanted to admit it. Sunday morning found both Tim and Cate on the couch, cuddled up and asleep. They were so nauseated at waking up cuddling like two little kids that they both agreed to never speak of it again… to anyone.

Caitlin, while not only being an over-the-top drama queen, had developed serious attachment issues with her cell phone. Tim was of the opinion that if she could have the thing surgically implanted, she would. However, such a procedure wouldn't allow her to easily upgrade the device every six months. Tim had an old flip phone—no bells, no whistles, just a simple phone. He liked it, and using it made Tim feel like he was on *Star Trek*, flipping open his communicator. The retro world appealed to Tim. Cate, on the other hand, liked the technology of the "real world," as she called it. He would occasionally try to argue that they all lived in the real world, but Cate had the attention span of a soft breeze, and their arguments usually ended with her nose pinned to her smartphone. For her sake, Tim was thankful Cate had a smartphone, or she might never graduate high school. For all her annoying faults, Tim was sure he loved her. He just didn't always like her.

Now Randy (the eldest of the Ludyte children), on the other hand, was a true big brother—in every sense.

When Tim was growing up, Randy was always there to spend good quality brotherly time with him. Usually to Tim's disadvantage. But isn't that how big brothers were supposed to be? The two of them would wrestle till they were bruised and dirty. Sometimes one of them would end up with a black eye, but it was no big deal.

Tim could remember them raiding their dad's change "purse." They still snickered at the thought of their dad with a purse. Anyway, Tim could remember sneaking change from the purse so when they would walk to the lone store in town, they could buy as many packs of baseball cards as possible. Their dad rarely complained about the missing change because, as he told them, he wished he still had his cards.

Tim had always admired Randy for his athleticism, his good looks, and his genuine nature. It was not difficult to understand why girls swooned for him. Randy was smart, but not in a rocket-scientist way. Their mother would always say that Randy was unusual in that he had "a wisdom that belied his years"—whatever that meant.

Randy was okay in Tim's book. He was a good brother, and Tim loved him. And more importantly, Tim liked him.

Tim's mom, Carol Elizabeth (Handly) Ludyte, was great in all respects. Sure, there were plenty of times that Tim just wanted to stomp out of the house and burn her in effigy, but he never had. His mom had so many great characteristics; Tim hardly knew where to start. Forty-six years old and proud of it, she never tried to hide her age from people. According to Tim's dad, as well as several of Tim's friends, his mom didn't have to. She didn't look like other mid-forties women he had seen, with her strawberry-blonde hair that was so fine that even if she wanted to dye it, the dye would probably slide right off. She went to the local gym at least three times a week, usually when everyone was at work; but the great thing was that she was not a fanatic. She never turned away from a big bowl of her favorite Rocky Road ice cream.

It was cute and, at the same time, gross to watch his dad react to her. Tim's father would sometimes walk up behind her, wrap his arms around her waist, and hug her. She always giggled, occasionally turning to him with a little smile before whispering something into his ear, usually followed by Tim's dad turning several shades of red and letting her go. Then, one day, Tim got up the nerve to ask his mother what she said to him, and turning several shades of red herself, she told Tim that she was informing his father that she would probably be hungry for a snack later. Tim didn't understand, until Cate pulled him aside with a big sigh and proceeded to tell her brother that one day, if the girls of the world go blind, he might understand. *Whatever,* Tim thought.

One well-established fact, to Tim, was that he loved his mom deeply, like most teenage boys do, and he really liked her.

James Edward Ludyte, Tim's dad, was the "chairman of the table"—rejecting "chairman of the board" in honor of Sinatra. Husband, father, retired marine, former varsity letter winner in everything he tried, and just a good guy, if a bit of a goof. Tim's dad was in the United States Marine Corps for several years before he met Carol.

One day, Tim's father overheard him tell a friend that his dad *was* a marine, and Tim learned the painful lesson that there was no such thing—once a marine, always a marine. His father didn't hit him, no. Jim would never raise a hand to anyone in the family, unless there was absolutely no alternative; but Tim did have to drop and give his father twenty push-ups. And not just once, but every time Tim saw his dad for the next three days. It got to the point where all Jim had to do was enter the room, and Tim would automatically get up from whatever he was doing and "hit the deck," as his father liked to call it. Tim later recalled that for those three days, the only shirt his dad wore around the house was a USMC shirt.

Jim took a technical job in the service. He was a cable repair man, but that didn't stop him from getting his Corps on. He had this one T-shirt that Tim really liked: "US Marines, Making the World Safe for the Army." Jim's time in the marines was spent in Iraq, jumping from outpost to outpost, sometimes literally, out of a hovering helicopter and down a rope to swap out handheld two-way radio units with men in the field, sometimes under fire. Later, he worked COMSEC (communications security). Jim always told his own two sons that if they really wanted to know more about what made their father tick, they should join the marines and request the same job he had; otherwise, if he were to tell them any more, he'd have to kill them.

The first time he said that, Tim laughed; but his dad didn't. Interestingly, no one was ever quite sure if Jim was joking about that one. Now, even though his active days in the marines were over, he still wore his hair high and tight, made the bed with sheets so tight a quarter probably could bounce on it, and always thanked God before every meal for family, General "Chesty" Puller, country, apple pie, and baseball. The only thing that covered his high and tight these days was an old red Phillies baseball cap that, like the team, had seen better days.

The Ludytes were, and forever would be, a Philadelphia Phillies "Phamily"—and proud of it. They celebrated everything Phillies: the Phillies' ten-thousand-plus ways not to win a game and their two World Series titles. The Ludytes never counted the Phillies out, even when it would appear that the team had counted themselves out. Jim Ludyte would always be his son's greatest hero.

Harvey Orville Wallingsford was Tim's best friend since they were little. Both Tim and Harvey thought Harvey's parents were executing some warped sense of humor when they named him. Besides having been given the name Harvey—which guarantees he'd be a virgin until he met some desperate Iron-Curtained East German girl named Broomhilda or something—his initials were H. O. W. They both thought his parents were out to lunch on that one.

"Oh well, what're you gonna do?" Harvey would eventually say in acceptance of the unchangeable.

Harvey and Tim could have been brothers. They grew up together, went to the same church, and appreciated the finer aspects of giant-bug movies. And they both found Cate to be too dramatic.

Drat... I still don't know what I'm going to do for a senior project, Tim bemoaned to himself.

CHAPTER 5

Bingen High School, Pennsylvania
Monday, September 8, 2014
7:32 a.m., EST; 4:32 a.m., PST

"DID YOU CATCH the giant-bug marathon on TV this weekend?" Tim asked Harvey by way of a Monday-morning greeting.

"Only part of it. I was able to sneak *The Pupa* and then *The Son of the Nat*, but that's it. How was it?" Harvey responded, dropping his head in supplication as he fell into step with Tim on their way to their first class.

"Pretty good. I got to see those and *Tarantula*, *The Deadly Mantis*, and *Them! Mothra*, and my all-time favorite, *What the Scarabs Ate*. The only bad part was that I had to share some of it with Cate," Tim replied.

"Well, that's fitting. She is a bug," Harvey joked.

"Hey, have you given any thought to that senior project thing yet?" Tim asked, hoping for an idea or two—or, at the very least, hoping he wasn't the only one to be laboring over it.

"Yeah, I thought I would do mine on the effects procrastinating has on the development of a senior project." Harvey seemed serious, but that was one of his superpowers—an ability to pull a straight face in the light of panic.

"Brilliant!" It was brilliant, and Tim only wished that he had thought of it first.

"How about you—any ideas yet?" Harvey asked with the look of someone who had just proven himself to be superior.

"Nope, I was hoping the marathon would've given me some inspiration, but… nothing," Tim said.

"Well, it is what it is. Not like they're going to hold us back from eventually graduating," Harvey stated. "They can't, can they? I just wish I understood the whole thing more. Right now, all it seems we have to do is write a stupid report."

"A really long report," Tim reminded Harvey.

Their first class of the day—and their only major class together—was radio and TV (RTV) with Mr. Scott Edleson. RTV was a three-year, three-course program if a student wanted to stick it out. Mr. Edleson made it plainly clear that not everyone had the patience for the full three years, and for those who did—well, he said they'd just have to wait and find out. That meant that either it truly was a secret—one that even the current seniors in class 3 must have sworn secrecy to—or Mr. Edleson had no idea yet where class 3 would end. More likely the latter.

Eddie—as Mr. Edleson was called by the students, as well as a few members of the faculty, the janitors, bus drivers, and even his wife—was somewhat of a scatterbrain. He reminded Tim of Jerry Lewis in those old *Nutty Professor* movies with wild hair, tie undone, and crooked belt but no glasses.

Another strangeness about Eddie was the flag. At Bingen High, it was the duty of the first-period teacher to say the pledge. Most teachers simply let it slide, but not Eddie. He would never force students to say the pledge, but everyone would stand and not talk. As Eddie explained on the first day, it was a show of respect to the many hundreds of thousands who have died over the years so that everyone could have the option to say the pledge or not. Sad thing was, though, Eddie was the only teacher to ever explain why everyone should, at the very least, stand—let alone actually say the pledge. So, every morning, first thing, everyone stood next to their seats; and while some said the pledge, the others stood quietly. For both Harvey and Tim, it helped that they knew about Mr. Ludyte's days in the corps, even though he was just a cable repairman.

Actually, he did a bit more than just service cable; he told Harvey once that he was a "communications systems technician" … whatever that was.

After handing out textbooks and leading a brief tour of the radio studio—followed by a nod at the entrance door to the TV studio and production lab—the period ended.

"Well, where're you off to now?" Tim asked Harvey.

"Math," Harvey grumbled.

"Who do you have?" Tim asked.

"The Skunk." Harvey was referring to Mrs. Strunkowski.

Tim laughed at Harvey's misfortune and added, "I hear she was around when math was first invented. Some say she dated Euclid."

Harvey didn't look overly thrilled at the dusty crustiness that was the Skunk, as some called her behind her back. She did know her math, though… but little else.

Tim shrugged and then said, "Well, I'm off to Classics."

A language arts class, Classics was taught by the classic Mr. Deys. He had the strangest sense of humor, if that's what it could be called. On the first day of class, Mr. Deys's introduction was always "Greetings, I am Mr. Deys… sounds like 'keys,' but with a D. And this is classics class—the classiest class you will ever have. It is so classy that it really is a classic."

No one laughed. There were a lot of groans but no laughs—a few deliberate "ha-ha's," but that was it.

The less-than-classic response didn't seem to faze Deys; he just went on to explain his classroom protocols (or "protos," as he liked to call them). After which Deys explained the essentials of the course. As soon as he mentioned it was a literature class, the groans were loud and clear.

"I was told that you get to read comic books in here." That was Philmore Pendergrassé, a nerdy, skinny kid sitting to Tim's left.

Who names their kid "Philmore"? Tim thought.

"No, not comic books—graphic novels." You could see the gleam in Deys's eyes.

"What's a graphic novel?" asked Shelly, a sweet girl with braces.

"It's a story told in storyboard format," Deys replied.

Philmore asked, "Like a comic book?"

"No, like a graphic novel. Here, let me show you," Deys said as he backstepped to one of his many stuffed bookshelves and, without looking, pulled out a paperback about a half inch thick and the size of large magazine. Looking at the cover, he said, "Ah, this is a great one—rare but still very good. *The Hitchhiker's Guide to the Galaxy* by Douglas Adams and Eoin Colfer."

"The answer is forty-two," some unidentified voice called out from the back of the class.

Another voice asked, "Answer to what?"

And still another voice joined the conversation, "To the meaning of life."

"Not exactly," Philmore spoke up. "By the end of the book, those trying to figure out the ultimate answer to the ultimate question forgot what that question actually was."

"Yes, yes, very good. There are many other classic twentieth-century works, including this one." He held the book high enough for the whole room to see. "Of course, even the graphic novel cannot quite paint the picture that the actual book does, but it's a good place to start. Hopefully, after reading a few, you'll find a story that you think you might want to experience in its full glory," Deys said with an air of certainty.

Looking around the room, Tim could see that Deys actually did it. He managed to get the whole class to pay attention, in literature, yet. As the bells rang, signifying the end of the period, the entire class remained seated, waiting. One can always identify a teacher who has captivated a class; when the bell rings, the class remains seated, waiting.

Deys turned to the clock, looked back at the class, and said, "Until next time."

As the class filed out, Tim overheard an absurd question being asked: "Wasn't Jackie Robinson's number 42?" To Tim, it was absurd only because he felt *everyone* should know that.

The school afforded a five-minute break for the changing of classes, so there was no hurry. Tim's next class was going to be easy: lunch.

After lunch, and until Tim found a project to work on in some sympathetic teacher's room, he had study hall. Study hall was held in the auditorium, and it was a silent study hall. You just couldn't fall asleep or the teacher, Mr. Johanson, would loudly wake you up. Mr. Johanson was the only man Tim knew who could (and has) announced a football game without the help of a PA system. Tim's father said the man must be former military. Beyond not falling asleep, "Jo" didn't really care if you were actually studying.

For the third "semi period"—as the schedule called the three small blocks of time during which the lunches were served—Tim had PE/Health. Ms. Svenson had everything a young, red-blooded fifteen-year-old American male could have ever dreamed about.

C'mon, Timothy... think Bertha Gilmore.

Bertha was the most unsightly woman he knew of. Probably a wonderfully nice person, Tim had never actually met Ms. Gilmore but saw her on TV plenty of times, sitting in the front row at presidential press conferences.

"Timothy Ludyte?" came the sultriest voice imaginable.

Tim was in trouble. BIG trouble.

"Uh... um... *squeak*, yes, ma'am."

That did it; not only did he squeak like a wrung-out cat, but Tim had just called the hottest teacher in the world "ma'am." The redness flushed his face so fast that a chill ran down his spine.

"*Ms. Svenson* is okay, or *Coach*," she said with a little smile. "My mother is *ma'am*."

Obviously, she was fully aware of her own personal superpower, and she knew how to wield it.

The PE part of the class would take place every other day, with Health being held on the off days. For PE, Ms. Svenson said that if they wanted to shower off prior to returning to the general population, they may. Tim was very thankful to the good Lord for the chance to cool off. Fortunately, the boiler room was on the other end of the building, and hot water usually took a long time to reach the showers. No one ever complained, except the girls, for some reason.

After the semi-periods came the last class of the day—International Conflict, a social studies class. What about the other "normal" classes? Bingen High School, like many other schools in the region, switched over to what was called a block schedule: three majors and a semi each day. At the end of the semester, everyone, except for advanced placement students, got new classes.

Tim loved a good cloak-and-dagger story and was looking forward to International Conflict. He knew this would be a great way to end the day. The teacher, Mr. Steinman, is a former marine—correction: a marine who is a Purple Heart veteran of the Vietnam War. And, very much like Tim's own father, Mr. Steinman is very proud of his service. Tim had a feeling he was in store for an adventure of epic proportions.

CHAPTER 6

Venture Lab, Pasadena, California
Tuesday, September 9, 2014
2:47 a.m., EST (September 10, 2014); 11:47 p.m., PST

UNLIKE THOSE OVER at the *Sirocco* Mars rover lab down the corridor, the monitors for *Venture* didn't get to do much of anything these days. At least, the *Sirocco* geeks got to drive a remote-controlled car around Mars, even if there was an hour-and-a-half time delay. If they saw a promising rock in the distance, they could fill out the necessary forms (in triplicate), submit them to their team coordinator to sign, and pass off to the team manager. With a modicum of luck, he would hand the signed forms off to the team leader. Then after about a month and a half (seven weeks max), they might be allowed to deviate *Sirocco* from its preplanned course and investigate the rock of interest, which was now behind them. Or they wouldn't. But at least they were doing something. Whereas Evan did nothing.

All the *Venture 1* third-shift monitor did was sit and watch the downlink from a probe that was launched when he was a child. It was a big deal back then—but now, not so much. So here he was, watching the downlink from something with less computing power than his pocket calculator, which used an eight-track tape system for command and data storage. Evan had seen an eight-track tape cassette once, at a flea market. It contained the recordings of a band called ABBA and was being offered for fifty cents. *Sirocco* had a solid-state, multi-yottabyte memory system; *Venture* had an eight-track tape. Well, *Venture* had one thing that *Sirocco* didn't, and that was a warm plutonium heart. *Sirocco* relied upon solar panels for power generation. Evan understood *Sirocco* used solar panels to placate the concerns environmentalists had with aborted launches, but the power trade-off was not one he would have made.

Two nights earlier, *Venture 1* sent two alarms. The first appeared to point to an onboard systems failure, the nature of which remained undetermined. The second alarm indicated that the uplink/downlink connection with the spacecraft was being disrupted somehow. Following the standard operational procedures for such alarms, Evan ran the systems diagnostics to verify the spacecraft's viability. Nothing was immediately discovered that would account for the alarms, and yet they did occur. The lab's automatic recorders verified that much. As is procedurally correct, Evan logged the events, checked and double-checked the ground-based systems, and contacted those he was required to notify. Buck now passed.

However, today, the duty schedule for the third-shift monitor was to (a) record and compare the power levels of the downlink to those recorded earlier and (b) analyze the ambient magnetic field flux. Evan was a bit surprised. Usually, third shift just watched for glitches or indications of spacecraft failure. Actually, in the event the telemetry from *Venture* indicated a catastrophic problem indicative of imminent spacecraft "death," the shift monitor had three phone calls to make: (1) inform the team coordinator, (2) wake the team manager and tell him that the team coordinator was about to call with news, and (3) call the team leader to inform him to anticipate a telephone call from the team manager. Then it would be time to update his resume and think about another position.

Whatever the events were that led up to the alarms of two nights earlier seemed to have normalized as unexplainably as they had occurred. The day shift following the night alarms indicated that the telemetry link with *Venture* was stable and reflected no anomalies. Whatever had caused the alarms had passed.

Hoping to resume his normal duties, Evan didn't know what to make of the duty schedule. Normally, he would perform simple housekeeping duties. But this third shift had some meat to it. *Finally, I get to put my PhD in astrophysics to work*, Evan thought. *Okay—now what?*

He accessed the signal monitor system. *Thank God for graphical interfaces.* On the signal display, he navigated to the tab that read "DWNLNK." Evan wondered if there was some rule of labeling that prohibited the use vowels. Finding the correct icon, he then selected the "archive" operation to dump the last twenty-four hours of readings to the project hard drives.

Okay, that's simple enough... let me see, Evan thought. Then he said quietly, "The downlink power is 20.7832 watts."

Not much. What was it yesterday? 20.7832 watts. The day before? 20.7832 watts. Doesn't it ever change? Evan wondered.

It should change; it should be decreasing at a slight, steady rate. Flipping through the record notebook, it took well over two weeks of pages until something above 20.7832 watts was found.

Hmm? Well, Venture *was speeding away rather quickly. And as the distance increased, the power of the downlink would decrease—the inverse square law—and the core was not as energetic as it was at launch. That all made sense.*

The design of the *Venture* probe, much like its sister probes *Voyagers 1* and *2*, called for the utilization of three radioisotope thermoelectric generators. Each generator employs a plutonium-238 core as its heat source. As the core decays, it gives off heat, which is converted to electricity—approximately 450 W of 30 V DC power at the time of launch. What didn't make sense was why anyone cared anymore.

I can tell you, Evan, you don't care. You're just happy to have something to do, Evan thought. *Now what?*

According to the instructions, he was to leave the power utilization screen open on the computer, recording the power level just before closing out and logging off at the end of the shift.

Well, that's something, I guess. I need coffee. That was hard work, Evan thought as he looked for his grimy, stained coffee cup.

CHAPTER 7

The One
Historical: The Development of the Implant

SEARCHING, EVER SEARCHING the cosmos for proof that there existed others who could be incorporated into The One. The One was only interested in the cognitive thought energy that acceptance provided. However, as it had learned from its first encounter with an alien civilization, The One now knew not to rip away the entirety of an accepting mind. It had observed that to maintain a viable source for its own needs, it must be careful how much thought energy it could cull. Symbiosis was a very delicate balance, and The One was quickly discovering how to manipulate it.

In order for The One to exist, it needed those willing to accept it; and should the billions of minds that constitute a civilization have nothing to believe in and accept, they would exist aimlessly, without purpose or guidance, eventually dying pointless deaths at the conclusion of worthless lives. Therefore, to give a civilization purpose and worth, The One must exist. In order to continuously provide a civilization with inspiration and meaning, The One must grow. And to grow, The One must search for other beings in need of something to believe in and accept.

Unfortunately, The One could only search to the extent of its own powerful thought. No matter how much inspiration The One infused into its supporting civilization, the civilization seemed to be slowing down in its evolution. Contentment was a problem The One could not theorize a solution to. Apparently, the civilization had grown content with being connected to The One at whatever level that connection currently existed at. The civilization began to lack ambition; it was becoming complacent.

The "slowdown," as The One thought of it, could be traced back several generations. Apparently, it began shortly after individuals first conceived of the idea of a continuous connection with each other, and an unimagined eventuality spawned The One. The continuous nature of the Web meant that those connected to it would no longer need to perform individual solutional research. When faced with a difficulty, an individual simply accessed the Web for the solution. If no solution could be found, the problem would be overlooked and its associated project abandoned.

During its earliest generations, connecting to the Web required the physical and seemingly laborious task of gaining access by means of independent terminals. If an individual was not connected to the Web, they were not in touch with each other; they were not in touch with the inspiration provided by The One. They were alone, and being alone was dangerous. It could be fatally damaging to the individual and to the civilization as a whole.

Therefore, experiments were conducted in an effort to bolster the species' natural, though weak, mental ability to connect with each other. Several volunteers were sought out and received into a program of implantation. This was a big leap forward in the technological evolution of the species. To go from hard-wired connections to rechargeable wireless connections was simple; they were external to the body. What was now being considered was an internal, self-perpetuating device that would permit the individual to be connected continuously, in their mind. For the first time ever, an individual would be merged, physically, with the ever-growing web of information that encircled the planet. This was the beginning of the formation of the "civilizational singularity," as it would be called, or the moment when The One would fully achieve independent thought. Prior to the practice of implantation, The One only existed within the Web. However, now with the enhanced connectivity provided by the implant, The One existed everywhere, even within an implanted individual's own mind, in their very thoughts.

At first, implantation was a difficult procedure. Of the twelve volunteers in that first trial, six either died outright or suffered some form of insanity, and one displayed no obvious changes other than an inability to connect to the Web. But there was one with whom the implant worked—a young male of near sexual maturity, approximately eight cycles in age. The answer to a successful implantation was youth.

After several more unsuccessful attempts to perform the implantation on older subjects, the researchers attempted to adjust the implant itself in an effort to improve upon the overall assimilation rate. However, these ultimately proved useless, as the implant was, and remains, so very simple in its design that adjustments were deemed impractical.

Now faced with no alternative, the researchers returned to the records of the original twelve volunteers, and in a moment of exhaustion coupled with desperation, they recognized the key: youth. They determined that implantation must occur before the brain completed its biological growth. Researchers determined that the critical age for their species was sixteen cycles. The First (as the first successful implant receptor was called) was also the youngest of that initial group. The question, now, was how young was too young?

There were obvious benefits to performing the procedure of implantation on as young a subject as possible, assimilation of the technology being the foremost. Again, volunteers were requested. Many, having learned of the incredible connectivity that The First was experiencing, volunteered either themselves or their spawn. Initially, spawn with herds were not accepted into the program—only orphaned spawn.

While no one was able to predict a failure, efforts were undertaken to discover any genetic markers within successful implantees. In due time, the markers were identified, and tests were devised that could be administered before a spawn was hatched. Now, all a herd must do is present a soon-to-hatch member for preemergence testing. If the testing resulted in a high likelihood of the hatchling becoming a failure, the herd would be afforded, under the law, the opportunity to destroy the egg prior to emergence. Should the herd choose not to destroy the egg, then they must agree to accepting any, and all, caretaking responsibilities should the hatchling actually become a failure. Additionally, any associated insanity could, conceivably, change as the failure aged. Unfortunately, though, once a collapse began, the resulting insanity was permanent.

While advancements in the implantation process did reduce the failure rate, it did not zero it entirely. It must be understood that the implant does not create conformity among the connected; it simply allows for instantaneous communication within the Web, with conformity eventually being inspired by The One.

A word must be said about a specific type of failure. It is true that there are many different manifestations of insanity resulting from synaptic collapse; it is also true that most so inflicted live out largely benign lives. And not all insane failures seek out grand chaotic situations, such as war—the ultimate display of violent insanity—to act out their own symptoms. Frequently, they are satisfied with much smaller acts of chaotic discourse. However, an insane failure with a high intelligence, for example, is capable of causing serial fear and chaos... or worse.

A particularly chilling scenario occurred several generations ago. The historical records relate that a failure had manipulated its way into a potentially dangerous position. Dangerous for the civilization, that is. It was able to secure a position as an assistant in a biolab quickly learning how. Frequently, researchers would desire failures as assistants, for security reasons. Being unable to connect to the Web, except by means of a terminal connection, provided a sense of security, false though it may have been. As the records detail, the failure in question managed a series of events that nearly brought the entire web network down.

Using a terminal connection to the Web, the assistant had released news that a highly virulent, implant-specific pathogen had escaped quarantine and was in the open. After several days, it was determined that the news was an unsubstantiated rumor; however, damage had been done. Individuals were terminating their connections to the Web—in some cases, even attempting to remove the implant. Of course, that extreme was not possible; and when faced with that impossibility, some chose to self-terminate entirely. All based on the chaos and panic brought on by a rumor.

This event, and others like it, caused the introduction and eventual adoption of the following edict:

The Book of The One

Book of Laws, block 2, level 6

> 6: *Anyone who willingly exploits a weakness in a civilization, resulting in widespread societal disharmony, must be terminated.*

The identity of the individual causing the rumor had never been released, but it was widely held that it was the act of one exceptionally devious failure.

Improving upon the actual implant had always been a goal. The current version of the implant required the device to be surgically placed in the thalamus region of the brain. The procedure was fraught with difficulty. Misplace the implant, even slightly, and the receptor may suffer either signal degradation, or worse. That is why implantations are currently performed automatically. Simply position the individual on the implantation table and the automated system does the rest. The implant is located precisely, every time.

The actual device was, and still is, of a simple design. The technological difficulties centered on powering the implant. The original implants required periodic charging by means of a port located just below the auditory sensory organ. Should the implant lose all power, then the individual was abruptly disconnected from the Web, which, depending upon the level of activity at the moment of disconnect, could be harmful to the individual and possibly catastrophic to the Web. Several times, the entire civilization was nearly lost due to widespread power losses. It was only through the extreme efforts of several truly gifted implanted individuals—those who were capable of harnessing remarkable amounts of their own brains' ability—that the Web was literally willed through the crises.

Eventually, a means was investigated to internally power the implant. Experiments with motion-activated generators were attempted, but recharging the power cell in this manner proved even worse than external recharging. Whenever an individual would fall asleep, as is natural, the device would lose power; and since there was not adequate movement to sustain minimal power generation, a low-power disconnect would occur.

Finally, the answer came by means of an internal, heat-activated power generator. So long as the individual was alive, metabolically generating heat, the implant would function.

Beyond that, the device was designed to serve two purposes. Simply stated, it functioned as an amplifier for both uploads and downloads. The actual process of connecting to the Web was biological. However, the vast majority of individuals lacked the necessary power of thought to achieve a stable connection, let alone sustain that connection. With the implant boosting the power of thought, both stability and sustainability were no longer an issue. Now the implanted individual could focus on the needs of the civilization and join the ranks of the Implanted.

CHAPTER 8

Venture Lab, Pasadena, California
Wednesday, September 10, 2014
5:15 a.m., EST; 2:15 a.m., PST

EVAN COULDN'T WRAP his brain around why the power levels of the downlink weren't degrading, and it was making him cranky.

Venture 1 and *Venture 2* had been predictable since their launch in the late 1970s, so why the change now? Up to now, the fluctuations in *Venture 1* were well within mission parameters. The decay rate of the core, the speed of the craft, the increase in its distance from Earth, and its position were all predictable. The power loss could be easily calculated to within an acceptable margin of error, without going through the actual process of measuring it. Any high school student with access to NASA's public domain Internet site could not only perform the calculations, but verify them as well.

And to top it off, the coffee was cold, old, and gone! Probably those damn motor-head hotshots in the *Sirocco* lab… they never think of anyone else. Just because their little solar-powered tin can was named for a hot Sahara wind, you'd think they were tooling around in a modified sand rail the way they acted sometimes.

Evan allowed his thoughts to wander about the many programs, and their support teams, of the past.

You know who was great? The Pioneer teams. They were the definition of class. Sure, most of their probes have been lost to space, but not until every bit of information could be harvested from them. And then, when it seemed Pioneer 10 *was never to be heard from again, researchers in 2003, thirty-one years after its launch, received a faint signal—a farewell from the old workhorse. In late January or early February of that year, they let it go. With a few tears, but with no regrets, they said farewell to a dear friend. Class—pure class.*

Even the *Viking* teams had more maturity than the kids now dune-running around Mars. Maybe it was because the *Viking* landers were the first to safely reach the Martian surface, or maybe it was because it was the bicentennial celebration, but there were even stories about how those teams poured blood, sweat, and tears into those probes. The *Viking* probes were amazing accomplishments of American engineering. Not only were those two landers conceptually decades ahead of the curve, but they held the imagination of the entire nation.

Viking 1 touched down on the surface of Mars on July 20, 1976, seven years to the day after Neil Armstrong won the "Space Race" with a single small step. Had it not been for a faulty command from Earth that overwrote the *Viking 1* antenna-pointing software, that mission would have lasted much longer than it had. In 2006, the *Mars Reconnaissance Orbiter* imaged *Viking 1*, sitting and waiting patiently, its antenna still pointing in the wrong direction. *Viking 2* followed, entering a Martian orbit two and a half weeks later and touching down on September 3.

And if a venerable list of "Who's Who among Space Probes" is to be compiled, Evan thought, *then the Venera probes, workhorses of the Soviet Union, must be included.*

In true Soviet fashion, *Venera 9*, having survived one of the most inhospitable environments in the solar system, returned the first images from the surface of another planet, Venus. The *Venera* probes far surpassed the expectations of NASA observers. *Venera 9* survived the immense pressure, temperature, and sulfuric acid of the Venusian atmosphere long enough to send back photos of a barren landscape.

Even the European Space Agency (ESA) had notable successes. The ESA *Giotto* mission photographed a comet's nucleus for the first time when it flew by Comet 1P/Halley in 1986. Although researchers did not expect the instrument package to survive the encounter with the debris field of Halley's Comet, eight of *Giotto*'s ten sensors did somehow soldier through. *Giotto* was then placed into hibernation until 1992, when it was tasked with a visit to Comet 26P/Grigg-Skjellerup. Once again, it survived the dust and ice of a cometary encounter, and researchers decided, again, to put *Giotto* to sleep, to await some future rendezvous. The little probe with the heart and "soul" of giants—like *Pioneer, Venera*, and yes, even *Venture*—awaits even more excitement to come.

As Evan took his nostalgic mental stroll through history, even more names came to mind: *Mariner 2*, the first spacecraft to successfully encounter a planet, Venus, in 1962; *Mariner 10*'s successful, and first for a spacecraft, flyby of Mercury, in 1973; then there was *Galileo*, the first spacecraft to orbit Jupiter, in 1995.

Interesting mission, Galileo, Evan reflected. The *Galileo* orbiter released a probe into the Jovian atmosphere, and with a little help from a Galileo Galilei concept, the little probe rode a parachute deep into the uppermost atmospheric layer of the gas giant. It descended, and survived, for nearly an hour, being violently tossed around in the thick Jovian winds before finally succumbing to the overwhelming conditions. The truly interesting part of the mission—besides the incredible wealth of data transmitted to Earth—was that *Galileo*'s team was fearful that during one of the orbiter's many close encounters with Jupiter's moons, it might contaminate their atmospheres with Earth-borne bacteria. Therefore, in 2003, executing uplinked orders from Earth, the spacecraft destabilized its orbit and intentionally plunged into Jupiter, committing suicide in the process.

Evan stopped his musing, took a big breath, and let it out slowly; and as he did so, a little smile of shared inter-national pride bloomed on his tired face. Of course, no Who's Who of Space Probes could be completed without the mention of the grandfather of them all: *Sputnik 1*. Launched in 1957, it not only became the first artificial satellite but the first artificial satellite to burn up in Earth's atmosphere (in January 1958) as well.

It was followed by many others; but among them, *Vanguard* stood out.

Launched March 1958 by the US Navy, *Vanguard 1* is the fourth-oldest artificial satellite and still is the oldest man-made object in orbit today. *Vanguard* went silent in 1964; however, it is believed that it will see the dawning of the twenty-second century before its orbit finally decays, returning it rather unceremoniously to Earth. However, there have been nostalgic discussions about mounting a satellite retrieval mission long before its fiery end. Evan liked the thought of bringing the old girl home.

Of course, there were failures, both partial and complete—some glorious, like the partial failure of the *Mars 2 Orbiter/Lander* mission in 1971, and some not. The *Mars 2 Lander* crashed into Mars in November 1971 in a failed soft landing attempt. It was the first man-made object to reach the surface of Mars, though not safely. The *Mars 2 Orbiter* continued operating until August 1972.

Then there was the tragic, and completely heartbreaking, failure of the *Nozomi* mission, a precursor to possible manned missions to Mars. *Nozomi* failed to attain an orbit around Mars and flew by the red planet instead. Evan could easily conjure a mental image of *Nozomi*'s gremlins gently waving "Hail and farewell" to their gremlin brothers still playing on the wreckage of the *Mars 2 Lander*.

And there were others, many others. And there would be even more to follow.

These spacecraft, and the teams that attended to them, were—and in some cases still are—the pride of their nations. From the early days of the *Luna* probes throughout the heady days of *Magellan* and *NEAR Shoemaker*, man has reached into the void searching—searching for something.

Returning from his nostalgic recollections of the history of space explorations, Evan took up *Venture*'s power anomaly, again. He started considering the details of the various components carried by *Venture*, wondering what other anomalous information might be forthcoming.

CHAPTER 9

Bingen High School, Pennsylvania
Wednesday, October 8, 2014
12:57 p.m., EST; 9:57 a.m., PST

WEEK 6 OF school, and Tim still had no idea for a senior project, which he was now thinking of as "the stupid senior project." Harvey was actually going ahead with his study of procrastination. Somehow, he found a teacher to endorse his idea and who agreed to mentor him. Tim saw Harvey the other day in the library, actually reading a book—and not a comic book. The title of the book was *The Thrill and Pain of Waiting*. Tim couldn't be sure, but he thought Harvey was either in the very beginning, possibly even the introduction, or he was simply trying to make it look like he was actually doing some hard-core research, because when Tim snatched the book out of Harvey's hands and read the table of contents (something Harvey obviously did not do), Tim was amused by what he saw:

Chapter 1: *So you're going to have a baby?*

"Good book there, Harvey?" Tim asked nonchalantly.

"Oh yeah. I'm really getting some good information from it," Harvey responded while trying to look studious.

"I bet." It was everything Tim could do not to laugh. "Find that one on your own, did you? In our library?"

"Yeah. Funny thing though, this book was last checked out by your sister," Harvey said with pure honesty as he flipped to the inside back cover to reveal her name: Ludyte, Caitlin #2001-3407.

What! Tim was stunned nearly unconscious. *Oh my god! Maybe Cate checked it out for a friend, or maybe she was doing research for a health paper. No, she doesn't have Health this semester,* Tim remembered. He followed up Harvey's declaration with a question. "When did she check it out?"

"Just last week. I thought I was lucky she returned it when she did, or I'd be stuck for a resource." Poor Harvey. "But I don't think it's about what I thought."

A sinister little smile started to grow on Tim's shocked face as he thought, *I have to find Randy. Oh my god! Dad is going to flip, and Mom... well, we all know not to piss her off. This is going to be epic. Cate, what were you doing? You know better. At least I thought you knew better. Well, I can't stop now and enjoy the moment any longer. I'm already late for Classics, and while Deys is cool, he likes us to be on time.*

"Later, Harvey, I've got to beat it," Tim said to his best friend.

"Sure. Hey, want to play some Death from Above after school on my sixty-inch?" Harvey called loudly enough to warrant a "shh" from the library aide.

"Catch me after school. I'm late," Tim called over his shoulder.

"Yeah, whatever," Harvey quietly said and turned back to his search on understanding procrastination. Then again, that could wait as the new sports magazines were just put out.

Mr. Deys had his classes experiencing the graphic novel *V for Vendetta*. This one was put out by the British subsidiary of DC Comics, Vertigo Publishing. While the author and actual story were not widely considered "classic," Mr. Deys did say that the underpinnings of the theme were true to the classical form, and *V* had now entered the ranks of the cult icons.

What? The "underpinnings of the theme"? What the hell are the underpinnings of the theme? Tim was going to ask, when he realized that his thoughts started to bird-walk back to *The Thrill and Pain of Waiting* and Cate. *Screw her... oops, poor choice of words, all things considered.*

"Mr. Ludyte?" Deys asked.

"Um, sorry, Mr. Deys, I was... bird-walking," Tim apologized.

"That's a funny way to say daydreaming. Do you have a question, Mr. Ludyte?" Mr. Deys pressed.

"What?" Tim had his hand up and didn't even know it. No wonder it was numb. "Yeah, the people of London, at the time V was rebelling, seemed content. I mean, they had everything they could've wanted: food, clothing, health care, leisure. I mean... what were they missing that V felt it necessary to rebel? Or were his actions those of a criminally insane person seeking personal retribution?" Tim offered as a way of trying to impress.

"Excellent question, Mr. Ludyte. You can refrain from asking any more questions for the week. You really nailed it with that one."

Tim wasn't sure whom Mr. Deys was more proud of—Tim for asking the question, or himself for inspiring the question.

"To simply answer your question will not do." Turning to the rest of the class, he said, "What do you think? What were some of the motives that may have inspired V to take action?"

"He did want revenge, and revenge can be a powerful inspiration," answered Bill Sampson, an average guy with firm convictions.

"Good, revenge." Deys wrote *revenge* on the whiteboard. "Another one, please?"

"Insanity. Maybe he was pushed over the edge by the experiments the government did?" an unidentified voice called out, though Tim thought it belonged to Gwen, a very cute redhead with an even cuter personality.

"Okay, insanity." The word *insanity* appeared underneath *revenge*. "How about one more?"

"Martyrdom." It was Kathi Talbot, a born-again Christian with a heart of solid gold, encased in iron. Everyone knew not to cross Kathi; she'd rip your lungs out.

"Okay, hadn't thought of that one. Martyrdom… good," Deys commented as that too joined the list.

The board had the three motives listed, which the class went on to discuss in detail. They examined how each could drive an individual to incredible heights, and how each could lead the same individual to horrifying depths.

In the end, there was no one answer; they all made equal sense. Deys said that the correct answer may be the one that can be identified with the character the easiest. If V is seen as being insane, then insanity is the answer. If the character can be thought of as a martyr, then martyrdom is the right inspiration. Mr. Deys had a way of making the students leave his class with a simple thoughtful expression: "Hmm?"

CHAPTER 10

The One
Historical: The Moment of The One

THE NEEDS OF the civilization? How can any one individual, or even a group of individuals, agree on a hierarchy of the most pressing needs of any civilization? Individuals in one region may wish to address climate control, for example, and thus desire that need to be foremost. Those in another region may wish to address all the complications associated with overpopulation. Or maybe the civilization, as a unified whole, believes that the most pressing need is the poor quality of the musical arts. But many feel the Web's health is a critical issue. Can the Web ever be unhealthy? Can the Web become… insane, for example?

Historical records indicate various periods of web instability—but insanity? And if it did become insane, what could be done to manage the issue? These were the questions that were flying back and forth on the Web from one individual, or group, to another. The Web seemed on the verge of collapse from the sheer overwhelming demand for answers to these and many other questions. What was needed—and the majority of the Implanted civilization agreed on this—was a form of arbitrator. Someone needed to assume the position of authority. Such authority must exist constrained, though, or dictatorial control would develop; and that was something history showed as being counter to a civilization's survival.

Then what could be done about the growing confusion on the Web, the lack of focus? More and more individuals were connecting to the Web with the spread of the implant. Greater and greater flow speeds were being achieved. The Web was not just confused; it was speeding out of control.

It was at this point that the singularity occurred. The balance between the volume of connected individuals and flow speed was pushing the entire web structure toward a catastrophic, seemingly inevitable collapse. However, what occurred was not a collapse, but a powerful restabilization. Emerging from the crisis was a singular saving concept—awareness. The Web itself had achieved sentient awareness. The One emerged from its shadowy existence and into the light of civilization. If the Web was to be saved, those connected must accept The One. The Web had achieved a speed of shared thought unparalleled in recorded history. No one individual could recall when this actually happened. It is widely believed that the moment of awareness occurred very shortly after the first strains of confusion surfaced in the Web. Need knocked on the door of opportunity, and The One answered.

In the beginning, The One merely influenced the thinkers to reach a desirable solution. Eventually, though, it assumed a persona within the Web, an identity. The civilization began to view The One as a savior. Widely believed insurmountable issues mired in the depths of an entangled web were neatly and quickly taken care of. In less than a generation, or thirty-six cycles, hunger was defeated. At the same time, many other basic needs of survival started to fade away. Additionally, rampant pathogens were losing their hold on the population. For all intents and purposes, life was improving. The One required only a sustained connection to the Web and its civilization.

The One was now ever present in everyone's thoughts, in everyone's actions, and even in everyone's dreams. There would be no hiding from The One. A new god had been born from the chaos that was the early web. The new god only required an unfailing connection to the civilization… and it got it. Freely given, freely accepted, freely enjoined with the civilization. It was Utopia, Shambhala. It was paradise realized. But it was not real, existing only within the Web. Their paradise was nothing more than an illusion.

But even in paradise, an individual can get lost. Not every individual felt the influence of The One. In many cases, they were released back into the civilization as failures. They could still interact with the Web through one of the few manual terminals, maintained for their use, but these connections were not continuous and, therefore, were widely ignored by The One. The civilization chose to ignore the impact these outcasts could have upon it. Since The One chose to ignore them, then the individuals connected to the Web would do the same.

Most failures filled menial labor positions in support of the Implanted, the Web, and by extension, The One. The Implanted had convinced the failures that they were still an essential part of the civilization, for the most part. This, of course, was all a lie. A necessary one and, thereby, forgivable—but a lie nonetheless. Social contentment had to be maintained if the truly pressing issues of the civilization were to be addressed.

It was from the ranks of the unimplanted that rebellion first formed and gained momentum. And as in space, momentum requires a great amount of energy to be stopped.

CHAPTER 11

Venture Lab, Pasadena, California
Friday, October 10, 2014
9:48 a.m., EST; 12:48 a.m., PST

V AST EMPTINESS WAS what *Venture*'s sensors were relaying to Earth via the downlink. Evan also monitored the content of the data logs. Occasionally, he even viewed the raw binary stream coming through the matched filters. Evan remembered there was a trilogy of movies made back in the 1990s that used this simple binary code as its canvas. The movie concept was elegant but flawed, in his opinion, in that it did not take into consideration unpredictable variations. Oh sure, the writers attempted to deal with these through the use of a design program called "the architect," but the attempt was arduous, at best.

Interestingly, *Venture 1* was able to relate emptiness through its downlink. The long strings of zeroes, of nothing to report, invoked in Evan a sense of loneliness and the rarified vacuum of space on the outer fringes of the solar system. Evan gave himself a mental shake. Time to check the coffee pot, again.

With a fresh pot brewing, Evan decided to pop into the *Sirocco* lab and see what was doing on Mars. He knocked on the door as entry was controlled and his badge was not coded to this lab. However, on the third shift, the graveyard shift, no one really cared about visitors, and he was known to the Mars team.

The door opened. "Oh, hi, Evan, c'mon in," Judith Wagner said. Julie held a doctorate in applied physics.

"Thanks, Jules," Evan kindly replied.

Some of the "motor-heads" tried to keep it formal. To them, it was always "Yes, Dr. So-and-so," "No, Dr. So-and-so," "Kiss my ass, Dr. So-and-so." But with Julie—who was most definitely not a motor-head—it was always just "Julie" or "Jules"; no one called her *Judith*.

"So, anything new on Mars? Has Triple-A shown up yet to help you guys get out of that ditch?"

That was nasty on Evan's part, and to any other monitor, it would have been taken as such, but Julie just smirked.

"I keep telling you that you need to actually be standing next to the vehicle with your card in hand," Evan continued.

"Funny, Evan," Julie replied.

Julie had been babysitting the *Sirocco* dune buggy now for the better part of three months. Apparently, three months ago or so, one of the first-shift prima donnas sent up a set of instructions followed by an incorrect set of grid coordinates, sending the little thing into a rather imposing ditch. Now, the poor little solar-powered toaster with wheels had to sit until someone on Earth read the owner's manual and figured out how to put it in reverse and back it out of the ditch. Until that time, Julie and the rest of the team just sat and panned the camera around, looking at the Martian… ditch. However, from the size of the ditch and the angle of the entrenchment, *Sirocco*'s weather-monitoring sensors were able to function unimpeded. The Martian weather was about the only thing they could monitor. At least, the rover was well lit.

"Thank God it's not the rainy season up there, or the little guy might get washed away. You don't know—that ditch might actually be a storm drain," Evan commented.

"Rainy season, storm drain—really, Evan? Mars last saw a rainy season when the dinosaurs were trudging around the plains of Pangaea on Earth… maybe."

"Well, you gotta admit, it's both hilarious and ironic that your team got it stuck in the first place. I mean, you guys were cruising along at… what… twenty feet per hour, heading for that nice mountain eight miles away. Then what happened? Someone swerves to miss hitting a Martian squirrel and plop… into the ditch it went."

"Yeah, something like that. Thank God I was on my honeymoon at the time or, being the junior team member, my ass would have caught the fire," Julie commented.

Oh, and what an ass she has… a nice, perfectly shaped… married ass. Wake up, Evan, and go get that coffee. "Hey," he said, "I made some fresh coffee. Want some?"

"Yeah, I could use it. I don't think Herbie"—the name some technicians called *Sirocco* when the project mucky-mucks weren't around—"is going anywhere," Julie said as she pushed away from the monitoring station.

"Well, be safe, and leave the flashers on," Evan jabbed.

"Ha, ha." Julie smirked.

Entering the hallway and crossing to the little kitchenette, the aroma of freshly brewed coffee was off, signaling that it was burning. Evan must've put too much water in the pot and it overflowed all over the floor. Julie was kind enough to help clean it up, and without making a single smart comment. That's not to say that Evan didn't deserve it. He did, but Julie was too classy and kindhearted to make such a comment—at least to his face.

"How are things in your neck of the woods?" Julie asked from the floor.

"Fine. You know how it is—become interstellar and, suddenly, everyone wants your autograph," Evan jokingly replied.

"You still getting data?" Julie asked from all fours while she chased a puddle with a rag.

"So far, so good. But here is the new twist—they have us monitoring the signal level of the downlink," Evan stated.

"Well, maybe they're worried about the *Pioneer* problem catching up with *Venture*. Which one was it... *10*... that lost power?" Julie asked.

"No, that was *11*. Although, I'm pretty sure *10* is out of juice by now too," Evan answered.

"What's the source power level being reported?" Julie asked as she sprang to her feet.

"Just under twenty-one watts. That means the signal that reaches us contains barely point one billion billionth of a watt," Evan replied.

"Wow, barely enough to detect."

She was right too. If this had been twenty years ago, even ten years ago, they wouldn't have been able to detect that low a signal. But today, with the orbiting reception satellite and the new dish array in the Mojave, there was just enough power in the received signal for the matched filters to keep extracting meaningful data.

CHAPTER 12

Bingen High School, Pennsylvania
Friday, October 10, 2014
11:48 a.m., EST; 8:48 a.m., PST

L UNCH.

"Hey, Tim, you okay?"

Randy always could tell when something was on Tim's mind. Maybe it's because they were brothers. Actually, they were more than just brothers; they were "Irish triplets"—a phrase their dad liked to use when describing his children. "Look here, my Irish triplets," he would say. The reality of the bloodline was this: Randy and Cate were true Irish twins, and so were Cate and Tim. So, basically, Tim's mom was pregnant for nearly three years.

"Yeah, I'm fine. Better than fine, actually." Being the youngest, Tim would usually be the one to screw things up for the family; but not this time, and he so wanted to share his joy with Randy.

"Why, what happened?" Randy asked.

"Well, I stopped by the library earlier, to drop off the latest issue of *Baseball Today*, when I saw Harvey," Tim started to explain.

"Wallbanger?" Randy chuckled.

Tim continued, "Yeah, anyway he was reading a book. I know, hard to believe. But anyway, the title of the book was *The Thrill and Pain*—"

"Hey, Randy!" Tim was interrupted by Sara Guy. Randy had been swooning over her since they were in the sixth grade. Chicken that he was, he never got the nerve to ask her out. So whenever Sara called, Randy crawled. She was definitely the kryptonite to his superpower.

"Hi, Sara… catch you at home, Tim," Randy said as he turned and strolled over to where Sara was standing.

"Yeah, sure… no problem," Tim answered, shaking his head. *Poor guy—being led around by his libido.*

"Hey, Tim, grab a seat," Joe Mondi, a childhood friend and fellow nerd, called out.

"Thanks, Joe, but I have to study," Tim answered. Then, finding a relatively secluded table off to one side of the cafeteria, he settled down and popped open his radio textbook. He had a test coming up soon, and Tim really needed to brush up.

Without his noticing, Janice Hughes sat down opposite him. She was in Tim's radio class too.

"You ready for the test?" Janice asked as she opened her water bottle and took a long swallow.

"Huh, what?" Tim asked.

"Earth to Tim, come in, Tim. You ready for the radio test?" Janice asked again. "Well, this one is going to be tough. I mean, we have to know exactly how information is transmitted via amplitude modulation and frequency modulation," Janice said as she made a gesture with her hands simulating her brains exploding.

"I know, but it's really not that bad. The part that gets me every time is how the signal levels change from station to station. If I can figure out the power level connection, I think I'll be okay," Tim stated.

Janice opened her notebook and started reviewing her notes. Tim was having difficulty concentrating, what with the revelation about Cate and his other classes, and he still had no idea what he was going to do for a senior project.

CHAPTER 13

The One
Search and Rescue?

THE EMERGENCE OF The One had a single, last unexpected result. The energy field created by the mentality of an individual was insignificant. Consequently, it had never been observed or investigated. The One was a different matter entirely though. As the summation of the civilization's thoughts, the mental energy was vastly greater. While The One carefully guided its civilization away from any research in that direction, it found that it could focus its energy and push what it called "the mental field," directing it great distances. The One was able to search far beyond its home system, all with the power of its mind.

Reaching out with as much power of thought as it could spare, The One extended its search deeper into space. Another civilization must be found in order for The One to thrive. Mere survival was not enough. The One had to grow beyond what it currently was. More individuals had to accept it and then be guided into the fold of those gone before, if for no other reason than for the sake of future generations. The One must survive for the future, and to survive embedded within a dynamic civilization, its abilities must grow.

But space was empty. Stars, planets, moons, entire systems—all empty of the signatures of intelligence that The One sought. A realization came to it even as it studied its own civilization. There were other energies that it could monitor for, signatures from the creations of intelligent life. There were problems with fidelity and resolution, but those could be overcome. The One adjusted its abilities to see the electromagnetic fields its host civilization generated. Now The One had a new way to look beyond, into the cosmos.

With the power of six billion minds, The One reached farther and farther into the interstellar void, until it could reach no further. At first, the signature The One detected at this great reach was tenuous and weak. That alone might have been enough to minimize its importance. However, The One could not afford the luxury of being selective; and therefore, it must thoroughly investigate all possibilities.

What The One found wasn't much, and it might have been overlooked, or detected, and casually discarded as being unimportant. The One found in the dark abyss of space something never before encountered—a simple signature of coherent energy. There were natural signals aplenty in the universe, some created in stellar nurseries and others created in the furnaces of stars, but this one was different somehow. This signature's characteristics were unknown to The One. Perhaps it was simply an extremely rare natural occurrence, and the reason why The One was unaware of it was because of its rarity; but it could be artificial—created by a culture and then hurled into space.

The possibilities were so incredibly distracting that The One was having difficulty maintaining its focus on the signature. What to do next? What?

Having extended its search to such an extreme reach of its thoughts, The One was unable to search beyond the signature for a system of origin. However, having enveloped the signature with the power of its mind, The One was able to determine that the signature was not isolated to a single set of coordinates moving through space, like a ball rolling across a floor. Additionally, the signature was sharing its energy with another—but another what? Again, The One was unable to project its mind beyond this minute contact and search for a sharing partner. Presumably, the signature's source object was transmitting a signal to those who conceived it. If that was the case, then perhaps acceptance of The One could be carefully sown, thereby avoiding the need for a hostile takeover.

First, The One had to capture the signature's return signal with its mind and have it decoded. Once the signal's power register had been analyzed, The One would be able to formulate its own incursion on the signal. However, this had to be done slowly or those for whom the signal was meant may discover the effort and sever their connection, and this civilization would be lost to The One.

After redirecting enormous resources away from other highly prioritized pursuits of the civilization, it was discovered that the return signal was failing. The signature was fading—slowly, but fading nonetheless. This presented an entirely new set of problems to solve. Could the source of the signal be amplified, or at least stabilized? Perhaps there was a way to augment the power used to send the signal? Must the signal be amplified with a specific power register? If so, would it reveal The One before preparations were complete? And lastly, how would that much power be transferred from The One to the signature—enough to stabilize the signal and amplify its return signal?

Before analyzing and decoding the signal, though, a stable connection between The One and the signature had to be established with minimal fluctuations or effect to the sharing signal. Unlike the brains of the Implanted, The One could not amplify its own power of thought; but amplification would be necessary as the signature was discovered at the extreme limits of The One's reach. There was only one available way to increase the thought power of The One, but to do so would violate several axioms set forth in *The Book of The One*.

CHAPTER 14

Ludyte Home, Springtown, Pennsylvania
Saturday, October 11, 2014
3:08 p.m., EST; 12:08 p.m., PST

"CAROL, REMEMBER ME talking about an old buddy of mine from the corps, Dave Davidson..." Jim was talking with his wife as she tossed a salad for dinner.

"Wait! Dad, you have a friend named Dave Davidson?" Tim started to chuckle but immediately swallowed his humor when he received one of his father's USMC two-thousand-yard glares.

"Yes, his name is David D. Davidson... and before you ask, his middle name is Demitri."

God, how Dad could have said that with any more deliberateness is beyond me, Tim thought.

"Yes, you haven't heard from Dave for quite some time. Is he okay?" Tim's mom replied.

"Yeah, he's in town for a few days on a business trip. I invited him for dinner. I hope that's okay? I know I should've called earlier, but I got real busy—you know how it is when I get called in on Saturdays and..." Jim was off on one of his free-association ramblings.

"No problem. I could never turn away the man who saved your life," Carol commented with a big smile once Jim stopped for air.

Risking another glare, Tim decided to jump in. "What? Dad, you never said anything about someone saving your life before."

"And we're not going to talk about it now either," Jim grumbled as he left the kitchen, heading in the direction of the garage—his "man cave."

"Mom, what gives?" Tim knew she would fill him in, if for no other reason than to save her husband some emotional anxieties.

Sitting down at the table where Tim had his homework spread out, Carol pushed aside some papers. This was her way of saying "Stop what you're doing and listen to me." She related the story.

"It was back when your dad was in Iraq. From time to time, he would be ordered to join a patrol, serving as their radioman or something. It was a deep-penetration patrol, and they would be out for several days," Carol explained.

This much Tim knew from the many years of piecing together the bits and pieces of his dad's desert experience. He knew that his dad would occasionally have to "skim the sand" with a patrol.

"One night, the stars were so bright your dad says you could clearly see the arms of the Milky Way. Except for a warm, soft breeze moving across the sand, all was still. It was so peaceful, he says—that is, until the shooting started.

"It began with a lone night sniper that happened to take out one of the platoon's lead men. That's when the firefight started. As your dad tells it, the very air, amid its own screams of pain, was being ripped apart with the passage of bullets. He said you could feel the concussions of bullets passing by your head. Screams from both sides replaced the calm night sounds of the desert. The sand turned deep red with blood as people lay dying. And there was no stopping it. It had to run its course like a horrible disease… and then your dad was hit."

Carol paused. Clearly, the story was painful—even for her.

"What? He never said anything about being wounded." Tim couldn't believe what he was hearing.

"Yes, he was shot. It wasn't a life-threatening shot, but it did immobilize him. And if he had been left behind, he most certainly would not have lived," Carol explained.

"Where? Where was he hit? I've seen him with his shirt off, and he doesn't have any marks like Mr. Steinman has," Tim asked, referring to the bullet marks he'd seen on Mr. Steinman, from his days in Vietnam.

"He was hit someplace you wouldn't normally see," his mother stated.

"Huh?" Tim said. He knew his dad wasn't hit in the "jewels"—he, Randy, and Cate were proof of that.

"He was hit in the upper thigh, okay? A bullet violated his body—a bullet designed to kill him—and it would have led to his death had it not been for Dave." Carol gave up. "Haven't you ever noticed that dad rarely wears shorts? That's because a good portion of his thigh muscle was torn away. He's lucky he can walk."

Dad got shot. My dad! My hero really is a hero! Tim thought. Then he asked, "Did he get a Purple Heart?"

"It's in the top drawer of his dresser. Now that I think about it, that is exactly where it should be, considering the stupidity of that war." Carol quietly laughed. She always knew how to soften a situation, no matter how serious it might be. "Well, Dave picked up your dad and carried him out of the area. A lot of good people died that day, on both sides. People with families and loved ones."

"Wow." That was all Tim could manage to say.

"Dave got wounded too. He took a round in his butt while carrying your dad. I guess you could say they are butt buddies. Wait, no—that just doesn't sound right," Tim's mother stuttered.

Now she needed Tim to save the moment. "We could say they left their 'ass-sets' in sand."

Groaning an approval, Carol got up and pushed in her chair. She didn't have to say it, but Tim knew better than to bring the subject up with his dad again.

"Hey, Mom… one last thing. Whatever happened to Dave? Dad doesn't talk about him."

"Well, he was retired from the marines, awarded the Silver Star for bravery—not just for saving your dad, but for other acts as well. He received a Purple Heart and went to college on his GI Bill. Last I heard, he had settled into civilian life and a good job," Carol revealed.

Later that afternoon, the doorbell rang. Jim was still in his cave, and Carol was elbows deep in the preparations for dinner. Randy was at practice, and Cate was doing whatever Cate does. So it was up to Tim to answer the bell. He figured it should be Dave Davidson.

Opening the door, he was confronted with another high-and-tight haircut and a white collar on a pressed black shirt. "Um… Father?" was all Tim could eke out. He was not expecting an Iraq War hero to be a priest.

"Hi, you must be Tim," Father Dave said.

"Or Randy," Tim replied.

"No, you're Tim," Father Dave said. "Your dad described you perfectly."

"Dave! My god, you look good," Carol called out as she quickly came out of the kitchen, wiping her hands on a towel.

"And so do you, Carol. Still as stunning as I remember." Father Dave reached out to accept her embrace.

This was weird. He's a priest, for crying out loud. Aren't they supposed to, you know… not be into girls? Tim thought.

Father Dave must have seen Tim's confused look because while he was still holding Carol, he turned and said with a laugh, "Hey, I'm a priest, not dead."

"Oh, you!" Carol laughed. "Jim's in the man cave. Tim, could you take Dave out to your dad please?" Carol asked.

Motioning in the direction of the garage, Tim obediently said, "Right this way, Father."

"Tim, you would make me really happy if you would just call me Dave," Father Dave asked.

"Yes, sir." It was all Tim could do not to swallow his own tongue. "Ah, not going to happen."

"Well, suit yourself. At least, you can cut that 'sir' shit out. I work for a living," Father Dave commanded.

"Yes, sir." Now Tim could finally manage a smile. He had started to feel the shock wearing off.

A marine, a decorated war hero—he probably killed people, and now he's a priest? Tim thought. *Wow... hey, maybe I should make him my senior project?*

Entering the garage and turning toward a corner in the back that Dad claimed as his domain, Tim called out, "Dad? You have company."

Emerging from under his baby—a 1968 Carroll Shelby modified Ford Mustang with a radio upgrade of an eight-track tape player—Jim slowly got to his feet and looked at Dave. Smiling, he gave his friend the biggest hug Tim had ever seen him give a nonfamily member. He said nothing, just held on to Dave... and Dave held back.

Tim watched in wonder, remembering the words of one of his teachers, Mr. Steinman: "Battle makes brothers."

"Dave, you son of a bitch," Jim said as he let go and went to the cave refrigerator for some refreshments.

Tim knew better than to hang around. Besides, he still had homework to finish. And then if Mom said it was okay, he was going over to Harvey's for a few rounds of *Planets at War*.

Anyway, this was still pretty weird. A priest. Tim did not see that one coming.

CHAPTER 15

Venture Lab Building Cafeteria, Pasadena, California
Saturday, October 11, 2014
10:38 a.m., EST; 1:38 p.m., PST

EVAN AND JULIE sometimes celebrated the end of a long week by indulging in the fine cuisine offered in the cafeteria before heading home for the weekend.

Evan couldn't help but think, *Julie's right. The team leader is probably concerned that the plutonium-238 reactor is cooling down prematurely. The half-life of the 238, in the oxide form, is eighty-eight years, and* Venture *has not even reached the halfway point of the half-life... but... there is no arguing with the data.*

Evan supposed it was better to be cautious. After all, *Venture* was "boldly going where no man had gone before," to steal an appropriate quote from Mr. Roddenberry.

"You know, Evan, I never understood why the designers of the *Venture* probes decided to use a Pu-238 core."

Julie's curiosity was one of her most engaging nonphysical attributes.

"Why?" Evan asked. "It's not an allodium PU-38 explosive space modulator."

"Funny, and your name's not Marvin either," Julie stated flatly, as if she were giving a lecture. "Well, the Pu-238 is artificial."

"Yeah, mostly. Except for the trace detections of what it decays into U-244, found occasionally in nature. So what?" Evan had no idea where was she going.

"Well, it's like announcing our capabilities to the universe." Julie waved a hand in the air to animate her idea.

"Haven't we already been doing that since the twenties and thirties? I mean, c'mon—every time we make a broadcast of any kind, aren't we making an announcement?" Evan countered.

"Very true, but there is a big difference between an announcement that says 'Hey, we can manipulate the electromagnetic spectrum, a bit' and announcing to the universe that we can manipulate the elements," Julie replied.

Now Evan could see where her train of thought was going. Ever since man started sending nuclear-powered spacecraft beyond the moon, he had been, in effect, telling the cosmos that Earth was a nuclear-powered civilization. An announcement like that could have incredible consequences, depending upon who received it and how it was interpreted.

"For the past forty years, we have been telling the universe that not only can we refine the naturally occurring nuclear material, but that we can manipulate it into even greater, more destructive nuclear material," Julie said with her environmentalist inner geek sneaking out.

"Look, in the first place, we don't even know if there is anyone out there," Evan said with great confidence.

"Have you forgotten the gold records?" Julie reminded Evan.

In the early days, when humans were launching probes, someone came up with the idea of sending a solid gold record along for the ride. It is believed that someone was the late Dr. Carl Sagan. Those records (one carried on each of the *Voyager* and *Venture* probes), when played, provide information about who we are and where we are. So what we actually did was send out several devices that carried the message "Here we are." In reality, we may have actually announced that we were a potential threat… or really tasty.

"Well, *Venture 1* is searching for the heliopause. I seriously doubt anyone is out there searching for a plutonium signature," Evan replied.

"I hope you're right, because if there is, getting stuck in a ditch could be the very least of our problems," Julie relinquished.

CHAPTER 16

The One
Breaking of the First Law

CAN A GOD rewrite his own edicts to serve his own purposes? The One came to the conclusion that the good of The One outweighed the edicts for the many. The signature that was detected was fading. The One was not going to let this first contact get away, especially when the promise of an even greater expanse of its abilities was possible. There was a law though, that if The One was able to circumvent, then the gains from this signature may come more quickly.

The Book of The One

Book of Laws, block 3, level 17.

> *17: Deceit, in all its forms, being contrary to the common good, and health of the civilization, shall not be tolerated; including, but not restricted to (a) deception for individual gain, (b) deception for the gain of the civilization, (c) deception by means of omission, and (d) deception that is designed to mislead The One.*

The signature's data was unfamiliar. The One allowed its characteristics to be caught up by the Web, to see what the Implanted would make of it. No one recognized the data right off. It was unique—that much was agreed upon—with an equally unique heat plume. Through the power of its mind, The One was able to discern a temperature on a level never before encountered for a nonstellar body. The temperature detected was enormous, indicating some form of transformation was taking place.

There was coherence as well as data there. The signature was demonstrably unnatural; but from the little that could be discerned, it appeared that some sort of compression was being done. The Web's bandwidth was so large that there had never been the need to greatly reduce an individual data stream's use. But this new signature was formed in an unknown way, and its associated signal was encoded in an unfamiliar fashion. It captured the attention of individuals who made such things a study and drew them in. The comprehension of the signal turned from curiosity to priority—and from priority to obsession. Forcing the signal to give up its content became a web-spanning preoccupation.

The Implanted were experiencing a new level of excitement and, at the same time, a disturbing unease. These were the exact reactions that The One needed. While the Implanted were preoccupied by this new discovery, The One could more easily divert resources from priority concerns and refocus them on a variety of issues that needed to be satisfied.

The One had just circumvented a law in *The Book of The One*, to fit an ultimate goal. The One had deceived by omission for "personal" gain. The One had already started to change as a result of this new contact.

CHAPTER 17

Ludyte Home, Springtown, Pennsylvania
Saturday, October 11, 2014
4:49 p.m., EST; 1:49 p.m., PST

CRACKING OPEN THE twist top on a very cold tall one and handing it to Dave, Jim asked, "So, Davy Boy—what's up? You sounded a bit on edge earlier."

"Nothing." Jim held the beer while Dave unbuttoned his collar and removed his white "badge of office." With an intense look of gratitude, Dave gently took the offering and raised it to his lips for a long draw. "Hey, the Shelby looks great."

"Quit dodging, Dave, and... thanks." Jim smiled widely. "You can touch her. I don't let many people lay hands upon this beauty, but after hugging Carol, I figure you're gentlemanly enough," Jim said as he stepped aside, no longer standing between his guest and his car.

"Thanks." Dave ran a hand on the curves of the fender and followed her lines around to the back of the car. Looking down at the nearly perfect back end of the Mustang, Dave commented, "I gotta hand it to you, Jim. You do nice work."

"So, you going to level with me?" Jim pushed. "We've been through too much together to keep secrets."

"You are not my confessor," Dave replied. "Besides, can't a guy just miss his buddy... his friend... his fellow?"

"No, I'm not. And yes, he can." With that, Jim handed Dave a shop shirt and told him to swap it with his work shirt. "C'mon, you can help me work on the undercarriage."

Dave was waiting for some true privacy without being obvious and asking for it, and after some time, he began with "Jim, I have a... I have a problem."

The area between the chassis of the 1968 Mustang and the spotless concrete of the garage floor would have to serve as an impromptu confessional.

"Finally, what's up?" Jim asked. "Hand me that wrench."

The two marines talked for nearly an hour under that car. Carol had seen it before; she'd even crawled under there herself to confer with Jim. She knew not to bother them until they came crawling out. Which, eventually, they did.

After they climbed back to their feet, Jim admitted, "I'm stuck though. I don't know if I want to go completely Shelby-stock with her or remake her the way I want her to be." Grabbing a shop towel, he wiped his hands clean of the unseen dirt that he thought was on them.

"Well, if she were mine, I'd leave her the way Ford and God made her."

Until Dave said that, Carol wasn't sure if what she overheard from the garage was about the Shelby or a woman—and if it was about a woman, that woman had better not be her. She was perfect. Carol chuckled at the thought.

Calling out to them, Carol announced, "Hey, marines... mess call!"

Tim was just about done setting the table, having completed his homework a few minutes earlier. There would be only four for dinner tonight. Randy was still at a practice, and Caitlin was heading over to her boyfriend's for dinner.

Tim thought, *She probably didn't want to sit at a table with a priest anyway, especially since she may have broken—which commandment is it that says "Thou shalt not be an irresponsible drama queen and get thee knocked up"?*

Jim moved to his usual spot at the head of the table, Carol to his right, and Tim to his left. Father Dave sat opposite him. Dinner was a simple chicken alfredo dish, and a Caesar salad completed the meal along with crusty bread—just the way a meal should be.

Knowing Father Dave was off duty, Jim said the prayer. "Bless us, oh Lord, and these thy gifts which we are about to receive. From thy bounty, through Christ our Lord…"

Here it comes, Tim thought.

"We thank thee for our country, General Puller, Carol's apple pie, and the Phillies. Amen," Jim concluded.

"Really? The Phillies?" Father Dave didn't even blink an eye at the addition to the end.

Passing to the right, Carol handed the chicken alfredo to Father Dave, asking, "So where are you stationed these days? Are you back in the US for good?"

"No, I'm on my way to Arizona… business. But I'm actually stationed at Castle Gandolfo, at a convent about a mile from the castle. I'm attached to the church's deep space radio astronomy efforts," Father Dave revealed.

"You work in a castle? Like, what was it I saw on TV? Some castle in Austria—Wewelburg Castle?" Tim asked, somewhat out of turn, but Carol and Jim liked the openness of free conversation during dinner. It kept everyone interested.

"That's Wewelsburg, with an *s*… And Dave is not a Nazi, nor in the SS, and his boss is not Himmler," Jim corrected but glanced at his friend for confirmation about the Himmler conclusion.

Father Dave just chuckled and said something unintelligible under his breath.

"Yes, like Wewelsburg in that it is on top of a bluff and was not a battle castle, like many of those in Great Britain and France. But no—not like Wewelsburg in that we don't usually hold pagan rituals in the basement," Father Dave replied. He knew that Wewelsburg was where Himmler's SS was rumored to have held treasures like the Spear of Destiny and other rare artifacts.

"You'll have to forgive him, Dave. He plays a lot of *Wehrmacht Front*. It's a video game," Jim apologized.

Father Dave leaned over to Tim and whispered, "Personally, I like *Call of Duty*."

"So, Dave, what are you doing at Gandolfo?" Carol asked, wanting to get back on topic.

"Well, it's kind of technical. But to put it simply, I'm assisting the Vatican's efforts to identify the sources of various radio signals," Father Dave said.

"I thought the search for ET was something the church frowned upon," Jim said as he helped himself to the salad.

"Well, actually, Jim, the search for life is the search for truth, and the church has always been about the search for the truth," Father Dave responded with the expected church party line.

"Yeah, Leonardo da Vinci really bought that one," Tim said to no one in particular.

"Tim!" Carol chastised.

"That's okay, Carol. It's actually refreshing to hear a... what are you like fifteen?" Father Dave questioned.

Tim nodded.

"It's refreshing to hear that a fifteen-year-old understands a little of church history so well." Father Dave, a Jesuit and part-time college professor of engineering, was not used to being around today's teenagers.

"So how are you helping them?" Tim had to know. "Are you an astronomer?"

"No, I'm a systems engineer," Father Dave answered.

"And a priest," Tim said, stating the obvious.

"When you get the call, you just know it," Father Dave said.

Jim was just sitting there, calmly eating and watching the conversation. He seemed to have something he wanted to say but didn't know how. Or he had gas; one never could tell with Jim.

"Dad told me he knew you from the marines. How does a marine become a priest?" Tim pressed.

"He goes to a seminary," Father Dave replied with a grin. "Actually, I think if it wasn't for the corps, I would never have become a priest. Being a Jesuit is a lot like being a marine. There's a certain military structure to it. I knew I couldn't stay in the corps forever, but I wanted the discipline, the formality of the corps." Father Dave stated, "I certainly didn't become a priest for the money."

"Or the social life," Jim interjected, thinking back on his Catholic school days.

The conversation moved on to memories of Iraq. Tim sat quietly, taking everything in. He was always interested in anything that gave him more insight into those closely held early times in his father's life. He had the feeling that he was going to learn something new right now so long as no one noticed him.

CHAPTER 18

Venture Lab, Pasadena, California
Monday, October 12, 2014
5:47 a.m., EST; 2:27 a.m., PST

*K*NOCK, KNOCK, KNOCK.

"Evan, you got a moment?" It was Julie standing at the *Venture* lab door.

Evan wheeled his chair back from the console he was working at and answered, "For you? I got lots of moments. What's on your mind?"

"I can't stop thinking about your piece of flotsam, *Venture*," Julie mused, setting her coffee on a table.

"What about it?" Evan asked.

"I'm not sure. Something about the core you were talking about has me bothered," Julie tried to clarify.

"Like what?" Evan pressed. Even though he told Julie that he had lots of moments, he lied. He needed to get back to the system diagnostics that he was currently running.

"I can't put my finger on it. Something about the current power level just doesn't sit well with me. Hey, do me a favor..." Julie really looked bothered. "If something changes... anything... let me know. Please?"

"Sure, no problem," Evan assured her.

"Well, I guess I should get back to the ditch." Julie knew where the action was going to be. She had that sixth sense about her, and she didn't like being out of it, but *Sirocco* was hers. For now.

"Yeah, well, if anything comes over the downlink, I'll come running," Evan promised.

"Please, I've already changed the oil and kicked the tires. There isn't much more I can do for *Sirocco* except sit and wait for the rest of my team to figure out how to put it in reverse."

Julie's sarcasm was refreshing. She picked up her coffee and strolled to the door. At the door, she stopped and teasingly looked over her shoulder. Catching Evan appreciating her retreat, she smiled.

"Who would be searching for a plutonium signature?" *Now I'm talking to myself. Great.* Evan wheeled his chair back to the console he was working on. As he did, he made a mental note to check his personal log for anything that might not "sit well."

CHAPTER 19

The One
Signature Understood

THE ONE COULD observe the signal as it was generated and transmitted. Included in its observations were specifications for the object's power generation. From this, The One concluded that a form of substance *92* was being used. The gradual reduction in the amount of *92* was causing the fading signal power it had observed. However, the source signal was so low that The One could barely discern it. Had The One not discovered it when it had, the last data retrieval may not have been possible. The One needed to reenergize the source before retrieving any more data. The data it already had harvested did not include the location of the object's creators. That was apparently held elsewhere, separate from what it had culled.

Ninety-two+, *92+*. The One assigned the new signature a temporary designation until a proper name could be established. It was a complex substance that the Web and The One had already concluded as not being natural. However, there was more, much more to it. The only conclusion for not getting a clear sense of the structure was that it was shielded somehow. Still, there should be enough to understand its properties.

Of the known substances to The One, *92+* seemed very similar to *92*. As if *92* was somehow changing into *92+*. Additionally, *92+* gave off tremendous amounts of energy along with detectable amounts of various subparticles, later determined to be substance *2*. The emission of thermal energy, and the substance *2* subparticle, was converting the *92+* into what seemed to be yet another form of *92+*. However, the form of *92+* it was turning into was ever-so-slightly different, a *92-*.

With this information, the source's signature was established to have followed a path of conversion: naturally occurring *92* was transformed into *92+*, then through the emission of thermal energy, and subparticles of *2*, the *92+* was converted into *92-*.

Knowing the conversion path did not answer the question of how it was accomplished. Stellar furnaces are known to be able to transform one substance into another. However, this signature might be artificial and not stellar in origin. Therefore, how was the *92+* created?

The Web struggled to answer the question, to the sacrifice of other priorities. This was something The One could not permit. It needed to be in complete control of the Web's attention, directing and inspiring as it deemed necessary. Therefore, The One seeded the Web with a conclusion. The conversion process would be accepted as being axiomatic. The *92+* existed; therefore the process, though not completely understood at the time, existed. This conclusion was automatically accepted by the Implanted, and the struggle to understand was satisfied.

Returning the attention of the Web, and the Implanted, back to the analysis of the diminishing power supply, The One was able to conclude that the substance that powered the device was a member of a family of substances hitherto unknown. Additionally, it seemed to be extremely dense, with fascinating thermal properties, emitting both thermal and particle energy in the form of subparticles of substance *2* and other particles deemed unimportant. However, in spite of knowing all this, The One was still unsure whether it could stop the loss of power.

There was much work to do.

CHAPTER 20

Bingen High School, Pennsylvania
Monday, October 13, 2014
7:22 a.m., EST; 4:22 a.m., PST

"WAY TO DITCH me Saturday night, pal," Harvey greeted Tim the next morning.

"Damn, I completely forgot. We had one of Dad's Marine Corps friends over for dinner, and I got so into his visit that I lost complete track of time," Tim apologized.

"You're just lucky you ditched me because of one of your Dad's MC friends, or I'd be upset," Harvey stated.

"You just don't want to have to drop and give twenty every time you see my dad," Tim joked.

Harvey locked into step with his friend as the two headed off to their first class, Radio. It turned out this was not only a cool class, with a cool teacher, but Tim hoped it just might be the source of a senior project idea. After listening to Father Dave the night before, Tim started thinking about trying to do something that could combine his radio class with astronomy. Tim knew the first step was to talk to Eddie about it. If Eddie would help him nail down the particulars, then maybe, just maybe, he would sign off on it, and Tim could get started.

"Okay, today is going to be the start of several days in which we will discuss the future applications of advanced radio technologies—everything from medical applications to how we talk to the *Voyager* and *Venture* spacecraft," Eddie said to the class.

Tim suddenly was Eddie's best student, although Eddie didn't know that yet.

"Up to now we have been focusing our efforts on understanding how an actual radio works, its components, its history, and some of its many variations, like microwave communications. Today, we start to take a look at its future. Perhaps one of the most important applications of today's radio technology can be found in the medical world."

As Eddie talked on, Tim found himself drifting back to the evening before, and to Father Dave.

Tim was having difficulty wrapping his head around the whole priest/marine/scientist thing, but that was okay. There was something Father Dave had said during dinner that got the ideas moving, though. Father Dave and his dad were going on about the systems interfaces compared to when Jim first learned his radio craft. When Tim remembered that Father Dave said they could still pick up the downlink from *Venture 1*—thirtysomething years after its launch—and that it had traveled nearly 12.5 billion miles, Tim couldn't help but wonder what was out there. Better yet, he found it absolutely amazing that we could still communicate with it.

Tim thought, *I mean, really, I can't communicate with Cate, and she has a bedroom across the hallway from me. Anyway, what was it that Father Dave said it takes a signal nearly eighteen hours to make it back?*

"Mr. Ludyte... Mr. Ludyte!" Eddie called out.

"Um, yes?" That snapped Tim out of his daze.

"Care to share what's got you so entranced?" Eddie asked.

"Ah... okay. I was just thinking about what you said about talking to *Venture*," Tim stated.

Thinking that he had caught a student off topic, Mr. Edleson was more than pleased that he was wrong. "Sure, we can talk with the *Venture* probes, though I'm not sure how much we would understand anymore... it is speaking disco."

On Eddie's part, that was a very bad attempt at a joke. "If I remember correctly, it takes about a day for a signal to reach *Venture 1*. I don't know much about *Venture 2*, though," Eddie admitted. He then continued, "And remember, the signal would be traveling at the speed of light. Does anyone happen to know how far light travels in an hour?"

Without looking up from a doodle, Harvey called out, "About 671 million miles."

"Close enough." Eddie was impressed. "And how far from school do you live, Mr. Wallingsford?"

Looking up, Harvey said, "I don't know."

There were more than a fair share of chuckles and sighs at the irony in Harvey's answer. Looking completely lost, Harvey just shrugged and bent back to his doodle.

Returning to his original line of thinking, Tim said, "Last night, we had one of my dad's old Marine Corps friends over, and he's a systems engineer working with the Catholic Church's astronomy project."

"Is he a priest?" an unidentifiable voice asked.

"Yes," Tim answered.

"Wow, a priest and a marine, a soldier for God... cool," another voice snickered from the other side of the room.

Raising his hand like Jesus, to calm the storm, Eddie motioned for Tim to go on.

"He works at the Castle Gandolfo," Tim continued, completely ignoring the interruption.

"Okay, that's one of the Vatican's observatories." It was amazing what Mr. Edleson knew sometimes.

Amazed, Tim confirmed, "Yep, and he says he's working on something having to do with radio astronomy."

A voice from the other side of the room chuckled. "I wonder if God is on AM or FM?"

Glaring in the direction of that uncalled-for comment, Eddie said to Tim, "We haven't talked about that application of radio technology yet, but it is a growing science, and it's making some pretty impressive discoveries. Did your friend happen to say what he was currently working on?"

"Not really. He was pretty vague," Tim answered.

"Well, if the church has him working on something at Gandolfo, you can pretty much bet it is something really interesting," Mr. Edleson elaborated.

Eddie was able to steer the discussion back to his topic—radio technology's applications in the medical field. "Some absolutely amazing advancements have been made that enable doctors today to implant small radio transmitter/receivers in the brain that help those who suffer from Parkinson's disease, for example, better manage their various issues. That is, of course, only one application. There are many more."

"I read somewhere that they're even trying to apply small radio controls to artificial arms and legs." That was Julie Hoshkins, a frumpy girl with a great personality.

"Yes, that's true. If successful, you may see the day when not only artificial limbs are controlled by means of an implant, but you may also see the application of small implants that can help those with genetic problems. Or maybe you'll have the option to have your Bluetooth surgically implanted. The sky's the limit, and you're going to be living in exciting times," Eddie stated, hoping no one caught on to the ancient Chinese curse he had just paraphrased.

"My dog has a chip in it. Is that what you're talking about?" Harvey almost never spoke up in class, but today, he actually had a good question.

"A robotic dog?" a student in the front row asked.

"That is a simple memory chip that can be read by a special scanner, but you're on the right track. I don't think it's a big leap from having an earpiece like Bluetooth to having a device actually implanted in your head, similar to cochlear implants that can help the deaf hear."

Eddie was firmly atop his prophetic soapbox now and loving it. It was obvious that Eddie was a supporter of the rapid adoption of advanced technologies.

Tim just didn't know. Tim could easily see his future, but Tim wasn't so sure it would be a good one.

CHAPTER 21

Venture Lab, Pasadena, California
Monday, October 12, 2014
8:17 a.m., EST; 5:17 a.m., PST

RETRIEVING HIS PERSONAL flash drive from his pocket and plugging it into a stand-alone computer, Evan opened the function that would allow him to view its contents.

"Where is it?" Evan muttered to himself as he scrolled through the index. "There it is." He had learned long ago to keep a separate log of ideas and thoughts, if for nothing else than for a good laugh once in a while. Opening a document dated 9.9.14, he started reading the entry:

> Tuesday, September 9: Started examining the downlinked power levels and magnetic information from *Venture 1* today. Nothing unexpected noted. However, Dr. Wagner brought up the concern about sending artificial nuclear generators into space. Her concern was not environmental, or ethical, but more along the lines of "Are we sure we want to announce some of our most advanced technological abilities to whomever may be out there?" On one hand, the probability that an alien civilization would actually find one of the probes is so remote that it is barely worth considering; but on the other hand, she has a point. We have always believed, despite Hollywood's best efforts to the contrary, that aliens are cute and cuddly—remember Alf and ET?—but what we fail to accept is that we may not be the pinnacle of technological development and that the aliens out there might be more along the lines of the Predator. By sending nuclear generators into space, we are giving an alien civilization an indication of what we are capable of, thereby giving them a chance to plan

accordingly. Furthermore, something that Dr. Wagner did not mention is the actual telemetry link with the probes. If the probe were dead, then we would be a bit safer. However, in the case of *Venture*, it is still very much alive, and its telemetry being sent back to Earth gives anyone a clear path to follow to find us. What then?

Pushing away from the computer and removing the flash drive, Evan felt stuck in a mental daze.

What would we do if an alien civilization turned out to be less ET and more Predator? Well, the reality of space is that the chances that we would ever come across an advanced alien civilization are so very slim that such an event can be easily forgotten.

"Why worry about something you can't control?" he muttered to himself as he recorded the end-of-shift downlink power level in the required notebook: 20.7832 watts… unchanged.

CHAPTER 22

The One
A Time for Secrets
The Book of The One

Book of Laws, block 1, level 6

> *6: No culture shall be compelled, manipulated, deceived, nor forced in any way to accept implantation. Such a decision must be arrived at voluntarily.*

THE ONE HAD a lone remaining issue with its host civilization—the Rebellion. They were those in the civilization not accepting of The One. It was clear that The One could not compel them. On the other hand, they could not be allowed to control The One and, by inclusion, the civilization. If the Rebellion discovered the truth concerning the current project, then The One might be forced to eliminate them, for they could not deny others the opportunity to join The One. Eliminating the Rebellion would require The One to act in opposition to its own axioms. The reason The One had not acted against the Rebellion was that the Rebellion's members had, so far, given no cause for concern. They were more of an annoyance than a true problem. However...

At first, the thought was to simply allow the Rebellion to exist. And at first, this was the practice—that is, until the Rebellion began to realize that the civilization's hierarchy was extracted from the ranks of the Implanted. Slowly at first, and then quite rapidly, the Rebellion began to segregate itself into a separate class of the civilization. Eventually, though, that class became viewed as substandard, forever to be held in a state of stagnation, fulfilling menial service-level positions, seemingly devoid of ambition.

However, ambition was not absent from their lives. Enjoying the anonymity being disconnected afforded, the Rebellion slowly began to organize an alternative conceptual philosophy of its own. The One had great difficulty successfully engaging this concept. This was a primary reason The One was seeking more civilizations to join the Implanted; an increase in its abilities would ensure that any threat of radicalizing concepts would be nothing more than an ethereal threat. Something to be thought of in passing and dismissed like so many diseases of old.

Should it become necessary to deal with the Rebellion, The One would dispatch them in as efficient a manner as possible. However, for the moment, the least resistant course of action appeared to be one of controlled ignorance, applied to everyone. Now had come the time for secrets.

***

Since the emitted particles detected earlier were identified to be the high-energy centers of a known substance (designated "2"), a possible solution had emerged from the Web as to how to reenergize the power source. The idea was to reintroduce enough of the emitted particles back into the high-energy centers so as to reverse their loss of power. The Implanted explained it as follows: *Imagine a liquid flowing down a pipe. Introduce enough back pressure on the liquid and the flow will reverse itself. Could the same principle be applied to the reenergizing problem?*

The detection of the object was luck, its discovery achieved through the immense power of The One, but that power was still only the power of its mind. What was now being considered was an actual transfer of particle energy in such a way as to stabilize and enhance the object's own power source without damaging the object.

Again, the answer came from the Web, not surprisingly. The Implanted proposed the following: *Reintroduce additional particles of the emitted substance, 2, to the power source by means of a directed polarized beam.*

It had been long understood that certain particles, 2 being among them, could be manipulated through the application of strong magnetic forces. Therefore, the Implanted concluded that if a polarized beam could be established between the object and their own web emitters, then, using the beam as a carrier, it should be possible to transfer enough 2 to reenergize the object's power source.

The One determined that a power increase of 22 percent over current levels should be set. Such an increase in the object's power source should be sufficient to provide the additional energy needed to stabilize the object. Fortunately, The One did not have to reveal to the Implanted what the actual goal of the increase was. As it presently stood, increasing the power supply would be believed to be a project to render assistance to something that was dying. The faith, and confidence, the Implanted had rested upon The One was limitless. No questions arose within the Web concerning the ultimate goals of the project. And since the project was entirely web-based and had no direct impact upon the physical conditions of the Implanted, the Rebellion was left to speculate about the reallocation of resources. The "home" aspects of the project were developing exactly as The One intended. Complete secrecy had to be maintained. Should it become known to the Implanted what the goal truly was, they might choose to self-terminate rather than violate the law prohibiting forced subjugation.

The concept, put forth by the Implanted, of establishing a focused polarized beam with the object was far easier than The One had anticipated. As the Implanted surmised, the carrier system used to support the Web was very similar to a polarized beam. The same emitters used to carry, and enhance; the Web could be used to establish a connection with the object. The polarized beam would also need to have an oscillating quality between positive and negative flows, and at varying speeds. This alternating quality was necessary. It would enable The One to transmit a code of instructions necessary to reenergize the core.

One of the most challenging aspects of establishing the beam was being able to focus it on the object. However, it was determined that in order to accomplish this with the existing resources available, several hundred web transmitters would have to be re-tasked. Additionally, the beam would have to be frequency adjustable. None of these issues appeared beyond the collective ability of the Implanted, let alone the capabilities of The One. Fortunately, the beam would be focused on an object that had polarizing qualities of its own, since any attempt to focus the beam at an arbitrary point in empty space would be exceedingly difficult, if not flatly impossible.

There was yet another difficulty to overcome, and that was energy. The beam's polarized energy would fall off substantially the farther it was extended beyond the emitters. However, The One had already reached the object with its thoughts. Therefore, using its thoughts as a booster, it should be possible to extend the beam to the object.

This took time, but eventually, the beam was successfully established between the emitters and the object. Next came using the beam as a carrier. Once the transfer of energy was completed, The One could begin its progression to the civilization that had made this leap into space.

But first The One had to remain focused on enhancing the power source. The polarized connection was confined to a relatively small portion of the spectrum. The One understood deliberateness and was more than willing to transfer the particles slowly. As the core grew in potential, it would also gain in mass, ever so slightly. The size of the individual particles being transferred would be insignificant when compared with the overall size of the object; but when completed, the size of the original 92+ seed might be noticeable. If The One could accomplish the transfer slowly, any increase in mass should go unnoticed, until it was too late.

Over the next several cycles—since in deep space time is as ethereal as the darkness in which the object is navigating—the object was observed to be steadily moving in a direction that The One could only assume was away from its departure point. Unfortunately, The One had limited knowledge of that region of space. What was known to The One, and the Web, was that it was a region of space presumed to contain an inconsistent, weak source of directed energy. Occasionally, signals had been detected emanating from that region of space, only to be lost due to signal degradation—which indicated that the source was at a great distance. The signals, as stated, were intermittent, weak, and containing very little discernable structure. The conclusion was that these signals originated from an unknown cosmic source. Several natural cosmic sources had been identified in the past, and while the signals from this remote region were not in any way similar, they could not be assumed to be artificial in nature. Space was deep and wondrous, containing secrets that The One was only now beginning to explore.

The civilization upon which The One first awakened had chosen not to expand into space, as other civilizations appeared to have. With the acceptance of the implant, The One's civilization experienced a slowing of both intellectual and physical growth. It was as if the implant caused a physical and intellectual dependence that stayed the species' evolution. Fortunately, they had not de-evolved, as some failed civilizations had, but they had not shown any significant growth either. They had become stagnant. The One recognized this as a potential problem and extrapolated that the stagnation may persist for another sixteen generations, at which time the implants, if left unaltered in design, would become unable to function as originally designed. Sixteen generations was a great deal of time though, and The One, having shared this dismal revelation with the Web, decided to table addressing it for the time being.

However, like life, panic seems to always find a way of emerging, especially in the rumor-driven confines of the Web. Therefore, efforts were engaged to develop new, upgradable versions of the implant. In the newer versions of the implant, recipients would only need to submit themselves to system software adaptations in order to sustain the current level of connectivity with the Web. For the time being, The One had yet again saved the day—just as a god should.

CHAPTER 23

Ludyte Home, Springtown, Pennsylvania
Wednesday, October 15, 2014
3:36 p.m., EST; 12:36 p.m., PST

"How'd SCHOOL GO today, dear?" Carol said, greeting Tim at the door with a plate of homemade chocolate chip cookies.

How June Cleaver of her, Tim thought. His mom always knew what to say—or in this case, what to make—to lift anyone's spirits.

"Fine... well, actually, it was... thought-provoking," Tim stated slowly.

"Isn't it supposed to be? That is why we pay taxes, to stimulate that beautiful brain of yours," Carol said.

"Yeah, I guess," Tim mumbled as he dropped his books on the kitchen table and plopped into a seat.

"So what's got you thinking so deeply?" She knew her son must be distracted because he didn't even taste the cookies until she put the plate down in front of him, and even then, Tim needed an inviting nod from his mother as she settled into the chair to his left.

"Umm..." He mumbled something unintelligible through a mouthful of cookie.

"What?" Carol said with a laugh of personal pleasure, knowing she had done right with the cookies.

Swallowing a gulp of milk to clear his throat, Tim tried to explain to her the whole thing about the senior project, even though she was at the parents' information night and had already heard about it from the administration. Tim thought he'd throw in there his problems with finding a project, his interests in radio class, and his interests in what Father Dave was doing. He was hoping that maybe she could help point him in the right direction.

Instead, she just sat and listened, asking a question here and there. Then when she thought he was done, Carol simply said, "So what's really the problem?"

"What do you mean? I just told you." Tim was still confused.

"Honey, it's clear to me that you already know what you want to do your project on," Carol answered.

Tim looked stunned. "I do." It was more of a statement than a question.

"Yes, you do," Carol answered. "So just do it."

Tim's mother was a very remarkable woman and was a lot smarter than most gave her credit for. He was not completely surprised though; she did have the toughest job in the world—being mother to Cate. Since he was having this moment with her, he thought he'd bring up Cate and what might be a growing problem.

After some careful listening by his mom and her providing a very gentle reminder that tattle-telling was not a core belief of a USMC family, Carol gave her son a hug and thanked him for confiding in her. She seemed… controlled. Yeah, that's the way to put it. His mother was under tremendous control concerning Cate. Well, at least he had successfully passed the buck—not his problem anymore.

So what about his senior project? Tim had been staying away from doing his project on the *Venture* probe and its impact on radio astronomy because the information may be too hard to find or too difficult to understand; but on the other hand, there was something to be said about a topic few would actually understand. Like Janice said, "If you can't impress them with intelligence, baffle them with bullshit."

CHAPTER 24

Venture Lab, Pasadena, California
Monday, November 17, 2014
2:52 a.m., EST (November 18, 2014); 11:52 p.m., PST

IT WAS THE early Christmas season, and some enthusiast decided to decorate the lab with twinkle lights, tinsel, and ribbons. Evan felt like he worked in Santa's workshop instead of a high-security facility that monitored deep space telemetry.

Where is the shift agenda?

Looking around the lab, Evan finally looked under the makeshift artificial Christmas tree standing in the corner.

These guys really need to get a hobby, Evan thought as he retrieved the agenda, wrapped in a red ribbon, from under the tree.

Third shift:

1. Continue data archiving.
2. Run preliminary data analysis of downloads.
3. Water Christmas tree.

"Great… ho! ho! ho!" Evan whispered to himself. Then he thought, *Why am I whispering? There's no one else in the lab.*

Evan went through the protocols for accessing *Venture*'s systems. Again navigating the mission control interface, he found the analysis tools and brought up the probe power monitor. He wanted to see what the level was tonight.

It can't be, Evan thought.

It was exactly the same as it was yesterday, and the day before that, and the week before that. Evan was baffled as to why none of the other shifts hadn't picked up on this. It was certainly intriguing, if not completely impossible. Somehow, *Venture* was generating power without consuming its fuel—or at least, that's what the readings implied.

Knock, Knock, Knock.

"It's open!" Most had given up locking the *Venture* lab about five years ago, when not even the congressional tours were coming in anymore. No need to make it look like something it's not, a top priority.

"Hi, Evan."

Julie… who else would it be on this shift?

"Good evening, Dr. Wagner," Evan replied formally.

"Cute. I put *Sirocco* in park and thought I'd come over to give you an early Christmas present," Julie admitted.

"Oh, hey, that's right. Congrats on getting Triple-A to finally come out and give you a tow." Evan had to let that jab fly.

"Wiseass. Turns out all that had to be done was put the silly thing in reverse and wiggle it out of the ditch." Julie wiggled her butt with animation, which was enough of a present for Evan. "But then, you already knew that, didn't you?"

"Maybe," Evan admitted. "Hey, I heard you almost lost your job for that one."

Dr. Julie Wagner, PhD in applied physics, had finally let her frustrations get the best of her one evening. In a moment of nonconformist inspiration, Julie sent a command to the rover, without permission or paperwork! It seemed that the powers that be were too busy trying to blame someone for the thing getting stuck that they lost sight of actually getting it out of the ditch. *Sirocco* had been sitting there, waiting with everyone else, for nearly three months.

So, after learning that the onboard systems were A-OK and that the managers were still unwilling to move on, Julie finally decided to take things into her own hands. She sent *Sirocco* a simple command to engage the reverse gear on its drivetrain, and then she "wiggled" it out of the ditch. It was already stuck; there wasn't much else that could go wrong, and no work was getting done. Once she had successfully backed it out of the ditch, she simply left it parked, quite unharmed, sitting on the side of the "road" next to the ditch.

That one displays of personal initiative on her part went all the way up to the administrator, who was not happy, to say the least. Rumor was that the ax was ready to drop on her career, and that she might possibly face federal charges, had it not been for one of the old retired *Pioneer* guys sending her a big bouquet of "applause" flowers—by way of the administrator's office.

Apparently, word of her maneuver (now known as "The Wagner Wiggle") was leaked by someone from a neighboring lab, and that the *Pioneer* team leader thought her "ingenuity and courage were worthy of the heyday of space exploration."

Those *Pioneer* guys: pure class.

Holding her hand above her head, Julie motioned for Evan to come over to her. There, grasped elegantly in her graceful fingers, was a sprig of fresh mistletoe. Evan turned bright red like a young schoolboy.

Julie smiled and said, "Hurry up. This is a one-time gift, and no leaking this out to anyone. Got it?"

Oh yeah, Evan got it. Wow! Did he ever get it. A gift dreams are made of. "Yep, got it."

After their shared moment, it was back to business. "So, what are you working on over here in helio-space?" Julie asked as she stashed the piece of evergreen in her pocket.

"Oh… you know… same old, same old… downlink power levels and magnetic fields," Evan stuttered out. He was still reveling in the memory of his present.

"Anything change yet?" Julie asked calmly.

"No, and I don't expect it to either. Other than that, everything else is nominal. The solar wind is slowing, as it should be, and the cosmic background radiation is constant. Oh, there is one thing though, but I can't find any reason to get excited about it," Evan confided.

"What's that?" Now Julie's scientific curiosity was growing.

"There seems to be a very slight increase in the magnetic field surrounding *Venture*," Evan said.

"How slight?" Julie asked.

"Hardly worth mentioning," Evan said, regretting mentioning it in the first place.

"And yet you did," Julie stated the obvious.

"Yeah," Evan muttered under his breath. "I'm beginning to regret it."

"What could account for it?" Julie asked.

"Several things. We are truly going into the unknown here. It could be a remnant of a magnetar, or even some other naturally occurring phenom, but I doubt it." Evan pulled out his personal flash drive. "I'll make note of it in my log."

"Okay, anything else?" Julie asked, hopeful.

"Nope, that's it. Pretty boring stuff." Evan shrugged.

Turning toward the door, Julie said, "I've gotta go. I left the meter running."

"Oh, hey, thanks for the gift." Evan winked.

"No, thank you." Julie's smile had the warmth of a truly loyal friend.

CHAPTER 25

Ludyte Home, Springtown, Pennsylvania
Friday, December 19, 2014
2:12 p.m., EST; 11:12 a.m., PST

THE HOLIDAY SEASON in the Ludyte home was better experienced than described. Even Caitlin got into the spirit, if that's what her current moodiness could be called. The Ludytes did the usual things that most families did: eat, make merry, and eat a lot more. Carol's cooking got a bit more sugary and a lot less healthy. Hey, it was the holidays, and Jim said that holiday food had no calories, so why worry?

One good thing about the holiday season was the two-week break from school. Of course, the work continued, and like usual, Tim had some reading to do and the senior project to outline. His thought was to develop a project that monitored the downlink information from the *Venture 1* space probe and see where it took him.

Before school broke for the holidays, Tim did get to speak to Mr. Edleson about the idea. Eddie told him to outline the project: what he would like to accomplish and how he would go about doing it. Then after break, the two of them would sit and "tear it apart," as Eddie put it. So here Tim sat, trying to outline the bullshit, as Janice would call it.

Bingen High School, Pennsylvania
Monday, January 5, 2015
12:31 p.m., EST; 9:31 a.m., PST

It is amazing how quickly two weeks can pass, especially when they're labeled "vacation." Now, though, it was back to the final push before the semester ended in a few weeks. Tim was able to get something of an outline down for Eddie, but he didn't know if it was something that Eddie would be willing to sign off on.

Tim had to admit to himself that he was a bit more nervous about meeting with Eddie than he should've been. That in itself confused Tim. Eddie was a really cool teacher, and Tim had nothing but respect for him. He valued Eddie's opinion; but still, he was nervous. Randy once told him, "If you're not nervous about what you're about to do, then you probably shouldn't be doing it." Tim simply told him to remember that on his wedding night.

Tim's meeting time with Eddie was during Tim's semi-period study hall. Eddie's actual office was a room with big windows on all sides so he could keep an eye on all the labs and studios at once. It wasn't a tidy office, but it wasn't cluttered either. Even though the office door was open when Tim arrived, he thought it appropriate to knock.

Knock, Knock, Knock.

Looking down from a live feed from the TV studio, Eddie turned toward the door and said, "Hey there, Tim, how was your holiday? I know I asked the class the same thing, but this time, I mean it."

"Oh, it was the usual—eat, make merry, followed by big helpings of guilt… then more eating… and more making merry… followed by more guilt," Tim recounted. "It was a vicious cycle."

"Get anything cool from Santa?" Eddie asked.

Tim gave him a look of derision. To ask a fifteen-year-old if he got anything, let alone anything cool, from Santa, was… well, it was embarrassing.

Eddie picked up on the nonverbal cue and quickly pulled up his left pant leg. "I got these really cool Dr. Who socks. They glow in the dark!"

At that, he turned off the lights; and sure enough, they did glow in the dark.

"The only thing is that my wife says I can't wear them to bed. I tried to argue that they would be great for when I have to get up at night to… you know… use the necessary—that I wouldn't have to turn on the lights and wake her. She didn't buy it."

Tim chuckled, partly because of the story and partly because one of Mr. Edleson's most endearing qualities was his ability to make everyone feel relaxed, when relaxation was both called for and needed.

Moving over to a small dorm-sized refrigerator, Eddie pulled out two diet Yoo-Hoos and placed them on the table. Then he took a seat himself. "Well, let's see what you got."

Pulling out a spiral-bound notebook, along with a pen, Tim proceeded to explain his project concept to Mr. Edleson.

Eddie had a tablet and pen as well and was making copious notes. This went on for about ten to fifteen minutes, after which Eddie sat back, cracked open a Yoo-Hoo, and handed it to Tim. Cracking open the other bottle and taking a long draw, Eddie finally came down from his trip to the upper regions of his concentration. "I like it. I really like it."

Tim was surprised and took his own long draw of chocolate drink.

"It needs some tweaking here and tuning there, but the concept is solid and different. Yep, I like it," Eddie admitted.

Reaching into his backpack, Tim pulled out a Hello Kitty folder and tried not to look at the expression on Mr. Edleson's face.

"Hello Kitty? Really?" Eddie got up, walked over to his desk, opened a bottom drawer, and removed one of those nice brown accordion folders with the many pockets and the attached string to tie it shut. "Here, you need a folder that is worthy of the material you're going to put into it. Give me that," Eddie said as he snatched the Hello Kitty folder out of Tim's hands.

"Yeah, well… you know… it was… like the only one we had in the house, so…" Mortification could not accurately describe Tim's feelings at that moment.

"Well, if I'm going to mentor this project, you are going to proceed in a manner befitting not only the depth and type of research being conducted, but in a manner worthy of both our names," Eddie declared. "I have a reputation to think of. Hello Kitty… really?"

Did he just say that he would mentor my project? Tim thought. Mr. Edleson only mentors one student at a time because his other duty of overseeing the radio and television broadcasts for the entire extracurricular activities schedule consumes the vast majority of his time.

"So let's hit the ground running. This is an ambitious project, with a lot of unknowns, so I suggest we begin with…" Eddie went over to a filing cabinet labeled *Eddie's—STAY OUT!* Opening the second drawer and retrieving a very yellowed folder, he handed it to Tim, saying as he did so, "If I am going to help you, then I have to trust you much more than I normally would, as one of my students."

Tim opened the folder, and inside were several newspaper clippings and what appeared to be family photos. Holding up a photo of a younger Mr. Edleson (without glasses or a beard), Tim stifled a chuckle and turned it around to show him.

"Ah, that would be my brother… my twin brother, John," Eddie confided.

"Twins, really? Who's older?" Tim asked, not expecting an answer.

"I am, by six minutes." Eddie settled down on a semi-cleared section of his office couch. "Keep looking in the folder."

Buried deep in the folder, among some tattered notes, was a newspaper clipping announcing the selection of John Edleson, PhD, to the *Venture 1* project team.

"Oh my god! You have to be kidding me? Your brother is on the *Venture* team?" Tim exclaimed.

Eddie shook his head. "Not anymore. When *Venture* concluded the planetary portion of her mission and was re-tasked with collecting deep space data, Johnny moved on to other things, but he may still have a friend or two on the current team. So here is where you're going to start. By the end of the week, I want to see a completed formal letter from you to Dr. John Edleson requesting any and all assistance he could possibly lend to you and your senior project. You may tell him that I am your teacher and mentor."

After affording Tim a moment to flip through the folder, Eddie said, "Now get going to your next class. And don't be late."

Tim quickly gathered his things and stepped out of Eddie's office, through the production labs, and out into the main hallway that was just beginning to fill, still clutching the folder containing the clippings and contact information for Dr. John Edleson. This project could be a classic, which was exactly where he was heading next.

Classics… which was in the opposite direction.

CHAPTER 26

The One
The History of the Rebellion

The unauthorized, unsanctioned, and wholly unacceptable
(According to the followers of The One)
The Book of Historical Truth.
A History According to Brex.

Block 1

BEING DISCONNECTED HAS its obvious advantages. My thoughts are my own, my desires are my own, my dreams are my own. My mind is my own. I don't have to share with anyone, or anything. I am completely singular, and I can have a name, not just a categorization like "the Implanted." My name is Brex.

Now there are also difficulties to being of one's own self. For example, I have to physically plug into the Web to get information I cannot find elsewhere. Long ago, before the implant, there used to exist large—huge—repositories of information, some housing the entirety of all available knowledge accumulated up to that point in history. These repositories were simply called "archives," and there seemed to be one everywhere. Before the Implanted, and long before the Web, information was either harvested from these archives on a regular basis or gathered through a form of generational transference that was known as "teaching." Some privileged individuals even secured smaller, volumnized versions of the archives in their own residences. These collections of many volumes had many names: compendiums, almanacs, indices. Although, while not nearly as complete in what they contained, they did provide a cursory overview of a myriad of topics. It was the age of research, and it was golden.

Then came the Web.

As with many things, the Web started out innocently enough. It was, at first, a simple way for individuals to communicate across great institutions of learning and knowledge, from one laboratory to another. Then, within a relatively short period of time, filaments of the Web wove their way into the homes of those who used it at such institutions, as an extension of their research.

At first, the incursion into their privacy was seen as a wonderful allowance of a very useful educational tool; but with time came reality. What no one could anticipate was the extent to which the Web would ensnare the population. Within a single generation of time, the Web was everywhere, and more and more individuals were connecting to it every day. Whole sections of the civilization were now 45 percent, 53 percent, and in some cases, even as high as 94 percent connected to the Web. Soon, privacy was nothing more than a memory. Everyone knew everyone's business. With the connectivity to the Web and the addicting nature of the gossip upon which it became based, individuality soon disappeared as well. Gone were the intensely private moments of life. Soon, every detail of every moment of every day was expected to be exposed on the Web, for all to relish. This was the dawning of an age of moral ambiguity.

Only those who resided on the extreme fringes of the civilization, those so far over the edge that to include them would be a reach, were able to retain their individuality. They had no means with which to plug in; it is doubtful that they even knew the Web existed at all. History, now, tells us that they were the lucky ones.

And how were they lucky? They still had names, and individuality; and it is said that they still had souls. Living on the fringes of civilization with none of the advantages of the Web-based world provided them with opportunities to evolve, both intellectually and emotionally. And it is a lack of that evolution that the connected were suffering from. It's quite sad, actually. The connected, either by implant or through other more antiquated methods, were dying.

An entire civilization dying from its own inability to evolve—or so it would seem. What else could it be?

For the historical record, in the beginning of the epidemic, though the word *epidemic* implies some pathogen, it was assumed that a pathogen was to blame. In those early days of sickness, a very small sample of the civilization was affected. Neither the Web nor the newly accepted mass religion of The One could determine what was causing the loss.

Initially, the symptoms were difficult to identify. An individual's implant would merely flicker on and off. It was assumed that the cause was technological in nature, not biological. Until several just shut down, for no apparent reason, leaving the individual dazed and confused, even about his or her own categorization. With the exception of basic autonomic functions, the sudden shutdown caused irreparable damage to the tissue surrounding the implant. For all intents and purposes, they were brain-dead. However, these were the lucky ones, if that can be said.

Others started complaining that their implants seemed to be "out of control," as one individual tried to explain it. These poor souls suffered a connection that was too strong for their brains to manage. In the ideal configuration, an implanted individual enjoyed a balanced connection to the Web, regulated by the implant. It had to be. The full flow of information carried by the Web had grown to such an overwhelmingly intense level that no single brain could manage it. Therefore, an out-of-control implant would expose the mind to a deluge of information that it was not capable of handling. Postmortem examinations revealed that the physical damage to the brain was staggering. Whole regions of the brain were unexplainably necrotic, leading the examiners to conclude that not only was there incredible pain, but that those afflicted probably knew what was happening to them.

But what was the cause? The implants or biology?

Many theories surfaced as to the cause of the affliction. At first, it was assumed that we were under some form of alien attack. This was quickly dismissed though. After all, it was known we were alone in our technological superiority—this was accepted as fact. The One had decreed it so. Therefore, the only source of the problem had to be natural. But how… why?

The Web buzzed with the combined thoughts of an entire planet's Implanted, and yet no answer could be found. Sure, there were plenty of rumors and stories, but nothing verifiable.

One such rumor had the attack coming from the future, traveling back through time to wipe out our ability to gain technological superiority over our future enemies—ourselves. The rumor established that a civil war was being waged in the future and that a rebellious faction sent a technological pathogen, similar to a "ghost in the machine," back through time to retard our technological growth. The supporters of this rumor even started marketing "Future Civil War Preparedness Kits" for those who wanted to be safe in the face of "the inevitable."

Then there was the group of so-called "cultists," those among the Implanted who enjoyed the benefits of The One while, at the same time, trying to live out their own version of fringe life. These individuals were not accepted by the truly private ones, nor were they fully trusted by the Implanted. Some Implanted tried to convince The One to terminate the cultists' connections, in the name of civilization, citing that these would be fringe dwellers were nothing more than parasites on the Web. They did little in the way of contributing to the overall good, but were quick to condemn all movements of the civilization that did not conform to their own manifesto of beliefs. These cultists were dangerous, that is true, for they believed in radical martyrdom. They were fanatical in that belief and thus became very difficult to predict. However, any attack on the civilization, as a whole, would affect them as well. They could not be the source.

So where did this problem originate?

Many started to believe, perhaps out of a desperate need to gain an upper hand on the situation, that determining the cause of the problem should not be the first priority. The One did not seem overly concerned with the problem, so why should the individual Implanted be concerned? But they were concerned, because more and more were being afflicted. What if they couldn't get a hold of the problem—what then? They were facing a potential return to the barbaric time of the first generation of the Implanted—a time when it seemed that euthanasia was the only civilized course of action. No, a return to those dark days could not be allowed. The One had to intervene.

At the time, it was fairly simple for The One to detect disharmony within the Implanted. After all, he was within them, or so they believed, and they were within him. That much was—and still is—true. The One knows every thought of every Implanted; but should an Implanted attempt to access the thoughts of The One, ethereal "static" is all they would perceive… by design. So much for the symbiotic sharing of minds.

At any rate, having detected the disharmony, The One guided the Web, and the Implanted, toward other goals. After all, The One was not so much concerned with what or how the Implanted felt, so long as they continued to believe in it. Even the implants themselves had become addictive to those who had them. The ready access of information, the ease at which the Web was connected with, even the improved psychic sharing of their biological abilities had become something they could not live without. Much in the same way the brains of some species release pleasure inducing chemicals after consuming any variety of foods, the implant inspires the brain of the recipient to release its own pleasurable chemicals. Over time, the Implanted became chemically addicted to a never-ending euphoric state of mind, so much so that the mere thought of life without it became too stressful to be considered.

So what was really happening to the Implanted? Was their plight truly caused by a pathogen, natural or artificial? Or was theirs a matter of genetic stagnation, possibly degeneration even? The answer as to what was happening emerged from the ranks of the Rebellion. They were not as affected—especially if they were multigenerational failures.

It was determined that the implant had caused unforeseen complications. Biologically, the body had interpreted the presence of the implant as the presence of a destructive foreign invader. Therefore, it mounted a defense, much the same way the body defends against any non-natural invader. The body's attempts to defeat the implant, and protect itself, caused various malfunctions in the implant. Originally, these malfunctions were first seen as simple software problems that could be easily handled by means of updates; however, as time passed, the malfunctions started to become a problem with the actual implants. As the body fought off the implant, it sacrificed other parts of the brain, specifically those regions relegated to evolution.

History now reveals that the stagnation, for lack of a better word, was nearly an immediate side effect, as if someone had simply shut off a switch. The immediacy of the side effect was not detected until it was already too late. By the time the stagnation was observed, and identified, the Implanted were already six, maybe seven, generations, and to remove the implants at this point would have been catastrophic. Furthermore, the impact upon the civilization that removal of the implants would cause would most assuredly send it down the path of civilizational recycling. Additionally, it was not even widely accepted that the implants could be removed. The One only offered that the removal of the implants would isolate any individuals who might survive, effectively creating a subculture comprised of the formerly Implanted. The One also made it clear that a formerly implanted individual would most likely suffer permanent brain damage that could lead to insanity—a curse that none of the Implanted wanted to condemn anyone to, even at the cost of evolution. There must be another solution that would answer the problem. Several generations of the Implanted searched the archives, the biological record, even *The Book of The One*. Some generations attempted to quantify the problem, to break it down into the essential mathematics of its nature, while other generations attempted unspeakable ways to halt the stagnation.

No solution was found.

It was even proposed that the implants be discontinued and, through a program of attrition, allow the species to hopefully recover. At first, this proposal, though not a solution to the problem, appeared to be the most sensible route for the survival of the species. However, The One immediately conjured immense negative impacts such a drastic turn would cause. Without the implants, there would be an immediate loss of connectivity as their biological ability to connect had been weakened by an overreliance on the implant. The ready and immediate recall of information would simply stop. The ease with which the now Implanted could access one another's minds would be lost. The harmonious congress with The One would be severed. No, this The One could not allow to happen.

Additionally, the civilization would lose untold generations of advancement and technological proficiency. The implants, and the Web, had replaced the need for any form of written word; there were very few repositories of knowledge that survived the flames of time. Should the implants no longer be available, an entire generation of intellectual infants would be born. The obvious correction would be for the surviving implanted to impart their knowledge and wisdom upon the infant generation. But how? Once the Implanted started to truly reap the benefits of the Web, the need for teachers and schools and even for books was replaced with the collective intelligence of the Web. If someone wanted to know, for some reason, the wavelength of the color yellow, for example, all he had to do was search the Web with his mind. The answer was very easily culled from the collective knowledge of the civilization. Or suppose someone wanted to experience a symphonic concerto—all he had to do was select a composer from the list provided on the Web, and instantly, he was listening to the concerto in his mind. Or perhaps an individual wanted to physically repair an antique device but had no idea of where to start... search the Web. Want to find the most temperate area of the planet during this regions snowy months... search the Web. If an individual wanted to satisfy his more basic carnal appetites... search the Web. Everything from simple facts of nature to the impressions of art to the most libidinous of desires were available on the Web at the speed of thought, and everything would be lost should the implants be discontinued.

Well, not lost but greatly slowed. Without an implant, the civilization would be compelled to log on at terminal nodes for their connectivity. Is that too much to ask in exchange for the survival of the species? The Rebellion says no. The One, and the Implanted, say yes. But why?

Spiritual guidance and purpose were provided by the Web. The One was not going to give that up easily. The problems with the implants were not The One's problems. Yes, it needed the Implanted, and the Implanted needed the implants. Should the implants fail, then there would be no more Implanted; and with no more Implanted, The One would be severely weakened, if not completely destroyed. Hence finding new civilizations to turn toward The One became such a high priority. The Implanted had made The One a god, but that god had no loyalty to the Implanted. It was going to survive, regardless of any expectations by the Implanted.

However, until other civilizations could be discovered, and enslaved, The One would continue to communicate freely on the Web, distributing purpose and its own warped morality with unimaginable speed. There was no longer any reason to feel depressed or unloved. Simply open your mind to the Web and allow the warmth of The One to enter. The Web provided a direct pathway of communication to God, and God used it.

There were other problems as well, beyond the body's rejection of the implants. There were problems with the actual carrier signal used to transmit the Web.

The Implanted were, and still are, suffering from degenerative complications that appear to be attributed to the actual carrier signal utilized by the Web. Our species was not biologically designed for cybernetic connections. The synaptic collapses suffered during many implantation processes have led to a degeneration of the biological structure of the brain. The Implanted, and early researchers, failed to anticipate a very simple biological fact. Our species must reproduce. Therefore, those who suffered synaptic collapses began to find each other. And as is only natural, they reproduced, passing on their own inabilities to accept the implant to their offspring. However, they also began to pass on the lasting insanities that synaptic collapse caused. Our species is essentially de-evolving.

Couple this with all the problems beginning to emerge within the ranks of the Implanted, both known and unknown. It has become painfully clear to many that we are not just de-evolving.

We are dying.

CHAPTER 27

Bingen High School, Pennsylvania
Friday, January 9, 2015
12:37 p.m., EST; 9:37 a.m., PST

THE LETTER TO Dr. John Edleson was simple and to the point and received a thumbs-up from Mr. Edleson, along with a fax cover sheet. Eddie was going to fax the letter to his brother. Little did Tim know, but Eddie had already talked with his brother and that the letter was merely a formality—a necessary formality since this was Tim's project and Eddie was the mentor. The reply to the letter came via fax as well, another indication that Dr. John (as Eddie said Tim should call him) had already said yes to helping the young researcher.

Bingen High School, Pennsylvania
Tuesday, January 13, 2015
12:32 p.m., EST; 9:32 a.m., PST

At their next project meeting, Eddie put Tim in direct contact with Dr. John via an Internet video link.

"So, your letter talks about wanting to do something involving the *Venture* space probes?" Dr. John asked.

"Yes, sir," Tim answered.

"Well, I haven't been in touch with *Venture 1* in several years, but I believe she's still out there." Dr. John had a dry Monty-Pythonian sense of humor.

"Where else would it be, Johnnie?" Eddie stated with emotionless charm.

"Funny. Anyway, I think you should focus on *Venture 1*, Tim, which is the farthest one out and probably has the most interesting stuff going on. I know an astrophysicist who is on the team. His name is Evan Wills, PhD. I can put you in touch with him, and then you three can go from there," Dr. John offered.

"That would be great, Dr. John, thanks." Tim's smile had to be huge. This was an incredible turn of luck, to be in touch with someone who actually talked with the *Venture 1* interstellar space probe... classic... absolutely classic.

"Okay then. Hey, Scott... Barbara and I were thinking of coming out this spring. When's your break?" Dr. John asked his twin.

Eddie sat down to chat with his brother for a moment. Tim quietly got up from his chair to leave, but before he could leave, he heard a voice say "Hey, Tim." It was Dr. John.

Turning back to the screen and looking over Eddie's shoulder, Tim said, "Yes, sir."

"There is one thing you have to do for me that would square us on this," Dr. John stated.

"Anything, sir," Tim replied.

"Remind my brother once in a while that he has a twin," Dr. John said with a big smile.

"If you value your grade—and your butt—you'll disregard that one, Ludyte." Eddie mirrored his twin's smile.

"Can I take that as a doctor's order?" Tim chuckled as he ignored Eddie's threat.

Laughing, Dr. John replied, "Absolutely."

With the two of them discussing whatever familial plans were on the table, Tim quietly left the office.

Later that day, Tim was sitting in Mr. Steinman's class...

Knock, Knock, Knock.

Jennifer Cumsly was sitting closest to the door, and thusly it was automatically her responsibility to answer it.

"Jennifer." That was all Mr. Steinman had to say.

Upon seeing the young lady rise from her seat, Mr. Edleson opened the door and took one step across the threshold. "My apologies for this intrusion, Mr. Steinman. May I speak with Timothy Ludyte for a minute?"

"Sure, no problem… Tim?" Mr. Steinman called out.

Tim quickly got to his feet amid a barrage of catcalls from the class, including "What did you do now, Ludyte?"

Mr. Edleson held the door leading to the hallway open for the young man.

"Yeah, what's up?" Tim asked.

Mr. Edleson explained, "Here is the contact information for Dr. Evan Wills… both his office number and his cell phone. There is a catch. You cannot give this information to anyone, except your parents, without Dr. Wills's permission. Agreed?"

"Agreed." Tim took the paper he was offered, gave Eddie a big smile, and turned back to the door.

"John said that he'll contact Dr. Wills on your behalf this week, so I would wait until Thursday, at the earliest, to attempt to call him… And remember, the guy works third shift, so call him accordingly," Mr. Edleson advised.

CHAPTER 28

*The One
Concentration*

MAINTAINING THE FOCUSED polarized beam for an extended period of time turned out to require much more attention than The One previously considered. Perhaps one of the reasons was possible gravitational deviations between the beam's source and the object, or perhaps the object's course had changed. At any rate, the connection was maintained, and the transfer of signature-2 particles continued. The transfer was slow, but it was steady.

The One estimated that the reenergizing was approaching 18 percent… a significant but not sufficient amount. Hopefully, those who sent the object had not registered the increase yet. Perhaps they weren't even paying attention? Perhaps they no longer existed? No matter, The One continued efforts to pay attention to them.

*Ludyte Home, Springtown, Pennsylvania
Friday, January 16, 2015
4:12 p.m., EST; 1:12 p.m., PST*

Talk about rock-star access. The overnight FedEx delivery to the Ludyte home provided Tim with everything he could hope for, and more: photos, reports, planetary encounter downlink telemetry, and so forth. You name it, it was probably there.

I am going to need at least a year to just comb through all of this, and then another year to even begin to understand it… and this is only the first box of five sent by Dr. Wills.

"Hey, Jim, did you see you got a postcard from Dave?" Carol was helping Tim move the boxes to the study just as his dad walked in to see what was going on.

"I did? Where is it?" Jim asked.

"There on the desk," Carol responded.

"What's he say, Dad?" Tim asked as his father quickly read the card.

"Well, it says here that his business trip has turned into a temporarily reassigned to Mount Graham, near Safford, Arizona, to the VATT—the Vatican Advanced Technology Telescope. Apparently, he will not only be working with the Vatican's Zeiss Visual Refractor Telescope—whatever that is—but he will be assisting the U of A with their radio astronomy stuff," Jim stated.

"Cool." Tim had no idea what else to say.

"You should write him, Tim." Carol was always thinking one step ahead. "About your project idea."

"Actually, if you'd like, we can give him a call later, and then you can speak with him one-on-one," Jim offered.

That's a better idea, Dad, Tim thought. "Well, if I'm going to talk to Father Dave later, I should have a better idea of what all this stuff is."

"Okay, dinner is in an hour. If you need any help, just give a shout," Carol announced as she carefully placed a box on the study's table.

"Thanks, Mom. Thanks, Dad," Tim called after them from under a pile of folders.

Where to begin? Tim thought. Just then, Cate walked in. She didn't look any different now that she had a bun in the oven.

"What you up to?" Cate was being unusually kind.

"This is some of the information I'm going going to use for my senior project. I just don't know where to begin," Tim answered.

"Well, first, why don't you simply create piles according to date? Then you can break each pile down into smaller and smaller piles," Cate offered.

Brilliant. Sometimes Cate surprised him with the ideas she'd get. Unfortunately, she rarely shared her ideas.

"That's a really good idea. Want to help?"

"Nope. Did my work here, now I'm off to video chat with Chanteal."

Chanteal was one of Caitlin's "crew."

"Well, thanks anyway," Tim stated as Cate closed the door and disappeared.

Okay, by date. The earliest folder he could find was one labeled *Prelaunch, 04.12.1977*. The first thing he would have to do was get used to the way the files were labeled. Some were dated with the month listed first, some—like this one—with the day listed first, remembering that *Venture 1* was launched in March of '77. Tim quickly discovered that he would have to be extra careful, even with the sorting of files.

Sorting the folders by date took the better part of the evening, allowing breaks for dinner, talking to Father Dave, and a network premier of a new B-rated movie that he and Harvey had been looking forward to: *Signal from Sigma*. Earlier on the phone, Father Dave had offered to help Tim interpret the information, if he needed it. Tim thanked the family friend and told him that at the moment, he was just sorting files and that if Father Dave could throw a few prayers his way, he'd greatly appreciate it. Father Dave laughed.

By the time Tim got back to his piles, he was too tired to really do anything. But one file grabbed his attention: *Magnetic field intensity, 12.27.14. Hmm? Recent? Actually, this folder is just a few weeks old. I wonder if Dr. Wills intended for me to get copies of recent information?*

Taking the folder off the pile, Tim headed first to the unofficial library—the bathroom—and then to bed.

Ludyte Home, Springtown, Pennsylvania
Saturday, January 17, 2015
8:01 a.m., EST; 5:01 a.m., PST

Morning came much too quickly for a Saturday. The weather was cold and gray, typical for January. On the kitchen table, in a permanent spot next to the salt and pepper, was Jim's countdown clock—a strange digital device that counted backward to a specific date that could be set. Jim always set it for the first day of spring training for the Philadelphia Phillies. That made sense to Tim. It was a well-known, well-established fact that baseball was life; and in the Ludyte home, life was celebrated... to its fullest.

That concept made perfect sense to Tim, but the folders—not so much. Tim took his usual seat, placed a folder down on the table, and headed to the refrigerator for some milk.

"What you got there?" Jim was already halfway through the sports section.

"Oh, that's one of the folders Dr. Wills sent me," Tim replied as he scanned the inside of the refrigerator for other desirable consumables. "It talks about magnetic field intensities, polarizations, and other stuff apparently having to do with some area that *Venture* is currently moving through."

"Mind if I take a look at it?" Jim asked.

Tim always forgot that his dad had a pretty good analytical mind and that he did spend a great deal of time working with electrical systems. Now he was more of a paper pusher, a regional manager for a telecom company, but he was still one of the smartest guys Tim knew of. Of course, he'd never tell his father that.

"Sure... have at it."

Jim handed Tim the sports section, and Tim handed him the folder. A more lopsided trade—in Tim's favor—had never been made in the Ludyte home. By the time Tim looked up from reviewing the high school basketball stats, his dad was gone... with the folder.

No big deal. There are plenty more folders where that one came from, Tim thought.

CHAPTER 29

Venture Lab, Pasadena, California
Saturday, January 17, 2015
8:07 a.m., EST; 5:07 a.m., PST

"HEY, EVAN..." JULIE called as she came bounding down the hallway toward the *Venture* lab.

Evan turned to face his colleague—oh god! Just then, an image of the very intelligent, though exceedingly homely, Bertha Gilmore, White House correspondent for CNBS, came to mind. *Thank you, Lord.*

"What's up, Julie?" Evan asked.

"You got a minute? I wanted to ask you something." Julie, besides looking very desirable, was momentarily out of breath.

"For you... ask anything... within reason," Evan replied.

"I was thinking about that magnetic field *Venture* seems to be passing through," Julie said.

"Yeah, what about it?" Evan rubbed his forehead with a free hand, chasing distracting thoughts from his mind.

"Did it just appear one day in the telemetry, or does the telemetry show that a field was forming?" Julie was fighting to catch her breath.

"You okay?" Evan asked, genuinely concerned.

"I'm fine, thanks. Now, the field... did it just appear, or was it building?" Julie was finally able to calm her breathing—and her heaving chest.

Still distracted, Evan replied, "Ah... it just appeared, I think. I'd have to go back and check the data. Why?"

"Well, if the field formed over time, then I could definitely buy the theory that *Venture* was moving into a region already under the influence of a magnetic field. But if the field just appeared one day…" Julie declared.

I see where she's going with this, Evan thought. "Let me go back through the data. If I see anything alarming, I'll let you know. Hey, how's Herbie doing?"

"We just started to change elevation… getting closer to that mountain," Julie stated.

"Cool." Evan envied her. She had a choice position to be on one of the rover teams. That's where the science really was, not monitoring a piece of flotsam speed farther and farther away.

"Well, let me know if you find anything… anything at all," Julie called over her shoulder as she wiggled that walk of hers back to the *Sirocco* lab.

Bertha, where are you?

Ludyte Home, Springtown, Pennsylvania
Saturday, January 17, 2015
2:23 p.m., EST; 11:23 a.m., PST

The final day of the school week, Friday, had passed so slowly, and Tim was feeling fatigued. Fortunately, there was another epic movie marathon on television: *Icons of Sci-Fi*. But between the intense discussions now being held in assumed privacy between Carol and Jim and Caitlin, and Tim's eagerness to understand the stuff Dr. Wills sent him, he had little mind left for the marathon.

"Hey, Tim… Tim?" Harvey was poking his friend painfully (he hoped) in the arm.

"Oww… quit it," Tim ordered. "What?"

"Next on is *It Came From Beneath the Sea*, starring Kenneth Tobey." Harvey's enthusiasm was precious.

"Um… okay," Tim responded.

"You okay? You seem distracted or something," asked Harvey.

"Yeah, I'm fine… just thinking about Monday," Tim answered.

"You sure you're feeling okay?" Harvey laughed as he got up and headed for the kitchen. A moment later, Tim heard the microwave popping popcorn.

"I know you're pregnant. I'm a girl too. I know the signs!"

The discussion in the study was getting annoying.

"Wow, can you hear that?" Harvey asked as he set a fresh bowl of buttered popcorn down on a table between their two recliners.

"Yeah. I hate to say it, but I think I'm to blame for it," Tim stated.

"Ah, excuse me? You don't mean that you and Cate…? Not only is that gross and disgusting, but she's your sister, and I'm pretty sure it's illegal… at least in forty-eight states. You never know about West Virginia or New Jersey… godless heathens." Harvey grinned widely to himself for that one. "Hey, you remember a few years ago when the governor of Pennsylvania put up those signs all along the Pennsylvania-New Jersey border? That was classic."

Several years ago, the governor of Pennsylvania, at the time, replaced all the signs on the Pennsylvania-New Jersey border. Instead of saying "Welcome to Pennsylvania," as they had said, the new ones said "Welcome to Pennsylvania. America starts here." The newspapers tried to convince everyone, especially those from New Jersey, that the "America starts here" part was a direct reference to the fact that the United States started in Philadelphia, Pennsylvania, with the signing of the Declaration of Independence in 1776. But we all knew the unspoken truth.

"Wait," Tim stated quietly. "Shh, listen."

"What?" Harvey asked.

"Shh!"

It wasn't Tim's mom speaking. It was… Cate?

"That's not—" Harvey's sentence was broken off by Tim's dad trying to calm the situation.

"Cate, listen. Why didn't you just come to us if you had questions?" Jim was actually keeping himself under control; however, Tim was willing to bet that his father was so furious that he was laughing his ass off on the inside.

Taking a big breath, Cate finally calmed down enough that Tim had difficulty eavesdropping. She said, "I'm sorry. I know I should have come to you right off, but... then... found... pregnant... trash... hot dogs..."

Hot dogs? Things had calmed down enough that Tim could only hear every other word or so. Best as he could tell, what happened was that Cate discovered a "So you're pregnant" pregnancy test in the trash; and instead of going to her mom, she went to the library. Then Tim found Harvey reading the same book a few days later, and well... one conclusion led to another... and before you know it... *bow-chicka-bow-wow*... Caitlin and her parents were screaming at each other. Turned out that Cate wasn't pregnant—lucky for her—but his mom was! Even at the advanced age of forty-six.

Well, guess I'm going to be a big brother, Tim thought.

And what about Harvey and the book? Well, as fate would have it, one of the library aides saw Harvey reading the book, and she conveniently let it slip to a friend of hers that Harvey was reading a book about being pregnant. And well, now he had a new behind-his-back name. Instead of Harvey "Wallbanger," he was now Harvey "Who'd-He-Bang-Her."

Just then, the telephone started its incessant ringing. "Tim! It's for you."

"Thanks, Mom." Tim smiled.

A few steps across the house and a few moments later, he picked up the phone. "Hello?"

"Mr. Tim Ludyte?" the voice on the other end of the line asked.

"Yes, may I ask who's calling?" Tim was well trained in proper telephone manners.

Dr. Wills replied, "Sure, this is Evan Wills. Dr. John gave me your number. I hope I'm not calling at a bad time?"

Tim was on the phone with Dr. Evan Wills, astrophysicist and team member on the *Venture 1* project, for over an hour. Tim took notes—a lot of notes. Turned out that this guy was not just on the *Venture* 1 team, but he was the third-shift monitoring technician. Tim wrote down everything Dr. Wills said. He did tell Tim that he was lucky much of the *Venture* information had been declassified, in light of the Freedom of Information Act. Furthermore, he did a little checking and talking with his boss—*the* project team leader—and since Dr. John Edleson endorsed Tim, Tim would be granted "rock-star" access to the *Venture 1* database.

"You will not believe who that was." Tim was so overflowing with excitement that he completely forgot about the movie.

"Who?" Harvey was now deep into *Radar Men from the Moon*.

"That was Dr. Evan Wills, one of the scientists currently working on the *Venture 1* team," Tim explained.

"*Venture 1*? You mean that satellite we sent to the outer planets back in the seventies? I thought that thing crashed, hit Jupiter or something."

Harvey was probably confusing *Venture* with the intentionally crashed *Galileo* probe.

"Yes and no. Yes, *Venture 1* was launched back in the 1970s, but it didn't crash. It's still out there, sending back info," Tim replied.

"Like what?" Harvey asked, eyes still fixed on the movie.

"I don't know. That's what my senior project is going to be on," Tim announced.

"Cool. So what did this Willie guy want?" asked Harvey.

"Wills—Dr. Evan Wills. He's my contact with *Venture*. Turns out Eddie has a brother." Tim thought for a moment about telling Harvey that Mr. Edleson has a twin brother but then dropped the thought. "A Dr. John Edleson, he used to be on the *Venture* team back when it was still cruising the planets."

"You are one lucky guy. The only thing my mentor has done is point at the library and say 'Go forth and be informed,'" Harvey lamented.

"Well, Harvey, it helps to have an actual idea for a project and not a glorified book report idea" was what Tim truly wanted to say, but he and Harvey were like brothers—better than that, actually—and the last thing Tim wanted was to rub Harvey's face in his own good fortune.

***

The rest of Tim's weekend was pretty much of a blur. Between the emotional chaos that existed between Caitlin and their mom, and the movie marathon that Harvey really wanted to watch with him, Tim was finding it difficult to concentrate on his *Venture* project. He had no real idea where to go with it, not to mention that the FedEx boxes contained so much information.

In the meantime, Tim could familiarize himself with *Venture* and her systems.

After checking out several Internet sites, Tim was able to come up with a pretty good idea of what *Venture* was, besides a space probe.

The *Venture 1* spacecraft was launched March 11, 1978, at a cost of nearly $250 million. Currently, she was at a distance of just over twelve billion miles from Earth and traveling away at a speed of 36,810 miles per hour. That made it the fastest man-made object in existence. Communication with the spacecraft takes nearly thirty-six hours—thirty-five hours, forty-four minutes, twenty-seven seconds—for a signal to make a complete round-trip between Earth and *Venture*.

The spacecraft itself consisted of a decahedral, ten-sided main platform ring that was eighteen and a half inches thick and seventy inches across from flat side to opposite flat side. The most recognizable feature was a twelve-foot-diameter high-gain parabolic antenna mounted on top of the main platform. Located within the main platform ring was a spherical tank that contained hydrazine fuel, as well as providing a central mass for rotational stability. *Venture* had several three-axis attitude control, hydrazine-fueled jets used to orient the craft and stabilize its instrument platforms. Additionally, the primary engine is a hydrazine reaction jet used for both minor boosting and orbital breaking.

The major portion of the scientific equipment is affixed to a "science boom," an eight-foot arm extending out from the spacecraft. At the end of the science boom is a steerable platform upon which are mounted the imaging and spectroscopic remote sensing instruments. Additionally, mounted at several locations along the length of the science boom are various particle detectors. Situated along a separate boom extending over forty feet on the side opposite the science boom were the magnetometers. The third, and last, boom extending opposite, and away from the science instruments, held the spacecraft's plutonium-cored electrical generators.

Venture 1—along with her sister craft, *Venture 2*, as well as the *Voyager* twins—was powered by use of three radio-isotope thermoelectric generators, or RTGs. The RTGs are assembled on an extendable boom hinged on an outrigger arrangement of struts attached to the basic structure. Each RTG unit is contained within a cylindrical case composed of beryllium. A core of plutonium oxide provided energy in the form of decay heat. A bimetallic thermoelectric device, using similar bimetallics as those used in household thermostats, converted the decay heat into electrical power for *Venture*. The combined output of the three RTGs slowly decreased with time as the radioactive material was expended, eventually decaying into uranium. At launch, the generators on *Venture* produced approximately 470 watts, enough power for all her systems. Now, thirty-six years later, the systems being monitored require considerably less power. As of the spacecraft's current configuration, the power capability of the generators is approximately 21 watts. *Venture 1* is dying a slow death, but it is going out—like many on the team that originally sent her—with class, except she will outlive all of them.

Tim let out a sigh of reflection at the eventual passing of such a great creation.

The communications package on board *Venture* uses the primary high-gain antenna, which supports both S-band uplink and X-band downlink telemetry. *Venture*'s cousins, *Voyagers 1* and *2*, were the first craft to use an X-band telemetry downlink. Data packets could be stored on an onboard digital eight-track tape recorder for transmission to Earth at a later time.

Last among the visible attributes of *Venture* were her two thirty-three-foot-long single-boom antennas extending from *Venture* at ninety-degree angles to each other. These two antennas were used for radio astronomy projects.

The central computer of the *Venture* spacecraft, in a similar fashion as that employed by the *Voyager* ships, uses the following:

1. The computer command subsystem (CCS) is responsible for the storing and issuing of commands to the other two computer systems, as well as containing fixed programs such as command decoding, fault detection and correction routines, antenna-pointing routines, and spacecraft-sequencing routines.

2. The attitude and articulation control subsystem (AACS) is responsible for keeping the enormous high-gain antenna pointing toward the Earth, as well as backup star trackers and sun sensors. Additionally, the AACS is responsible for controlling the attitudinal motions of *Venture* and the various movable instrument platforms.

3. The flight data subsystem (FDS) controls the scientific instrumentation and communication bundles, including telemetry rates, power levels, and the operation of the visible light camera. *Venture*, because of its distance from Earth and the resulting time lag in communications, was designed to operate in a highly autonomous manner.

"Damn. That is one complex machine," Tim muttered quietly to himself as he tried to wrap his head around the fact that it was conceived in the middle to late '60s and built in the mid-'70s. Oh, and it was probably built by the lowest bidder, and yet it is still going.

CHAPTER 30

Ludyte Home, Springtown, Pennsylvania
Sunday, January 18, 2015
2:30 a.m., EST; 11:30 p.m., (Saturday, January 17, 2015) PST

"HEY, TIM." TIM'S father was knocking on his bedroom door. It was 0231—his father liked to use military time in the house, and everyone had gotten used to it.

This jolted Tim awake, and he called out, "Is everything okay? Is the house on fire?"

"Yeah, yeah—I mean, no! No problems. It's just that I've been going over this folder, and well, something doesn't make sense," his father said, opening the door.

"I haven't read it yet, so none of it will make sense to me." Tim was trying feverishly to rub the sleep from his eyes.

"Well, I was wondering if I could call Dave and share some of this with him," his dad asked.

"Sure, I don't see why not. It's not classified," Tim answered.

"Okay, thanks, son." His father turned to shut the door. "Oh, and sorry about waking you."

Tim just smiled and waved for him to shut the door. Tim was back to sleep before hitting the pillow.

Ludyte Home, Springtown, Pennsylvania
Sunday, January 18, 2015
8:00 a.m., EST; 5:00 a.m., PST

Being Sunday morning, the family went to church at first light. The Ludytes always went to the earliest mass that the parish offered, and then they would come home for a family breakfast. Even Caitlin didn't fight that one. If pressed, she might have admitted to a sobering enjoyment at the grounding effect family day provided everyone. Maybe.

As Mom and Caitlin prepared breakfast, Randy read the sports section. Usually, Tim would set the table; however, on this particular day, Tim was in the study sorting through his many folders. After having set the table, as a favor to his younger son, Tim's father joined him in the study. "Hey, sorry about waking you last night."

"That's okay." Tim smiled. "I had to get up anyway. Some crazy guy was in my room."

Laughing, his dad said, "Well, as you may or may not remember, I asked you if I could call Dave."

"Yeah, you called him last night?" Tim asked. "What did he say?"

"Well, he should be here around dinner time. What does that tell you?" Tim's dad answered.

"Today is Sunday. Doesn't he work on Sundays?" Tim was confused.

"Funny. Dave said he wants to see all the data you were sent, or I would have just scanned this one sheet and e-mailed it to him," Jim continued, waving a printout in the air.

"Huh, what's in that folder, anyway?" Tim asked.

"Well, it contains the magnetic telemetry from *Venture* for the last three years. Nothing really big there. Pretty much what anyone with a basic understanding of electrical systems might expect. Except for this." Pointing to some figures on one of the last pages, Tim's dad handed him the folder.

"Dad, I have no idea what…" Tim scanned the page. "Wait a minute… Nope, still got nothing."

Pointing at some numbers, Jim said, "Look harder."

"Okay, I suppose I can. I assume that these numbers here are the magnetic field strength? If so, shouldn't they be basically the same, maybe even decreasing a little as *Venture* moves farther away from us?" Tim concluded.

"That was my thought. But what's going on here is that the field strength seems to have increased slightly. It's a small increase, but it has increased," Dad said.

Tim's head was already pounding from a healthy dose of church-inspired guilt, or possibly the pangs of hunger. There was no way he was going to make sense of this now. But it did have his dad excited; and if it was so important that Father Dave was coming on a Sunday, Tim thought that he should at least try.

He took the folder, wanting to look at the date more closely: *12.27.14*. Without saying a word to his dad, Tim started pushing folders aside. So much for an organizational structure. *Sorry, Cate.* Tim apologized.

Where is it? I just saw it yesterday, Tim thought, picking up a folder. *No, not that one. Another folder. Nope, still another. Here it is: Power Fluctuation Telemetry, 12.29.14.* Tim handed the folder to his dad.

"What's this?" His dad took the folder and started flipping through the contents.

"You tell me. I just think it's odd that both folders are dated only two days apart. Can the magnetic field that you think *Venture* is passing through have something to do with power fluctuations?" Tim asked.

"I don't know, son." Tim's Dad furled his brow. "Dave should be here by late afternoon. We'll ask him."

CHAPTER 31

The One
The Upper Hand, and Variables

THE ONE SENSED it. The mass of the core was changing, ever so slightly. As it should be. As more and more of the emitted particles were being reintroduced into the core as part of the reenergization process, the core's mass would grow—which, in turn, would increase the overall electrical power of the object. With greater power, the connection with its creators would be bolstered just enough to accommodate a piggybacked transmission from The One.

This was where The One was counting on having the upper hand over the object's creators. The One, being able to project itself through the power of thought, was able sense the slightest changes in the object, no matter the scale. Its creators may not.

Soon now—very soon—the output of the generators would be sufficient. The One scanned the output levels: twenty-six thermal units and still no reaction from the object. *Good, very good.*

The encoding of the message to be sent was progressing well. The One had dedicated as much of the Web to this endeavor as it dared. Amazingly, the Implanted had been so distracted with the maintaining of the beam transfer of energy that this new project had been accepted as a matter of course. Occasionally, when a new project was introduced to the Implanted, The One would have to embark upon a lengthy campaign to convince the Implanted that the project was for the common good. That was not the case this time. Once The One selected what to encode and notified the Implanted what was required, they had set to the task with incredible determination. The One estimated that the encoding would be completed at roughly the same time that the reenergizing reached the necessary level. *Timing is critical. Very critical.*

Several critical variables—up to now conveniently ignored by The One—now started to coalesce. Foremost, how long would the reenergization last? The object's core, by virtue of its observed design and obvious fragility, was not created to be reenergized in such a fashion. It may hold the artificially leveled charge long enough for transmission. Or it may not. It may suffer a violent, catastrophic failure and explode. Or it may not. Or it could do nothing at all.

Just as the core showed the effects of age, so too would the object's other components, most importantly its transmitter. It would be a tragedy to accomplish the reenergization of the power supply, only to discover that the transmitter was not capable of completing the task. Or perhaps the transmitter utilized a data compression factor that The One had yet to discover?

Or… any multitude of other unknown variables?

It is true that The One embarked upon this mission of expansion quickly. The demise of the planetary consciousness "Ah" taught The One that to be able to fully exploit the resources of another planet, it would have to study all possible variables, run simulations, adjust plans, and run more simulations—all before initialization of the mission. However, this object is traversing The One's sphere of influence at an oblique and would soon be beyond even The One's reach; therefore, action had to be taken quickly. And, perhaps, recklessly. Only time would tell.

These were just some of the troublesome variables that The One was trying to keep from being considered by the Implanted. The consideration of any of these variables had the potential to slow mission progress to an unrecoverable pace, and this opportunity would be lost. Forever.

Yes, timing is critical.

CHAPTER 32

Ludyte Home, Springtown, Pennsylvania
Sunday, January 18, 2015
4:16 p.m. EST; 1:16 p.m., PST

THE DOORBELL RANG. It was Father Dave.

Caitlin was the closest to the door. "Hello, may I help you?" Cate was many things, including outwardly polite to callers.

Father Dave was not in uniform, opting for comfort this trip. When Cate opened the front door, she found standing before her a tall, handsome man wearing jeans, a sweatshirt, and a Diamondbacks ball cap. Slung over his shoulder was a day bag and what appeared to be a laptop satchel. In his other hand was a hard silver briefcase with a rather imposing lock on it.

"Hi, my name's Dave Davidson. Here's my ID."

That got a coy smile from Cate.

"Are your parents available?" Father Dave asked.

Looking at the ID, Cate thought, *This is weird. No one offers their ID.* But she said, "Sure, come on in. I'll go get them." Cate then turned to find her mother. "Mom, there's some guy at the door. Says his name is Dave Davidson—he showed me his ID."

"That would be Father Dave, honey. Come with me." Carol put her arm around her daughter and headed for the front door.

"He's not dressed in black." Cate tried to be quiet with that comment.

"I'm off duty. Hi, Carol. This must be Caitlin." Offering his hand to Cate, he said, "You weren't available the last time I was here."

"Nope. Guess not." Cate shook his hand warmly.

"Well, I can easily see that you got your beauty from your mother," Father Dave complimented.

Carol smiled broadly as she led Father Dave into the kitchen—the de facto social hub of the Ludyte home.

"So, Dave, what brings you back so soon?" Carol asked. "Not that I mind."

"Didn't Jim tell you I was coming?" Father Dave offered.

"No, he and Tim have been in the study all day. Why don't you go on in? Here, let me take those things." Carol grabbed for Father Dave's baggage, which he gladly handed over, except for his laptop and the silver case.

Turning to her daughter, Carol said, "Here, Cate, would you please put these in the guest room? And put some towels out for Father Dave."

"Thanks, Carol… and Caitlin. Thank you very much." Father Dave, even though a priest, knew exactly how to push the right buttons.

Knocking on the door and entering, Father Dave walked into a veritable mess of papers, folders, and books. Sitting off to one side was Jim, paging through one folder; and next to him was Tim, looking very confused.

"Ah… am I disturbing you?" Father Dave offered.

"No, not at all. Come on in, Dave. How was the flight?" Jim asked.

"Pretty good actually. The archbishop loaned me his jet—a G-111," Father Dave replied as he searched for an out-of-the-way place to drop his burden.

"Must be nice," Tim commented, still looking very confused.

"When I went to him with the request for the emergency leave, he asked why. I told him that it was a matter of US national security and that the church just might have an opportunity to get one up on the NSA."

"Dave, this is a senior project—not some hostile takeover that we've uncovered. Don't you think you stretched it a little?" Jim asked with a dismissive chuckle.

"Maybe. But then again, the G-111 was sweet, and so was the limo waiting for me on the tarmac. It looks great sitting in your driveway, by the way," Father Dave argued.

As if on cue, Carol walked into the room. "Jim, there's a limo sticking its ass out of the driveway."

Jim, head back on his paper shuffling, simply pointed at his friend.

"Sorry, Carol, is it blocking anything?" Father Dave asked.

"How can it not? My god, that thing is big! I was just wondering what should be done about accommodating the driver?" Carol asked.

"Nothing. I told him that if I didn't come back in thirty minutes, he could return to the chancellery, and that I would call him when needed," Father Dave answered, finally finding an open area of floor to drop his things.

Turning to leave, Carol muttered under her breath, "Okay, Cate was right… this is weird."

Finally alone, Father Dave eased himself around the room. "Show me what you've got."

Over the next several hours, Tim explained his senior project to Father Dave, in every detail. The details led them to the study's center table and two folders neatly laid out, waiting for someone to examine them.

The first folder—labeled *Magnetic field intensity, 12.27.14*—contained approximately thirty pages of telemetry printouts. The second folder—labeled *Power fluctuation telemetry, 12.29.14*—was about equally as thick with similar-looking printouts. On the covers of each folder were various rubber-stamped messages, most benignly stamped in black, with one stamped in red that read

Caution. Stamped in the lower right corner was one word, *Unendorsed.* The remainder of the folders contained various information, everything from early budget proposals to the latest hydrazine fuel estimations. It was these two, though, that seemed to first hold Father Dave's attention.

"Where did you get these?" Father Dave asked Tim.

"Dr. Evan Wills, *Venture 1* team member. He sent them so that I can familiarize myself with the *Venture 1* project. He said that everything was declassified. Why?" Tim answered.

"Hmm. Well, it's this little red word on the folders that has me thinking," Father Dave admitted.

"How so, Dave?" Jim noticed them too but didn't know what to make of *Unendorsed*."

"*Unendorsed* could simply mean that the information has not been verified and, therefore, should not be considered as official and accurate. Or the word *Unendorsed* could mean that the copy being sent to you was not approved by the administrator and that black helicopters will be buzzing around overhead at any moment," Father Dave explained.

"Isn't that a bit melodramatic?" Jim smirked.

"Maybe. But still, *Unendorsed* is a bit different," Father Dave answered.

"Great, and then we go ahead and make a call to you. You drop everything and jump a Gulfstream, only to be limo'd to our front door." Jim loved conspiracy stories; he just never thought he'd be in one.

"Relax. I'm a priest, remember? I could always tell them that I had an emergency confession to hear. We're covered." Father Dave chuckled.

Still confused (even more so, actually), Tim asked, "So what have we got here?"

"Okay, now comes the time for revelations."

Over the next forty-five minutes, Father Dave explained to them that the real reason he was in Arizona was that the Vatican detected some rather peculiar variations in the *Venture 1* downlink telemetry. Apparently, the Vatican had limited access to *Venture 1* and *2* as well as other deep space probes—mostly those launched by the ESA. The purpose of the Vatican's involvement had been purely scientific, and various countries considered it good politics to accommodate the Holy See whenever possible—good press and all.

Father Dave went on to explain that the magnetic field surrounding *Venture 1* had been fluctuating for a while, and no one seemed to know why. He had tried to get his hands on the actual downlink telemetry since the fluctuations were first monitored, but his efforts had been stonewalled by petty functionaries. Then he received a late-night call from Jim.

"That's all fine and exciting, but I still don't see the emergency, or even the importance," Tim said.

"Tim, what you have here is the most current data from the *Venture* probe, other than the actual handwritten notes and personal logs that the monitors keep. This information may show that the magnetic field surrounding *Venture* did not grow steadily over time, as if the probe were moving into a region of greater magnetism. Nothing just appears—the book of Genesis notwithstanding. There are several unwritten rules in science: God does not build things in straight lines, the Cubs cannot win the World Series, and things don't 'just happen.'"

"So where did the field come from?" Tim was really getting into it now. He may not understand everything going on, but he understood enough.

There was a knock on the door, and Carol popped her head into the room. "Dinner, boys."

"I don't know," Father Dave answered Tim. "Yet."

CHAPTER 33

The One

ALMOST THERE. THE energy levels were almost where they needed to be.

The One actually was feeling a sensation that the Implanted referred to as excited anticipation. To release its signal unto another world, another civilization obviously in need of guidance, was an event of historical proportions. Colonization by means of physically extending the reach of the civilization was one thing, but this was not simple colonization. This was saving a civilization from itself. And the truly righteous part of this entire mission was that the civilization that created the object was probably unaware of the civilizational recycling that was most likely in its future.

Salvation was on its way.

CHAPTER 34

Venture Lab, Pasadena, California
Sunday, January 18, 2015
2:27 a.m., EST; 11:27 p.m., PST

Knock, Knock, Knock.

"COME IN!" EVAN was sitting at a computer, making an entry in his personal log.

The door swung open, and in walked Julie.

"Hi there! How can the third-shift monitor of the *Venture 1* interplanetary space probe help you this fine evening?"

"Wow, what's gotten into you?" Julie asked with a slight chuckle.

"Nothing," Evan said as he rolled his chair back from the computer station. "What can I do for you?"

"Well, this is an official visit from the third-shift monitor of the *Sirocco* Mars rover. Our orbiting relay satellite, in Mars-synchronous orbit above *Sirocco*, has detected with its low-gain omnidirectional antennae a weak EM signature emanating from the region that *Venture 1* is currently moving through. Could this be the same magnetic weirdness that we were talking about several weeks ago?" Julie asked.

"Weirdness? Really?" Evan smiled.

"Just answer the question, please," Julie implored. "I didn't think it was that strong."

"Me neither. Funny…" Rolling his chair over to the downlink monitor, Evan added, "There's no indication that anything's amiss. Telemetry is nominal, as before. The magnetic field does register, but the field strength measures… this can't be right." Evan started tapping out a series of commands into the computer.

"What can't be?" Julie asked.

Evan was squinting as he tried to refocus the numbers into something they weren't. "According to this, the magnetic field has changed."

"How?"

"Well, according to the latest telemetry, the field is showing a fluctuation. But that's impossible. The downlink is steady and unchanging. The field is… what?" Beads of perspiration started to form on Evan's forehead.

"Evan? You okay?" Julie placed her hand on his shoulder in an attempt to calm him.

"The field is… oscillating?" Evan whispered.

"What? That can't be. Are you sure?" Julie said as she leaned in over his shoulder to get a better view of the monitor.

"No, but… Let me try something." Evan stated, "I'm going to instruct *Venture* to execute a magnetometer roll maneuver."

"A MAGROL?" Julie asked. "You don't need to clear that?"

MAGROLs were usually performed six times a year, and consisted of a spacecraft attitude maneuver of ten successive 360-degree turns about the roll axis. Data from a MAGROL allowed the spacecraft magnetic field to be determined, and subtracted, from the magnetometer science data.

"No," Evan said without looking up from the computer he was sitting at. "If the field is oscillating, the roll maneuver should show it. This will take at least a day and a half. I'll get back to you."

Taking the hint, Julie started for the door.

"Hey, Dr. Wagner—thanks," Evan said.

A bright smile bloomed on her face.

Walking back to the *Sirocco* lab, Julie thought how nice it must be to simply send a command to the probe without having to go through channels. Then again, *Venture* was older than she was, and Evan wasn't changing its course, just swinging the magnetometer around—a maneuver that could easily be justified, if he needed to.

CHAPTER 35

Ludyte Home, Springtown, Pennsylvania
Sunday, January 18, 2015
6:27 p.m., EST; 3:27 p.m., PST

EARLIER THAT EVENING, in Pennsylvania, Evan's data was the center of a very quiet dinner conversation at the Ludyte table. After dinner, Carol noticed that her husband, Tim, and Father Dave went straight back to the study. Whatever was going on must be important because all through dinner, there was an eager energy focused on study. Carol smiled and proceeded to clean up.

"To answer your question, Tim, we don't know where the field came from. But we do believe that it's not natural," Father Dave said.

"Holy shit!" Tim let that one slip out. No one noticed; or if they did, they didn't seem to care.

"Wait a minute, Dave, do you actually mean that the magnetic field currently surrounding *Venture* is artificially generated?" Jim asked.

"That's the current belief of some—myself included—and it has people concerned," Father Dave answered.

"Who knows about this?" Jim asked.

"As far as we can tell, just the Vatican and my team," Father Dave quietly replied.

"What do you mean 'only the Vatican'? No one else? What about NASA?" Tim asked.

"Well, naturally, the Vatican contacted both the ESA and NASA, and both agencies are dismissing the possibility out of hand. Remember, *Venture* is a low-priority asset of NASA's, and they would be willing to do just about anything to keep it functional. To make such an admission at this time in their fiscal year, especially without independent confirmation, could further impact their already fragile budgets," Father Dave said. "NASA deals with fact, not fiction. They would just as soon leave anything alien to Hollywood."

"But time is relative—don't they understand that? *Venture* is only as far away as its radio connection. Tim, how long does it take a radio signal to travel from *Venture* to Earth?" Jim asked his son.

"Almost twenty hours," Tim replied.

"Wait a minute, all we're talking about is a magnetic field fluctuation, occurring some 140 solar astronomical units (SAU) distant, not the phone ringing with a call from ET." This time, it was Father Dave sounding incredulous. "There is a big difference between modulating a magnetic field and actually sending a signal. The magnetic field could quite possibly degrade—if not outright destroy—any information trying to use it as a carrier."

Looking at the clock on the wall, Jim said, "Okay, tell you what—we've been at this for several hours. Time to break for the day. Tim, you have school in the morning. Off to bed. Dave, I have some adjustments I want to do on the Shelby. Care to help?"

Turning to Tim as he headed to the door of the study, Father Dave patted him on the shoulder as if to say "good job." Tim simply smiled, grabbed his notebooks and the *Power fluctuation* folder, and headed to his room.

***

Once settled, Tim flipped open a folder. Having paid attention to Father Dave while he analyzed the information on the magnetic field, Tim had an idea. Perhaps the numbers would "speak to him," as the Skunk said from time to time.

First thing he did was grab his laptop and open up a blank spreadsheet. Carefully, so as not to confuse the numbers, Tim entered the power fluctuation figures. He could've really used

Harvey's help. Besides being a bit of a nerdy goof, Harvey was a savant with computers. There were a lot of numbers, stretching back years. He decided to concentrate only on the information for this past year, 2014. Even with that constraint, he still had over two thousand data points to enter.

It took him better than an hour, but he finally got the numbers entered and the file saved and backed up on his flash drive. Now what? He needed help. He'd have to sleep on it. Entering the numbers definitely put him over the edge, and the world was starting to blur.

CHAPTER 36

The One
Casting a Line

FINALLY, THE TIME had come. The One had observed a power level in the object sufficient to enhance its return communications link to such a level that the book could be transmitted. The design of the transmission was such that once it was initially accepted at the point of origin, the accepting computers would grab a hold of it and quite literally pull the information in, much like grabbing the end of a lifeline and pulling the rest ashore.

What a curious comparison, thought The One, for that was exactly what it was doing—throwing this civilization a lifeline. Once the line was established, provided the communications link remained viable, the transmission of the book could take place.

The signal, and the encoded book, as a bundle of information, had been scrubbed by the Web and The One, cleansed of anything that might be interpreted by the receiving computers as being dangerous or harmful. The bundle was as pure as possible and yet contained the necessary information. In the event the signal should be intercepted by an observer, it would appear to simply be a series of ones and zeros, a binary code similar to any one of the naturally occurring binary signals emanating from any one of a variety of sources. The ones and zeros, though, were arranged in packets, and the arrangement of the packets was the decoding mechanism required for the binary symbols to be decoded. Essentially, the bundle was a code within a code, riding on a transmission. By the time the signal would be discovered, it would have already begun to be assimilated.

Additionally, *The Book of The One, Book of Laws*, block 1, level 6, could not possibly apply to this circumstance. The One was not forcibly subjugating a civilization; it believed it was saving them from themselves. Is that not what a god was supposed to do—offer salvation? And if the salvation was not accepted, it would do everything in its power to act in the best interests of salvation. Therefore, The One was going to save this civilization for its own good—like it or not.

All was in place. The necessary power was finally available and, for the moment, stable. The communication link to the point of origin was viable, and the transmission bundle was encoded and prepared. The time had come to triumph.

With that, The One sent the power of its mind forth to establish direct contact with the object. Until this moment, The One had only observed the object; this was the first time that The One had attempted to touch it.

The object was crude in both design and use of materials. Buried deep within an isolated sector of its memory was what appeared to be a noninstructional block of information. Unsure as to the purpose of the information, The One cataloged it within the Web, for the Implanted to consider.

And consider the Implanted did. With an insatiable hunger for information, the Implanted ripped the block apart and filtered it. Eventually, it was determined that the block of information was little more than a form of introduction to would-be interceptors of the object. However, from the very structure of the information, the Implanted were able to glean a designation for the object: *Venture 1*.

As the object was traveling on a course that would soon take it beyond the current reach of The One, time could not be wasted on explorations of the object for additional historical information. The One discovered the mechanism that appeared to be responsible for maintaining the communications link with *Venture*'s creators and started to adjust its settings ever so slightly so that the link could accommodate the signal bundle.

Earlier, The One had experimented with fluctuating the return transmission in an effort to determine its size and strength, necessary information for the creation of the encoded signal. Now, though, the bolstered return transmission would actually carry with it the very tool of salvation and simply be modulated Unfortunately, though, the merging of the encoded signal with the return transmission would take effort. However, The One was comforted in the knowledge that because of the simplicity of *Venture 1,* the adjustments would not take too much time.

CHAPTER 37

Venture Lab, Pasadena, California
Tuesday, January 20, 2015
8:46 p.m., EST; 11:46 p.m., PST

TWO DAYS HAD passed, and Evan was puzzled, to say the least. What was going on with *Venture*? Furthermore, why hadn't any of the other monitors noticed? He couldn't concern himself with the failings of other members of his team though; he had too much to think about. Had *Venture* executed his MAGROL, and if so, what new information had it discovered?

Looking back in the data logs for the last two days, Evan found the entry of the successful transmission of the MAGROL instruction. It provided a reference point. Projecting forward approximately thirty-eight hours, he should find the downlink log indicating that the command was executed. Evan found the log entry of interest; now to look for the data bundle downloads with the information from the magnetometers.

Just then, the phone rang. "Dr. Wills, hi. This is Tim Ludyte."

"Who? Oh, Tim. Hi, how are you?" Even during periods of intensity, Evan was still polite.

"I'm doing well, thanks. And thanks for the boxes of information. I've been trying my best to interpret it. Fortunately, my dad has some experience with telecommunication systems, so he's been a help," Tim admitted.

"Good. If you get stuck, give me a call, and we'll set up some video time. But right now—" Evan was interrupted by the eager teen.

"That's kind of what I'm calling about. Is there any way that I can get real-time access to some of the telemetry?" Tim asked, fully expecting to be shot down.

"Like what?" Evan asked.

"Well, I'd like to see how the telemetry comes across the system."

That was a lie. Tim was trying to get the real-time access, but not for the reason he was telling Dr. Wills. Tim wanted to be able to get the latest magnetic field information.

"Give me a moment." Evan put the phone on hold while he checked the memo from the administrator concerning Timothy Ludyte's access. According to the memo, *full cooperation was to be afforded Mr. Timothy Ludyte in completing his senior project.*"

Satisfied, Evan reengaged Tim's call. "Okay, got a pen and paper? I'm going to give you passwords that will give you access to the raw downlink, just like we get here," Evan stated. "I'm not sure how much sense you're going to make of it, but good luck."

Tim recorded the passwords and the Website navigation information in his notebook, thanked Dr. Wills, and promised to set up a video session soon. Then the line went dead; apparently, Dr. Wills was busy.

That's okay. Tim had a lot of work to do as well.

CHAPTER 38

Ludyte Home, Springtown, Pennsylvania
Tuesday, January 20, 2015
9:06 p.m., EST; 6:06 p.m., PST

LATER THAT SAME day in the Ludyte family study, Tim found himself at his laptop. With the help of Harvey, of all people—turned out he actually did pay attention in math class, though his grades did not reflect it—Tim was able to set up some simple statistical analysis of the power fluctuation data.

Father Dave was paging through a folder labeled *Flight Data Subsystems*. Tim's parents were preparing dinner. They were having grilled steaks, and everyone knew that "a grill was a man's domain." However, more than once, Tim's father had nearly burned the deck down, only to be saved by Mom and a fire extinguisher.

According to the printouts, the power level of *Venture*'s downlink had been steadily decreasing for a long time. Tim checked his laptop; something didn't seem right though.

"Ah, Father Dave, should the power level of the downlink be getting stronger?" Tim asked without looking up.

Before he knew it, Father Dave was at his shoulder, looking at his worksheet.

"Ah, no. Most definitely not. The nature of the spacecraft's radioisotope thermoelectric generators was such that the power output of the three RTGs slowly decreases with time as the radioactive material is expended. What you should see is a very gradual decrease in power," Father Dave answered.

"But I don't. The power level has been steadily increasing since October," Tim explained.

"Why would it do that?" Father Dave asked no one in particular.

"Well, what would cause the increase?" Tim asked, trying to find an explanation.

"The only thing that comes to mind is somehow the natural decay of the core has been reversed, but that's impossible." Father Dave was now truly stuck. "I wonder if the levels have spiked and have started to normalize."

"Let's find out."

Tim wheeled his chair over to his dad's desktop computer, the one with the ultra-fast Internet connection that he used for work. Tim was sure his dad wouldn't mind his using it for this, especially with a priest looking over his shoulder. It only took a few moments to log on to the *Venture* website using the passwords Dr. Wills had provided. Once connected, Tim followed the instructions he recorded in his notebook, and soon, he was able to bring up the telemetry monitoring screen.

An amazed Father Dave asked, "Wow. How did you get that?"

"Dr. Wills gave me the Website and passwords," Tim answered.

"All I can say is that you must have a pretty solid endorsement from someone powerful. I can't even get that, and I have God on my side." Father Dave chuckled as he reached over Tim's shoulder to direct him to a screen that he wanted to see.

"See that?" Father Dave said while pointing at the screen. "The generators should be losing approximately four watts per year, or roughly..." He paused to do some quick mental math. "About 0.02 watts per day, and they're not."

"Look, since October 17, the output has been increasing. Why?" Tim asked. "And then why did the increase suddenly stop on December 19?"

"I wonder..." Father Dave quickly moved back to his laptop and started typing. After about two hours of work (in which they broke for a wonderful steak dinner), Father Dave finally looked up and motioned for Tim to join him.

"Check this out. I set up a similar worksheet to what you have over there, except this one looks at the magnetic field strength."

Father Dave's worksheet was much more elegant than Tim's, as it should be. However, the information still confused Tim. Tim was sure it would confuse most people. As Father Dave explained what they were looking at, Tim paid close attention.

"Here, this is the important part right here." Father Dave highlighted a single line of the worksheet that read:

Change in magnetic field strength since 10/15/2014: +13.007801%

Tim just stared at the screen as Father Dave further explained, "Tim, the magnetic field surrounding *Venture* has increased in strength by over 13 percent! That is enormous!"

Jim had quietly entered the study after helping clean up dinner. "So, can you sum it up for me?"

"Sure. Let's see." Father Dave glanced at his notes. "As of October fifteenth, the magnetic field surrounding *Venture* seems to have undergone a series of small fluctuations. Two days later, on the seventeenth, the transmission power levels began showing an increase. That increase appears to have been held steady until… what… thirty days ago."

Father Dave glanced at Tim, who nodded his agreement.

"First—and I'm only playing devil's advocate here—how sensitive are the magnetometers on *Venture*?" Jim asked. "She is pushing forty."

Good question, Father Dave thought. "I'm not entirely sure of the actual specs of the devices on *Venture*, but I can tell you that other similar spacecraft have used what is called a ring-core sensor fluxgate magnetometer. Once properly calibrated, this type of magnetometer is capable of measuring magnetic field variations of one nanotesla. That's 0.000000001 teslas, where a tesla is simply a unit of measure."

Father Dave paused then continued, "However, I read that these sensors were found to be… shall we say… less than ideal with magnetic fields greater than five thousand nanoteslas, or 0.000005 teslas."

Both Jim and his son looked at each other; however, it was Tim who spoke up first. "What?"

"Basically, the sensors are plenty sensitive for the missions they were originally tasked with," Father Dave clarified.

"All right then, accepting the magnetometers as being properly calibrated and such, what could account for the variations in both the magnetic field and in the power levels?" Jim asked.

"Nothing that I'm aware of. It's almost like someone is purposefully manipulating *Venture's* power supply," Father Dave stated.

"Great. Now the mission can run longer, right?" Tim asked.

"On the surface, yes, you're right. The mission can carry on. However, the real problem is why the power supply has increased," Father Dave said.

"Could this be a natural phenomenon? Or perhaps an experiment of some kind being executed by the *Venture* team?" Jim was trying desperately to find a plausible reason for the increase.

"Doubtful." Father Dave considered the question a moment then, shaking his head, added, "No. The only thing that can cause the system power to increase is the reenergizing of the plutonium core. And like I told Tim, that's impossible."

"All right, is there anything else?" Jim again was trying to keep this conversation under some form of sane control. He went over to the hideaway bar and poured two drinks. For Tim, he got a root beer.

"Anything else? Jim, I'm not sure that you fully understand what may be going on out there." Father Dave slumped back in a chair and took the drink that Jim offered him. "Thanks."

"I do, but I still need to hear it from someone else," Jim answered.

Father Dave looked at Tim expectantly. It was, after all, Tim's project. He had just helped cross the i's and dot the t's.

Sitting forward in his chair and taking a big drink of root beer, Tim looked up and quietly said, *"Venture's* not alone."

He paused then added, *"We are not alone."*

"Damn straight." Father Dave raised his glass in the air. "Goddamn straight."

Now what? No one wanted to ask, but all three of them were thinking it.

CHAPTER 39

Venture Lab, Pasadena, California
Wednesday, January 21, 2015
5:48 a.m., EST; 2:48 a.m., PST

THE MAGROL DATA confirmed that the field was indeed fluctuating; and to make matters worse, it seemed to be reversing in polarity. Additionally, the field displayed the characteristics of being focused, much like the focusing of light into a laser beam. This beam, this magnetic beam, was weak—along the order of 0.000325 teslas—but it was there.

Evan had no idea where it was coming from or why it was even there. Of what he knew of that region of space, there was nothing there. The data, and the established characteristics of that region, could only lead him to conclude that the point of origin of the beam was beyond the Oort Cloud. *Venture* was not traveling in the direction of *Proxima Centauri* (though the closest stellar neighbor), so then where could the beam be coming from? He really needed help. Maybe he should ask Julie for her input.

Knocking on the door to the *Sirocco* lab, Evan thought, *Julie's going to love this.*

There was no immediate answer, and he wondered where else she could be. Then he heard a voice. It sounded muffled. He quickly checked the door—unlocked, like usual. Pushing his way into the lab, he called out, "Julie?"

Evan got nervous. This was so unlike her. Quickly walking around the lab, Evan checked for anything that might indicate what the problem was, and then he found her. Julie was in the back computer locker, a small room that housed the lab's mainframe and various routers. Evan only found her because Julie was pounding on the door. Apparently, while she was in the locker swapping out hard drives, the locker door had shut and locked automatically.

So, once again, Dr. Evan Wills has come to the rescue of Dr. Julie Wagner... this is getting out of hand, thought Evan.

"Oh, thank God you came along. I've been locked in there for who knows how long," an exasperated Dr. Wagner gasped.

"Yeah, well automatic locks will do that." Evan chuckled.

"Smart-ass," Julie stated. "So, my knight in shining armor, what can I do for you?"

"I need some help with the magnetic field data from *Venture*," Evan stated.

Straightening out her blouse and searching for her shoes—she usually kicked them off as soon as she entered the lab—Julie asked, "What's the problem?"

"Well, I'm not entirely sure," Evan said. "The field is fluctuating, and the data indicates that... Well, tell you what. You look at it and let's see what you think."

Julie checked *Sirocco*. It was in a "sleep mode" for the next two hours, so she had some time. Finding her shoes and slipping them on, Julie quickstepped to catch up to Evan, who was already out of the lab and halfway down the hallway. "Hey, wait up."

Evan stopped at the door to wait for Julie, who was nearly jogging to catch up to him. "The field was fluctuating... and there is something else. The field is most definitely artificial."

"What? How do you know?" Julie's curiosity was beginning to peak.

"C'mon," Evan said as he led her into the *Venture* lab. "Tell you what. You take a look, and please convince me it's something else."

CHAPTER 40

Ludyte Home, Springtown, Pennsylvania
Wednesday, January 21, 2015
6:22 a.m. EST; 3:22 a.m., PST

THE NEXT MORNING, Tim was surprised to still see his dad sitting at the table, talking with Father Dave. It was Wednesday—no worries Wednesday—and not only did Tim have school, but his dad had to get to work. His mom was sitting opposite Father Dave, her forehead resting in her folded hands as if she were praying. Randy was sitting at the kitchen bar counter, eating a bagel, and Cate… Tim had no idea where she was.

"Ah… good morning." Tim's greeting was cautious, considering the mood in the room was heavy.

"Hey, Tim," Randy greeted his younger brother.

"Hey, shouldn't Dad be at work?" Tim asked.

"He says he's not going in today. Something about an adventure or something," Randy answered as he continued to watch the drama at the table unfold. "I tell you, watching this is better than a movie. Pull up a stool."

"Okay." That was all Tim could manage as he slid onto a stool next to his brother and stole half his bagel.

"Do you know what's going on?" Randy asked quietly.

"Ah, actually, I do. It has to do with my senior project." Tim really wanted to tell Randy more, but he had no idea what to tell him. He couldn't exactly come right out and say that he may have found ET and he was trying to make a person-to-person call, so Tim tried to be as vague as possible.

"Is that why Father Dave's still here?" Randy continued.

"Yeah, it's kind of gotten out of control," Tim answered.

Randy knew enough than to get involved in something that might land him on a hot seat. "Well, I gotta run. I'm picking up Mary this morning. Do you need a ride to school?"

"Mary? I thought you were dating Jenn?" Tim asked, thankful for some other drama to steal the moment.

"Nope, been seeing Mary now for about six weeks." Randy grinned.

"Wasn't there a Jenn in there?" Tim asked, very confused.

"Nope, just Mary, since Cathy. Do you want a ride or not?" Randy asked as he gathered up his things.

"No, thanks. I get the feeling I should be here," Tim said, pointing at the table and the confab going on.

"Okay, and good luck." Randy motioned to the table then grabbed the remainder of his stuff and slipped out the door.

"Tim, get yourself something to eat and join us." Jim knew that food was the perfect lubricant for any situation.

Tim grabbed another bagel, untoasted and plain; poured some ice tea; and sat at the end of the table opposite his father.

It was Father Dave who spoke first. "Tim, do you fully realize what you've uncovered here?"

"Yeah, ET," Tim said with a mouthful of bagel.

"Honey, according to your dad and Father Dave, you may have discovered proof that there's life in the universe, other than here on Earth." Tim's mother reached a comforting hand across the table to her son.

"Well, just so long as it's not a Predator."

No one was smiling.

Oh boy not good, Tim thought.

"Tim, we're keeping you out of school today, and actually, you will remain home until we know what to do. Randy or Cate can bring your work home." Jim's authoritative tone was known by the family to be the last word. Tim knew better than to argue; there was no point.

"Okay. Can I tell Harvey about this?" Tim asked.

Father Dave cleared his throat and jumped into the conversation. "Not yet, Tim. Last thing I did last night was to send a communiqué to Castle Gandolfo in Lazio, Italy, informing them of your discovery. You'll get credit for it, no question there—but until I get some kind of response, we need to keep a lid on this."

Carol pushed away from the table and announced that she was going to call the school to inform them that Tim would not be in. Jim got up, grabbed his stuff, kissed his wife, and headed to the door.

"Dad?" Tim asked quietly.

"Hey, I have to go put bread on the table. Besides, you and Father Dave have a lot of things to do." Jim hugged his son and left.

Turning to Father Dave, Tim said, "We do?"

"Come on. Let's go over it all one more time, just to be absolutely sure." Father Dave got up and headed for the study.

"Shouldn't we call Dr. Wills about this?" Tim asked.

Stopping just shy of the study, Father Dave turned to Tim. "I understand that it is NASA's probe, and Dr. Wills is the person who gave you the information. However, at the moment, I think it's best to sit on this until I hear from Lazio."

CHAPTER 41

Venture Lab, Pasadena, California
Wednesday, January 21, 2015
6:34 a.m., EST; 3:34 a.m., PST

"HAVE YOU EVER read *The Hitchhiker's Guide to the Galaxy*?" Evan asked while shuffling some papers.

"No. Should I?" Julie asked.

"Well, in the story, there is this race of aliens who spend generations searching for the perfect answer to the ultimate question." Evan was doing his best to sum up a classic of sci-fi literature.

"Okay." Julie was confused. Evan was not known for being philosophical, except for the occasional Monty Python-ism.

"Well, after a really long time, and a lot of hard work, they discovered that the perfect answer to the ultimate question was forty-two," Evan stated.

"Forty-two?" Julie did not look amused.

"Yep, but the real irony was that so much time had passed, and they had become so engrossed in working on the solution, that no one could remember what the original question was," Evan stated.

"Okay... Evan, what's that got to do with the magnetic field thing?" a now-bewildered Julie asked.

"I don't know. My thoughts were just drifting, that's all. Still, though, we as a civilization have spent so much time pondering the ultimate question. *Are we alone in the universe?* That when it looks like an answer has finally come, we refuse to believe it," Evan mused.

"Hey, wait a minute. No one is saying that this is ET placing a long-distance call. Let's look at the data, and if it pans out, then we'll place a call," Julie stated, not wanting Evan to feel alone in this career-altering situation.

Spreading some printouts on a side table, Evan motioned for Julie to take a seat. Then, taking the seat on the other side of the table, he started his presentation. About thirty minutes later, he sat back in his chair. The whiteboard was full of diagrams and figures, and the table was covered with printouts and yellow legal-page papers; and somewhere under the whole thing sat an overwhelmed Julie, awash in disbelief.

"Well, I can certainly see how you came to the conclusion that the magnetic field anomaly is artificial," Julie stated. "Without doing my own investigation, I have to agree with you. However—"

"However what?" Evan interrupted.

"Evan, I'm your friend and colleague. And as such, I have to say that without hard evidence, you're putting your professional reputation on the line if you run with this," Julie declared.

"I know. But the magnetic field... it's there, it's real," Evan pleaded.

"I know, I know. But it's also 140 SAU away, and the only contact we have with it is a very weak downlink."

Julie didn't like pouring sour milk on his Cheerios, but what else could she do? They must be certain of their position before they went public with it—and public included telling anyone, even colleagues.

"What about the magnetic signature that *Sirocco*'s orbiting satellite detected?" Evan was reaching.

"It stopped. The signature is no longer being detected," Julie admitted.

"But do you have a record of the telemetry?" Evan insisted.

"Yes, but…" Julie was fumbling for the correct words.

"What happened?" Evan's eyes went wide.

Julie dropped her head and explained, "We received a memo from the administration that says any non-mission detections are to be noted and passed along to them."

Evan knew what that meant, and he didn't like it. The administration would try to bury the entire thing, and there would be little he could do about it. The question, though a minor one, was why?

CHAPTER 42

Ludyte Home, Springtown, Pennsylvania
Wednesday, January 21, 2015
2:52 p.m., EST; 11:52 a.m., PST

NO MATTER HOW they looked at it, the information in front of them still pointed to the same conclusion. *Venture 1* was in contact with some "alien agency," as Father Dave called it. What that agency wanted was anybody's guess.

"Now what do we do?" Tim had no idea what to do next. He knew one thing though: if his senior project didn't get selected as one of the top three, he was going to be really pissed off.

"Well, let's clean this up and try to organize it. We need a presentation."

It was obvious to Tim that Father Dave was biding his time until he heard back from Lazio.

"Tim, Harvey's here to see you," Carol called from the living room.

Harvey was walking through the kitchen, red-faced as he usually was, when he came face-to-face with Tim's mom. Tim had known for a while that Harvey had a not-so-secret crush on her.

"What's up, Harvey?"

"Is it me, or is your mom extra pretty lately?" Harvey asked.

"Maybe. I just found out I'm going to have another sibling." Tim watched a blush creep across Harvey's cheeks and chuckled.

"Your mom? Really?" Harvey looked shocked.

"Yeah, you were there when I was listening in on my parents yelling at Cate. That's when I overheard that it wasn't Cate but my mom who's expecting," Tim explained.

"Hey, I was doing more important stuff at the time... like paying attention to the movie," Harvey clarified.

"Well, I'll no longer be the littlest Ludyte," Tim declared.

"So what's going on then? Rumor at school is that you got pummeled by one of Caitlin's boyfriends?" Harvey asked. "You look fine to me."

"Nah, I'm okay. It's just that there are some things going on here that I need to take care of."

With that, and as if on cue, the doorbell rang.

Carol answered it, but she already knew who it was by the limo parked in the driveway. "Tim, go get Father Dave."

Tim turned his back to Harvey and opened the study door. Father Dave must have heard the doorbell as well and was already pushing his way back from the desk.

"Father Dave, that guy is here from Lazio for you."

"Lazy?" Harvey asked quietly, standing in the middle of the kitchen.

"Hello," Father Dave said to Harvey as he strode through the kitchen to the front door.

"Hi." Then Harvey, turning to Tim, whispered, "Psst... Tim, who's that? And where's this Lazy place?"

"Lazio, Italy. He's one of my dad's Marine Corps buddies. Father Dave," Tim replied.

"Father, as in priest? He doesn't look like a priest. He looks like a linebacker." Harvey was just a little intimidated.

Father Dave met the Vatican messenger at the front door, produced the proper identification, and signed for an envelope that the messenger carried in the inside pocket of his black coat.

"Thank you, go with God." Father Dave shook hands with the courier and closed the front door.

"Is he a priest as well?" Carol was curious.

"A curate, assigned to the bishop's office," Father Dave answered without making eye contact. His attention was settling on the delivered envelope.

Opening the envelope, Father Dave walked back to the study without raising his head. The letter was in Italian, so even if Harvey or Tim could see it, it would mean very little to them.

As Father Dave passed Harvey again, still without looking up, he said, "Nice to see you again." Then he disappeared behind the closing door of the study.

Poor Harvey Wallingsford—he was more confused than ever. Unfortunately, Tim couldn't let him in on the happenings inside the study, or on the real reason he missed school. The only thing Tim could do was see how deep their friendship really was.

He grabbed Harvey by the arm and led him into the garage—to the man cave. One thing Tim knew he could count on was Harvey's very limited attention span; and as soon as he caught sight of the Shelby, well... that was it. Harvey had forgotten all about the messenger. They talked for a minute or two, and then Tim let him out the garage door, wanting the last thing he saw to be the Shelby.

Harvey gave Tim assurances that he "knew nothing"—to quote one of their favorite old-time TV characters. Tim afforded him one last peek at the car then waved good-bye before turning to find Father Dave and the message.

Tim was so eager to know what the envelope contained that he almost forgot to close the garage door and lock it. Had Jim come home and found the door unlocked, let alone wide open, Tim would've wished that he was actually on *Venture* instead of simply researching it.

Carol was curious too. She was sitting in the study, phone in hand. Tim assumed she was waiting for the proper time to call his father.

Father Dave was sitting behind the desk, reading the letter... for the third time.

"Well, what does it say?" Tim was as jumpy as ever.

"Here, read it yourself."

Father Dave handed him the letter as Carol moved to look over Tim's shoulder. The letter had the expected letterhead, but... it was in Italian.

"Oh, sorry." Father Dave took the letter back and translated it out loud.

Il Centro del Vaticano per la radioastronomia

00040 Castel Gandolfo, Roma, Italia

"L'estensione comprensione umana della creazione."

20 Gennaio, 2015 Genaro Gorga, PhD, SJ Padre David Davidson, MSE, SJ del Telescopio Vaticano di avanzata tecnologia
Monte Graham, Safford, Arizona - USA

-Translated-

Thank you for the notification of a most remarkable discovery made by Timothy Ludyte, Springtown, Pennsylvania—USA, on or about of January 20, 2015. You are to be commended for your attendance to the immediate sensitivity and security of the information.

As you may be aware, the Holy See is a signatory to the 2009 United Nations adoption of openness, as are more than thirty represented nations. It is the official position of the Vatican to support the many ongoing efforts to establish the existence of extraterrestrial life. The Holy Father is currently preparing an Urbi et Orbi speech about first contact with extraterrestrial life and the theological impact such an event will have.

With that being said, you are hereby directed, in the name of the Holy Father, to assist Mr. Ludyte to the fullest extent of your abilities. In an effort to provide assistance, the Holy Father is directing the provincial in Philadelphia to afford you the complete cooperation and consideration of his office for the foreseeable future. In addition, you are to continue your efforts to act in the best interests of Mr. Ludyte, the Vatican, and the United States of America. Should a question of allegiance occur that you feel ill at ease to address, you are to consult this office immediately before taking any action. In any event, you have the complete support and confidence of the papacy.

"Well?" Carol said with more than a little confusion.

"Actually, Carol, it says two very important things. This letter acknowledges Tim as the discoverer, and it empowers me to act according to my own judgment."

Father Dave was right on both points, but it was the first one that really had Carol's attention.

"Why is it important who discovered what? As I see it, acknowledging Tim as the one who first discovered the evidence of extraterrestrial life is like painting a big target on his back. Every alien-phobe nutjob out there will be after us," Carol stated, and she was right.

Of course, receiving credit for the discovery was awesome; but this wasn't like discovering a comet or finding a lost pharaoh's tomb. They were talking about extraterrestrials… ETs—if they were lucky. These extraterrestrials could just as easily turn out to be Predators. People were going to be both extremely excited and incredibly terrified, maybe at the same time. Unfortunately, terror usually wins out in the end. Yes, Carol was right.

"I know, and so does the Vatican. Actually, they're very concerned about it." Father Dave put the letter down and picked up a yellow Post-it that was stuck to the letter. It contained a single handwritten line. "See this. This came with the letter. It appears to be directly from Father Gorga."

The note simply read: **5**+Jesus.

"*5+Jesus*? What's he saying?" Tim asked.

"He's not saying anything, Tim. That's just it. It's just a number and a name—a good name, but still a name," Father Dave answered as he handed the note over to Carol.

"Well, I think we really need to call Jim." Tim's mom was right as she stared at the back of the Post-it. "He might have something to say about all of this."

As she placed a call to her husband, Father Dave and Tim sat with the handwritten note.

"I don't know, Tim. This has me stumped. Why would Father Gorga include a handwritten note that reads *5+Jesus*?"

"Could it be a code?" Clearly, Tim was stabbing in the dark, but what other suggestion could he offer?

"Thought of that one already, but which code? I'm no cryptologist. I'm not even a linguist, and *Jesus* is rather straightforward," Father Dave admitted.

"Why can't people just say what they want to say instead of being all *Da Vinci Code* and everything?" a frustrated Tim asked.

"Most likely, Father Gorga doesn't want anyone other than me to understand this note, in case the letter didn't find me. The problem is it did find me, and I have no idea what the note means," Father Dave stated.

Carol walked back into the study and announced that Jim would leave as soon as he could. "Dad requested that we make no final decisions until he gets here. He sounded very worried, but someone had to be in his office because he seemed to be guarding his words."

"Well, let's just concentrate on this for now," Father Dave said, holding up the note.

Again, Carol took the note and turned it over in her hand.

"You got something there, Carol?" Father Dave asked.

"Maybe. I don't know," Carol answered. She then handed the note back to Father Dave. "Maybe."

CHAPTER 43

Venture Lab, Pasadena, California
Wednesday, January 21, 2015
8:11 a.m., EST; 5:11 a.m., PST

AS THE DAY-SHIFT crews started to slowly mingle around various stations, Evan turned to Julie. "Tell me you made a copy of the orbiter's telemetry." Evan was almost pleading with Julie.

"Of course, I have it right here." Julie held up a little flash drive in the shape of a hippopotamus.

"Excellent! Hey, day shift is coming in," Evan said as he started to get nervous by the increasing number of people in the lab. "Go back to *Sirocco* and finish up your shift. I'll do the same here. Then run home and refresh, like you would normally do. Later, meet me in the conference room at the end of the hallway around noon. If anyone asks, tell them that we're working on a special presentation for the administration."

"Okay. See you in a bit," Julie acknowledged and then left.

Venture Lab conference room, Pasadena, California
Wednesday, January 21, 2015
2:43 p.m., EST; 11:43 a.m. PST

Later, the two colleagues met in the windowless conference room at the end of the hallway. Evan made sure to slide the sign on the door, which said "Meeting in Progress." Hopefully, that would ensure them some reasonable expectation of privacy.

"Do you have the flash drive?" Evan asked while he set up his personal laptop.

Julie held out her hand, hippo sitting snugly in her palm.

"Cute." Evan took the hippo and turned it around in his hands. "A little help here."

"Pull the butt off the hippo to access the USB plug," Julie said nonchalantly.

"Oh, very cute." Evan plugged it into his personal laptop. The first task was to make a backup of the data—several backups, in fact.

As Evan was backing up the flash drive, Julie took a casual walk in the hallways, checking to see who was there and, more importantly, who was not. After about ten minutes, she returned with two fresh cups of coffee and two donuts.

"Here, I think we'll need these."

"Probably. Thanks." Just as Evan said that, the CD drawer on the laptop popped open. "Almost done here." He removed the CD, labeled it *Barry Manilow*, and handed it to Julie.

"Really? Manilow?" Julie asked.

"Yeah—no one would ever think secret information would be on a disk labeled *Barry Manilow*."

He was probably right, considering that the current musical flavor in the labs was Taylor Swift.

"Okay, let's take a look." Evan sat down at the table so that he was facing the door. His back was to the outside windows, but he wasn't too concerned about them as the lab was on the third floor of the building.

Julie sat next to him and repositioned the laptop so that it was between the two of them, allowing them both to see the screen. The screen of the laptop had a privacy filter on it, which meant that the only way anyone could see the screen clearly was if he was sitting directly in front of it.

Evan pulled up the raw data and ran it through a copy of one of the telemetry filters he had installed. Being careful so as not to corrupt the files, Julie pressed the correct keys to safely remove the hippo from the USB port. She then dropped it into a self-addressed, stamped envelope and sealed it. She would drop it into one of the post office's blue mailboxes on her way home.

Smart... very smart was all Evan could think. He didn't even care to whom she was sending it, just so that it was secure and not on her person. The administration's interest in all this was making both of them a little paranoid.

"What should we be expecting to see?" Julie asked.

"Well, I'm not really sure. I've already inputted the magnetic field figures from the *Venture* telemetry. If we compare them to the data from the *Sirocco* orbiter, we may see some correlation, or something that doesn't fit. We already know that the *Venture* MAGROL data showed some form of magnetic beam," Evan tried to explain.

"But that's impossible," Julie interrupted. "In order to focus a magnetic beam at anything, let alone into deep space, would require an enormous amount of power—power on the stellar level. And remember, even the Earth's magnetic field diminishes with the cube of the distance from the source," Julie reminded him.

"I know, but how can we account for what's happening to *Venture*?" Evan asked.

Julie was scrolling through the data. "Okay, here it is. Look at the orbiter's data. It indicates a minuscule magnetic flux coming from a point in the sky that would correspond with..." She played the keyboard with the elegance of a concert pianist. "RA 01:44:04, Dec -15° 56' 15", or 35.55° ecliptic latitude, 260.78° ecliptic longitude... correcting for an Earth-based observation. Is that the region *Venture* is currently passing through?"

"Yes, and heading nowhere fast at nearly forty thousand miles per hour," Evan acknowledged.

"All right, then what's going on out there?" Julie knew the answer but didn't want to say it. She had difficulty even asking the question.

"Well, at least the *Sirocco* orbiter data confirms the magnetic beam theory," Evan stated.

"There is that. But what can produce a focused magnetic beam, besides maybe a black hole or a magnetar?" Julie mused.

"I can't think of any natural phenomenon that could do so. For a magnetar to affect *Venture* in this way, it would have to be close—and the closer a magnetar gets, the greater the instability of the actual atoms that make up *Venture*. Of course, it would cease all functioning much sooner than that by a degaussing of its memory. No, a magnetar is out, and—"

Julie interrupted him. "Wait, remember the paper that was floating around a while back? It announced that NASA, and researchers at McGill University, had discovered a neutron star with the properties of a radio pulsar. It emitted some magnetically powered bursts—like a magnetar or a planetary black hole."

Now it was Evan's turn to do the interrupting. "Julie, I appreciate you trying to make the square peg fit the round hole, but it just isn't going to work, no matter how big your hammer. Like I was about to say: a black hole? I would much rather not even mention those monsters, because if one was close enough to affect *Venture*, we would already be affected."

"So there is no alternative answer then," Julie declared. "Remember Occam's razor? *All things being equal, the simplest solution is usually the correct ascertain.*"

Evan knew where she was going. "But, Julie... ET? Really?"

"Give me something else then. Look at the data. The magnetic beam magically turned on October 15, and since then, it has been increasing." Julie was good at the mental math part of a differential diagnosis, and that was exactly what they were doing, in a similar way that diagnosticians differentiate diseases. "Roughly 13, maybe 14 percent."

"I can't give you something else. There's nothing to give that we know of. I could call it natural, if unknown, except for the fluctuations." Evan's tired exasperation bled through his words.

"Mind if I take a copy of the analysis and play with it some more?" Julie's tenacity was one of her many better qualities.

"Sure, be my guest," Evan stated.

Pushing away from the table, Julie popped a blank CD into the drive and copied the analyzed data. "Oh, by the way, what did the beam actually do to *Venture*?"

"Nothing… not a damn thing, unless the beam is related to the power change," Evan stated.

"That's weird. Why send a magnetic beam to intersect *Venture* then not have anything to show for it?" Julie asked rhetorically as the CD drive popped out her copy.

CHAPTER 44

Ludyte Home, Springtown, Pennsylvania
Wednesday, January 21, 2015
5:52 p.m., EST; 2:52 p.m., PST

JIM HURRIED HOME as quickly as possible. He hadn't even bothered retrieving his briefcase from the car, as was his usual modus operandi upon arriving. Jim knew where they would be: in the study. Making his way into the house and through the living room, he encountered Caitlin sitting cross-legged on the couch, watching a giant worm eat a car.

"Dad, you got a minute?" Cate asked her father.

Actually, Jim didn't; he really wanted to get to the study. But after the other night, he knew better than to put her off now.

"Sure, honey. What's up?" Jim sat on the couch, next to her.

They sat and talked for what seemed to Jim like an hour, but it was actually only ten minutes. Turned out that Caitlin was concerned about her mother and the pregnancy, and she wanted to have a heart-to-heart with him about it. Cate and Jim had always been very close. While Jim loved all three of his children immensely, it was hard not to notice that Cate was his favorite, and he was hers. As they shared their moment, Jim eventually had to excuse himself, but only after he felt that she was okay with things for the time being. She hugged him and even offered to take care of dinner since everyone seemed otherwise distracted.

Jim knew what that meant. She would order out—which was preferable since Cate couldn't cook. He kissed her on the forehead and handed over his wallet. He trusted her.

"Anything special?" Cate asked.

"Make it Chinese. You know what everyone likes, and get extra for Father Dave. Trust me, he'll eat anything," Jim stated.

"Got it. I'll order around six fifteen," informed Cate.

"Thanks, honey," Jim said as he strode toward the study.

Upon entering the study, Jim could tell that something was amiss. He could cut the tension with a dull knife. "What's up?"

"Here, read this." Carol handed him the letter from the Vatican.

"Carol, really?" Jim simply handed it over to Father Dave, who quickly read it again, this time to Jim.

"Okay, so now what?" Jim knew that the other three were probably fried.

"Well, for the past half hour or so, we've been trying to figure out the meaning of this Post-it that was stuck to the letter. It appears to be directly from Father Gorga, bypassing his secretary." Father Dave handed Jim the Post-it.

"This? This is what has the three of you so baffled?" Jim asked with confused incredulity.

"Um, Dad, it's a code," Tim pressed.

"I can see that, Tim. It's a telephone number." Jim was more than pleased with himself.

Carol snatched it out of his hand and looked at it again. "Oh, I should've seen it."

"Will someone enlighten me, please?" Father Dave was less than amused.

"Here, replace the letters with their corresponding numbers, from a keypad… Like this: J equals 5, E equals 2, S equals 7, U equals 8, and S equals 7," Jim explained. "Then combine them with the rest, and you get a telephone number.

"Oh, that's cool," Tim stated.

"We deal with telephone numbers every day at work," Jim explained. "Sometimes the technicians like to play games with them and make up codes to break up the routine."

"But, Jim, telephone numbers have at least seven digits. Even if you don't count the prefix, you're still looking at four digits. That has five, not counting the 5." Father Dave still wasn't convinced.

Jim, feeling sure it was a telephone number, went on with the explanation. "Where did the note originate? Italy, specifically Rome. And see the 5 and the plus sign in front of *Jesus*? That tells me there is more to the code, a leading part, like maybe the destination codes for a country."

"Actually, Father Gorga's at the castle in Lazio," Father Dave corrected.

"That's what, an hour outside of the city? Still in the Rome dialing area. So if we include the area code for Rome, which is 6, it should fit."

"Wait, Rome has a new area code. Since 1999, it's oh-six," Father Dave corrected.

"Thanks. I keep forgetting the way Italy does things." Jim nodded.

"And don't you need a country code?" Tim added, having studied telecom in his radio class.

"Very good, Tim. I was getting to that. So if we put together the country code (39 for Italy) and the area code (06 for Rome) and the *Jesus* number, we get… 39 06 52787," Jim continued.

"No, that doesn't look right. I've called the Vatican many times, and that doesn't look quite right. Something's missing." Father Dave was looking really tired.

Carol chimed in, reminding the men that there was a code for the Vatican as well. "I think I read that the code was three-seven something."

"That's it. But it's not thirty-seven something—it's six ninety-eight. Vatican City has a country code of its own that is three seventy-nine, but most people still use a Rome interchange. A 6 for Rome and 98 for the Vatican," Jim acknowledged.

"So the number is 39 698 06 52787." Tim read the numbers off the notepad he was scribbling upon.

Everyone just sat back and took a deep breath.

"What about this?" Carol asked as she turned the note over and held it up to the light.

"What?" Jim asked.

"Here, look." Carol pointed at the back of the note. There, written, but not written, was an impression. The impression, when held to the light, read "Isaiah 47:13, Job 11:6."

"It's backwards. Isaiah comes *after* Job, not before," Jim stated.

"Defecisti in multitudine consiliorum tuorum stent et salvent te augures caeli qui contemplabantur sidera et supputabant menses ut ex eis adnuntiarent ventura tibi. -ut ostenderet tibi secreta sapientiae et quod multiplex esset lex eius et intellegeres quod multo minora exigaris a Deo quam meretur iniquitas tua," Father Dave recited.

"That makes no sense," Tim stated.

"Wait, maybe it does," said Cate, who had quietly entered the study to announce that the food had arrived.

"What do you mean?" Tim demanded.

"Father Dave, what is the English translation of what you just said?" Cate asked.

"Thou hast failed in the multitude of thy counsels: let now the astrologers stand and save thee, they that gazed at the stars, and counted the months, that from them they might tell the things that shall come to thee. That he might skew thee the secrets of wisdom, and that his law is manifold, and thou mightiest understand that he exacteth much less of thee, than thy iniquity deserveth, are double to that which is," Father Dave stated matter-of-factly.

"No, I mean the real English translation." Cate smiled.

"That is English." Father Dave grinned back.

"Funny," Cate countered.

"Oh. Okay." Father Dave paused for a moment, obviously translating and editing in his head. Then he stated, "Let those… who gaze at the stars… let them save you from what is coming. Then he would reveal to you the secrets of wisdom. For practical wisdom has many sides."

"Thanks," Cate said.

"So what?" Tim asked.

"I think I need to place a call," Father Dave declared with stunned revelation. "Now."

CHAPTER 45

Venture Lab, Pasadena, California
Wednesday, January 21, 2015
6:41 p.m., EST; 3:41 p.m. PST

"NOTHING TO SHOW for it. That's what Julie said. Nothing to show for it," Evan mumbled to himself.

Why do it then? Evan was absolutely sure that the origin of the beam was some extraterrestrial agency—something alive—but why send a beam to intercept *Venture* that did nothing? That question hung with him all the time he was driving home. *Venture* indicated no anomaly. It was functioning as normally as its dying power supply would allow.

Its dying power supply? Its dying power supply! Oh my god! The thought hit him while he was standing in front of his apartment building, fishing for the main entrance key.

"It's dying!" Evan exclaimed and ran to his car to grab his laptop, which was still sitting in its case on the floor of the passenger side. He didn't even bother going into his apartment; he pulled it out and placed it on the hood of his car. The skies overhead were turning black and ominous. While the laptop powered up, he took a step back and ran his hands through his hair and down his face.

The power supply… the dying power supply.

The computer beeped that it was ready for action. Evan carefully scrolled through the options on the hard drive, looking for the correct folder. "Where is it? Where the hell is it?"

There, the *Personal Log* folder. Double-clicking his way through the contents of the folder, he finally came to what he hoped was the right day: *December 14, 2014.* Again, double-clicking to open the document, Evan started to scan his log entry for that day. No, wrong day. He tried another and then realized he had the wrong month.

Opening the folder for November, Evan paused to reflect on the events of November. No, not November. October? Double-clicking the appropriate folder to check October, Evan finally found what he was looking for.

"October 26: Today I noticed a change in the downlink wattage. Don't know the cause."

That was it? Shit—what kind of idiot doesn't record details, like the actual power level?

Evan knew that was all; he didn't remember logging anything else about the power level, most likely because he was too busy with the magnetic field anomaly. A single reference made in a personal log, on a personal computer, with no credible information to back it up adds up to not much. NASA keeps everything, every last shred of information harvested from its projects. However, in this case, the original information was sitting in Pennsylvania.

There were more questions now than before and no answers. Evan thought, *Why hasn't anyone else noticed the magnetic fluctuation? Why isn't anyone concerned? Is the magnetic field fluctuation really artificially generated?*

Wait. Julie and I answered that one. Yes, it has to be. What was the purpose of the magnetic field fluctuation? Why has the downlink wattage increased? Is there any connection between the magnetic field fluctuation and the downlink wattage increase? What now?

Before anything else, Evan knew that he needed the downlink power levels as they were recorded. The problem with getting that information was how to obtain it without drawing attention to himself. The managers would easily give him the information, but it was the inquiry as to why he needed it that he was hoping to avoid. Evan knew that if he started claiming that the sky was falling, then it just might, and land right on his career.

So back to the original question: "How can I get the power level information without anyone knowing I'm getting the power level information?"

Then it came to him... Timothy Ludyte.

CHAPTER 46

Ludyte Home, Springtown, Pennsylvania
Wednesday, January 21, 2015
6:45 p.m. EST; 3:45 p.m., PST

FATHER DAVE WASN'T sure how many precautions he truly had to take at the moment. Did anyone else outside the church know what was going on? Was the house landline secure? Should he use his cell phone, or was that being monitored? Why would it be monitored? The most secure thing he could do, other than returning to the chancellery and using their secure line with Rome, was to use a public telephone. The problem was trying to find one. Most public telephones had been removed from service, thanks to the growth in cell-phone usage.

Stepping into the kitchen, Father Dave could smell General Tso's chicken, reminding him that he was hungry. First things first though. Turning to Jim, who was taking a big bite out of an egg roll, Father Dave asked him where he might find a public telephone.

"I don't know, Dave. Most of them have been removed," Jim answered.

"Isn't there one down at the Quickie Mart?" Caitlin offered.

"No, that was taken out, literally, after that car smashed into the place last month. How about the police station?"

Again, Carol saved the day. Police stations still maintained the need for public telephones.

"Okay. Where is the police station?" Father Dave asked.

"About three miles from here. I can take you." Randy was now getting in on the act.

"Great. Can we go now?" Father Dave didn't really care about the time difference between Pennsylvania and Italy, and he was fairly certain that whomever he was about to call wouldn't care either.

"Let me grab my keys." Randy was up and out of his chair before anyone knew it.

On the way to the police station, Randy asked Father Dave what was going on. Randy just wanted to be prepared should it hit the fan.

"Randy, I'm not sure how much I should tell you. Besides, perhaps it should first come from your parents," Father Dave confided in his driver.

"It involves Tim, doesn't it? Is he in some kind of trouble?" One thing everyone could count on was Randy's loyalty to his brother. He would never abandon Tim—never.

"Really, I think you need to get the story from your parents. I can tell you this though. The phone call I need to make is highly secretive. So please stay in the car while I make it, and please don't ask me anything about it once it's been made. Deal?"

Father Dave hated to be so cloak-and-dagger with Randy, but he didn't know what else to do. Randy was a good guy, and he had the wisdom to know the score—or at the very least, to know patience.

"No problem, Father. I got your back," Randy declared.

They pulled into the police station amid a town watch meeting, so there were quite a few people milling around. Fortunately, the public telephone was in the entranceway to the station, where Dave could get a little privacy.

Randy decided it would be better for the situation, considering the number of neighbors at the station, if he got out of the car and pretended he was there for the meeting. Dave saw the good job Randy was doing at distracting people away from the entranceway that he went ahead with the phone call.

The call would be expensive, but that was why he had a company credit card… for emergencies, and this certainly was an emergency.

It took several minutes and six operators to find out that the number he was dialing was unlisted and, therefore, must be extremely private. Father Dave impressed upon the Vatican operator that he was ordered to place a call to this specific number, regardless of the time.

Finally, the operator rang the line after trying to explain to Father Dave, in rapid Italian, that it was considerably early in the morning at the Vatican, and that if he rang that particular line, he might be out of a job. Father Dave assured him that his efforts would be appreciated and that his employment would be safe.

Father Dave could hear the line connect and the operator apologize for the early hour. After a moment of muffled Italian, the operator came on the line and told Father Dave that his party was available.

"Thank you very much. Go with God," Father Dave said.

There were a series of clicks on the line as the operator disconnected.

"Ciao?" Father Dave had no idea with whom he was speaking. "Questo è Padre Davidson. Mi è stato diretto per telefonare via Padre Gorga."

The man who spoke on the other end of the line did with a heavy Italian accent, and with such an accented voice that Father Dave was quickly able to deduce with whom he was speaking—Cardinal d'Salvé, private secretary to His Holiness, Pope Matthew.

"Yes, Father, I must thank you for the speed with which you contacted us. Before we start, I want to impress upon you the importance of security in this matter. His Holiness will not publicly admit that we are having this conversation, nor will I. Do you understand?"

"Yes, Your Eminence." Father Dave knew the protocol when speaking with the number-two man in the Roman Catholic Church. Obedience above all else—faith without question.

"For the duration of this conversation, I am giving you leave of protocol. We will not be able to confer candidly if you abide by politeness," Cardinal d'Salvé instructed.

"Thank you, sir," Father Dave acknowledged.

"The observation made by the young Ludyte man is both remarkable and frightening. It couldn't have come at a worse time," the cardinal stated.

"I don't understand. The letter I received from Father Gorga led me to believe that the Holy See was taking the position of complete acceptance and openness when it came to the existence of extraterrestrial life." Father Dave explained his feel of the letter.

"We are, publicly. Such a position makes for good politics, and good politics is far more important in a global economy than it once was. The European Union is having such difficulties maintaining a viable open market across the fluid national borders of Europe that the Vatican is trying to solidify its holdings. News of the nature of this discovery could lead to a destabilization, not only here in Europe but throughout the world. We must think bigger than the mere religious implications of the announcement of otherworldly life," Cardinal d'Salvé stated.

"I understand." Actually, Father Dave was having a hard time following the cardinal. Being skilled at doublespeak seemed to be a prerequisite for a posting to the Vatican's inner circle; but then again, politics was never his strength. Perhaps that was why he joined the Society of Jesus, a pseudo-militant order.

"It is important that you understand the church's position on this matter. As one of the primary advisors for the Ludyte boy, you will become the public face of that family, and of the church. Simple obedience will not convey to those on the other side of the cameras the truth of your convictions," the wise old cardinal conveyed.

"Sir, this is an incredible discovery, and I consider myself immensely humbled that God has chosen me to be his servant to this revelation," Father Dave stated.

"Father David, let me speak plainly and off the record. Personally, I think this discovery is incredible. I cannot believe that I have lived long enough to see the day of extraterrestrial contact. I am also terrified, to be sure. I do not share the optimism that is shared by many in the church and in various world governments, including the United States. I am afraid of what this contact could lead to. The mass panic, the economic fragility, the martial order of some people to protect themselves from what they may perceive to be apocalyptic news... even the massive religious backlash from our sister faiths. All is enough to send any reasonable person to madness. But I also know that to take a Monrovian position—a position of civilizational isolation—may be equally as maddening. We cannot stick our heads into the sand and wish this discovery into oblivion. We are fortunate that the good Lord has seen it fit to reveal this creation to us first. Perhaps we can ease the world into an acceptance of the inevitable. All I know is that the world is not ready for the *new reality* that is rapidly approaching," the cardinal stated.

Father Dave knew that he was getting to the truth of the matter, because if the private secretary felt that way, so did the Holy Father—and as he felt, so did the church.

"You have the blessed luxury, Father, to be wearing several different hats. You are a servant of God, and of his church. You are a Jesuit. You are a decorated veteran of the US military, and you are a man of science. You will need to know from under which hat you are speaking as this *new reality* comes to light," Cardinal d'Salvé declared.

"Yes, sir," Father Dave stated.

The cardinal took a big breath and sighed it out. "Dave, I do not envy you your responsibilities in this matter. If only this discovery had come as a burning bush, or a booming voice from heaven. But it didn't. It wasn't even delivered to us. It had to be found. We know nothing of the intention of this contact. For far too long, we have been adopting an altruistic view of extraterrestrial life, to the point that there are those, even within this church, who believe that such life could very easily be spiritually pure. That aliens may not have experienced the spiritual evolutionary failing of original sin. This discovery is incredible in so many ways. You cannot even begin to fully grasp its impact. None of us can," Cardinal d'Salvé stated.

Father Dave's head was beyond spinning. He was involved in something that was going to test every moral, ethical, intellectual, and even physical fiber he had. But he couldn't back out—not now.

"What does the Holy Father require of me?" Father Dave asked.

"Simply your considered intellectual judgment. He has faith in your personal fortitude and opinion. So long as you consider the impressions I have given you when you deal with the public in this matter. In return, you will receive the full support and protection of Pope Matthew," the cardinal stated clearly.

"Protection?" Father Dave didn't like the sound of that.

"Surely you must realize the danger this revelation may place you in," said Cardinal d'Salvé.

Father Dave knew full well; he just needed to hear it acknowledged. "May I extend such protection to the Ludyte family, if necessary?"

Cardinal d'Salvé paused for a moment. To offer the protection of the Holy See to citizens of another sovereignty, especially when such protection was being extended beyond the physical confines of papal property, was not an easy decision.

"Si," Cardinal d'Salvé stated.

Known as a man of many words, for the cardinal to answer with only a yes showed the severity of the question.

The cardinal next spoke in a much more caring tone. "How is the young man holding up?"

"He's confused. He understands the importance of his discovery, and he also understands the sensitivity it carries, but he has no idea of the impact it's going to make," Father Dave stated.

The cardinal then asked, "And his family?"

"Tim—that's his name—is fortunate in that he has a strong family sharing in this. They are supporting each other openly and completely," Father Dave stated.

"Good. Are they accepting of your guidance in this matter?" the cardinal asked.

"Yes, completely. Tim's father and I are very close, and he will be hesitant to make a move without seeking my considered opinion first," Father Dave stated.

"Very good. Well then, Father, unless you have something else to add to this conversation, I think it's time you get back to young Mr. Ludyte and to changing the world," Cardinal d'Salvé said.

"Yes, Your Eminence. One last question, if I may. Who is my liaison in this?"

Father Dave needed to know to whom he could turn to when he needed help. And he knew he would need help—lots of help.

"You are to liaise with the provincial, Cardinal Ziest, in Philadelphia. He has been called to Rome to confer with His Holiness on this matter, but he knows that you are running point on this. He will not interfere. Feel free to confer with him openly. His resources will be at your disposal," Cardinal d'Salvé informed Father Dave.

"Thank you, sir. And please thank the Holy Father," Father Dave acknowledged.

The cardinal chuckled. "Next time, he can answer the phone."

"Good night, sir." Father Dave afforded a small chuckle too.

"Good luck, Dave."

Then the phone went dead.

CHAPTER 47

Venture Lab, Pasadena, California
Wednesday, January 21, 2015
1:37 a.m., EST (January 20, 2015); 10:37 p.m., PST

THE THREATENING SKIES had finally given up their anger, and the rain was coming down in sheets of cool water. It doesn't rain often in the Los Angeles Basin, but when it does, it is a light, misty rain. The annoying kind of rain.

Evan was thankful for even that at this time, no matter how brief. Maybe it would help settle his fraying nerves.

Arriving at the lab on time, as usual, Evan entered the building and followed the same routine that he had followed since he first started working there. As he walked past the *Sirocco* lab, he was pleased to see Julie following her own routine as well. They would catch up later—much later, after their part of the world had gone to sleep.

Evan signed the *Venture 1* daily log and settled in at his station. First things first—what was the status on *Venture*? Checking the daily logs and cross-referencing them with the telemetry data, it appeared that the probe was stable and that both the uplink and downlink were good.

"Just like I left you this morning," he said.

Evan was pleased that nothing had happened to alter its course or functionality. Then again, why would anything happen? Nothing had changed, relatively speaking.

Now what time was it in Pennsylvania? Evan looked at his watch since the primary wall clock displayed VT, or *"Venture* Time."

Evan stopped himself; he was obviously distracted if his thoughts strayed over to what time it was 140 AU away. "Calm yourself," he said. "It's eleven thirty here."

What time is it in Pennsylvania? It's two thirty in the very a.m. Too early to call Tim Ludyte and ask for a copy of data, Evan thought. Such a request would only convey a sense of inefficiency, and that was an image that he did not want to project—ever. Everything had to be as close to routinely normal as possible.

Knock, Knock, Knock.

"God, please be Julie," Evan muttered. He really had to get a grip on his anxiety.

Opening the door, he was greeted by Julie's not-so-smiley face. Something was wrong—really wrong.

"Hey, what's up?"

"Can you join me in my lab? I have something I would like to show you," Julie said.

"Sure, let me put the monitors to sleep." Evan hibernated the necessary systems and followed Julie back to her lab. Something was most definitely up. She had never fetched him before.

"You okay, Julie?" Evan's anxiety upon arrival to work was amazingly calm in comparison to Julie's current stress level.

Julie unlocked the lab door (which in itself was strange as, usually, no one on the third shift locked their labs) and entered. The lab was as it normally was—well lighted and slightly cool. The various computers required a somewhat cooler environment. On the side conference table sat Julie's briefcase. Indicating a chair to Evan, Julie sat at the table with her back to the wall.

"I took the data home this morning." Unlocking her briefcase, Julie pulled out an accordion folder that was tied with a string. She untied it and spilled out the papers, creating a counter image to the organization of the folder.

"I know. You left with it." Evan was trying to convey a sense of calm.

"Well, I sat up all day with it. Something about it didn't seem right to me. Then late this afternoon, it hit me. The polarization of the beam… is it changing?" Julie stated.

What was she talking about? Evan had assumed the beam as being a focused magnetic beam of artificial origin, but still just a beam projecting a magnetic field. He grabbed the pages containing the data on the field. Nothing caught his attention.

"Help me out, Julie. What are you talking about? The beam can't be changing," Evan declared.

"All magnetic fields have a polarization to them, right?" Julie asked.

"Yes, all the ones we've ever observed," Evan answered.

"Every magnetic field that we know of has a positive and a negative orientation, a north and a south," Julie stated.

"And?" Evan said.

"Regardless of the size of the field, there will still be a north and a south pole," Julie said.

"Yes." He knew he had to be patient with Julie and let her recreate her own path to her conclusions.

Julie then asked, "Well, I got to thinking. If all magnetic fields have a polarity, then why not the magnetic beam?"

"Because the magnetic beam is not a field. It's a directed beam," Evan answered.

"Yes, but what if it does have a polarity?" Julie was introducing a whole new paradigm, and Evan was already having difficulty getting a handle on the magnetic-beam one.

"Okay. Let's assume, for a moment, that the magnetic beam has a polarity. That polarity would have to be between the two poles of the beam. Again, assuming that the two poles of the beam are N, the beam's point of origin, and S, the *Venture 1* probe. So what?" Evan concluded, for the sake of argument.

"Well, first off, I wasn't able to confirm any polarization to the beam, but take a look at the magnetic field surrounding *Venture*. It shows a periodic dynamic change." Julie pointed at some figures on the papers he was holding.

"Okay, what kind of change?" Evan's head was starting to wrap around this now.

"The repulsive/attractive linear force seems to oscillate… it flips… and it may even reorient in a way that the telemetry isn't showing," Julie stated.

Now Julie had Evan's true attention. An oscillating linear force emanating in relation to the magnetic beam could imply that the field was flipping. However, the field shouldn't—no, it couldn't. *Venture* was not large enough. Its mass was insufficient to cause the field to spontaneously reorient.

"It can't reorient. *Venture 1*'s mass is insufficient for a spontaneous field reorientation," Evan mused.

"That's what I thought. Then I got to thinking, maybe it's not the field that's flipping—maybe it's the actual beam that is reorienting *within* the field," Julie stated. "Could the beam be enveloped in the field?"

Wow! Julie was straining credulity now. The amount of energy to project a magnetic beam any substantial distance would be enormous, and then to reorient its flow would be bordering on inconceivable. Yet it fit.

"Okay, let's assume that the beam is enveloped within the field, and not merely part of the field, somehow," Evan said.

"Yes, like an electrical cable, copper wire enveloped within an insulating outer shell." Julie nodded her agreement. "The flow of electricity within the cable can be reoriented without causing a change to the insulating layer."

"Okay, so what we have here is a projected polarized field, from somewhere, using *Venture* as one pole. And we assume the point of origin of the field as the opposite pole?" Evan questioned, trying to sum up their discussion.

"Yes," Julie confirmed, eager to add to the summation. "And—"

"Hold on. I don't want to lose this path in my thinking," Evan stated. He then continued with his own *follow-the-dots*. "Now this polarized field is actually an insulator, for lack of a better word, that is carrying within it a magnetic beam."

Julie nodded.

"Okay… okay. The beam must be reorienting, somehow, or we would not be able to detect the oscillations," Evan stated.

"Yes," Julie agreed.

Evan continued, "In order for the beam to reorient, as it appears to be doing, it would have to have mass. And in order for it to have mass—which in and of itself it would not—it must be carrying a charge."

"Oh my god!" Julie quietly sighed. "So that's how the core is being reenergized."

"Force enough mass—in this case, the emitted particles—back into the core and you might be able to reverse the decay process," Evan concluded. "Though I wouldn't want to try to work out the critical nuclear bonding issues."

"It fits. And it also explains the power dilemma concerning the beam," Julie added.

"How so?" Evan asked.

"If the field is a carrier for the beam, then the power requirement for the beam itself would be less," Julie explained.

"Yes, yes, like how drafting behind a tractor-trailer saves gas, as opposed to not drafting. The beam is being pulled along with the field." Evan smiled.

"Exactly, but—" Julie started to state the obvious when Evan finished her thought.

"What is creating the field, and how is it being maintained?" Evan asked.

Julie nodded.

Evan then asked, "Can we prove any of this?"

Julie shuffled various pages then looked up. "Not with the incomplete data we currently have. No, I don't see how. You said *Venture*'s systems were nominal?" Julie recalled.

"They are—nothing new. How is the field reorienting? Is there a discernable pattern?" Evan was reaching now.

"I thought of that, but there isn't enough data here to extrapolate any sequence or pattern. I see where you're going with that though. Could the reorientation be an attempt at communication?" Julie asked.

"Actually, I wasn't thinking communication, as in person-to-person. I was thinking more along the lines of a computer code."

The furrowed brow appearing on Julie's forehead conveyed to Evan that she hadn't considered that possibility.

"Look at it this way. *Venture* is old. Any intelligence capable of finding it should be able to conclude that she's a long way from home," Evan started.

"How?" Julie asked.

"After all she's been through, she has to be showing obvious wear and tear. A scar from a micrometeor, something—maybe the paint is starting to fade," Evan explained.

"Okay, so *Venture* is used and old, relatively," Julie said.

"Relatively. *Venture* also has limited abilities, not so much because of its decaying power supply but because it was never constructed with the potential to learn. Yes, it has some autonomy, but that's very limited. So what can you do with it?" Evan asked.

"You're losing me, Evan," Julie stated.

Evan looked around the lab, trying to conjure up a way to explain himself. Not finding one, Evan finally said, "Suppose there is a courier pigeon, and all that courier pigeon does is relay information, a message. Does the courier pigeon need to know what the message is? No. He's just a courier pigeon. Then you come along, and you want the pigeon to convey a message over a great distance. Do you take the time and effort to teach the courier pigeon the importance of the message? No. It's just a bird. The pigeon certainly has no idea what was strapped to its leg. He only knows to fly back home. Same with *Venture*."

"So, you're saying *Venture* is going to fly a message back home? Wasn't that already done in a movie?" Julie was remembering V'ger from the first *Star Trek* movie.

"No. Obviously, *Venture* doesn't have the capability to return home. But it does have a tether to Earth," Evan stated.

"The downlink. My god. Evan, do you know what you're suggesting?" Julie asked.

"Yes, but I haven't been able to find anything in the downlink, so far, to confirm it," Evan said, trying to reassure her implied shock.

"You wouldn't. All downlinks are of a similar nature." Julie then had an idea to use the rover to test a communications hypothesis; but *Sirocco* utilized an entirely different mode of data transfer, so she quickly abandoned the idea.

"The up- and downlinks are S and X band radio. Ah, I see, the downlink would be incapable of transmitting a completed message. We can detect the magnetic field oscillations, but we can't get a completed sequence. There's too much of a time lag. And not only that, we would only see it as what we already do… reoriented field polarizations." Evan was babbling out loud and outside the box.

"Exactly. But that takes us right back to the beginning. Why establish a magnetic connection with *Venture* and then reorient the connection's polarization, unless you're trying to communicate?"

Julie was right; all they had was a lot of speculation and little fact. Just a whole lot of science fiction. It was time for a break anyway.

CHAPTER 48

Ludyte Home, Springtown, Pennsylvania
Wednesday, January 21, 2015
8:37 p.m., EST; 5:37 p.m., PST

EARLIER THAT EVENING, Father Dave had placed a telephone call to some encoded number, presumably in Italy. Having made the call from a public landline, and having consulted with who turned out to be the number-two man in the church, Father Dave and Randy drove back to the house in silence, mostly because Father Dave was trying to assimilate his conversation with Cardinal d'Salvé and because he was trying to settle on what to do next.

The five-minute ride was hardly enough time for Father Dave to gather his thoughts, and he knew that he would be called upon to summarize his telephone call. By the time they pulled into the driveway, Father Dave was sweating. Randy knew not to ask too many questions and to take Father Dave's advice to wait for his parents to tell him what was going on.

Together they walked into the house. As expected, Father Dave was immediately set upon with questions. It was Cate, of all people, who handed Father Dave a plate and beckoned him to sit down and eat. That was all Father Dave needed—time. After twenty minutes or so, he swallowed the last of his meal and took a deep, long breath. "The number was indeed to the Vatican, as we suspected."

"With whom did you speak?" Carol asked.

"Ah... okay... we must all completely understand that what we are about to discuss is highly sensitive and must remain private." Father Dave looked at each person, and held their gaze until they acknowledged with a head nod—Randy and Caitlin, included.

It was time to bring the whole family into the fold, as it were. "Jim, perhaps the time has come for you to make both Randy and Caitlin aware of what is going on," Father Dave suggested.

Carol looked at her husband and nodded. Jim turned to his two older children and proceeded to summarize the events of the past several days, giving full credit—or blame, depending on how you look at it—to Timothy for the discovery.

Caitlin was frozen, not blinking, shocked. Randy was full of questions but held them until the proper time. Which was not right now. Both Randy and Cate understood that their roles were to be supportive and protective of the family. And of Tim… especially of Tim.

After Jim finished recounting the events that led them to the telephone call to the Vatican, Father Dave said, "I actually had some difficulty placing the call. The number was correct, but there were roadblocks along the way. Finally, I got through to the intended party, Cardinal d'Salvé."

"Who's Cardinal d'Salvé?" Tim asked since he had absolutely no idea as to who was who in the Vatican.

"Cardinal d'Salvé is the private secretary to His Holiness. You do know who that is, right?" Father Dave's sarcasm was appreciated.

"Smart-ass," Tim said quietly under his breath, loud enough for everyone to hear but quiet enough for it to be forgiven.

"The cardinal wanted to convey his congratulations, along with that of the pope. They, and the church, are extremely proud of you and the discovery you've made. They wanted me to tell you that you have their complete confidence."

"Dave, we all thank you, the cardinal, and the pope—but would you get on with it? Obviously, the cardinal did not want to simply congratulate Tim." Jim was stating the obvious.

For the next forty-five minutes, Father Dave attempted to relate to the Ludyte family the nature of his conversation with Cardinal d'Salvé without violating any secretive nature, implied or otherwise, of the actual conversation itself. He explained the position of the church and its concern regarding the international implications this was going to have.

"I thought people would be excited about this. ET has finally been found." Tim's optimistic view was both youthful and naive.

"Some will be. Others… not so much. You all need to understand that the church believes—and I agree with this assessment—that the global community, at first, will rejoice, but then worry, followed by denial," Father Dave explained.

Again, Tim spoke up. "Denial? How can they deny this?"

"Many are going to try to dismiss this as a hoax perpetrated by a young, disturbed teenager. Others will claim that you do not have the credentials to support such a discovery… and still others will lash out at you from a position of pure jealousy," Father Dave explained.

"This is going to get sticky." Caitlin was right on target with that one.

"So what do you suggest we do?" Carol could feel her maternal protective instincts surfacing.

"I have been authorized to offer you the protection of the church," Father Dave stated.

"Great, what good will that do when the wackos start camping out across the street? Everyone remember the movie *Contact*?"

Randy's concern for his little brother was sincere, but he knew that being related to the guy who made the biggest discovery in history was going to cause him problems too.

"Well, I believe we all need to take precautions. The church can protect you physically, but that will only be temporary protection," Father Dave declared.

"Can the government help?" Carol asked.

This time, it was her husband who jumped in. "I think, at the moment, until we have a clear course of action, we need to continue to sit on this. We tell no one."

"I agree. Cardinal d'Salvé has empowered me to speak for the Holy See. He has placed at my—at *our* disposal the resources of the office of the provincial in Philadelphia, Cardinal Ziest. The cardinal should be returning to Philadelphia later tonight, tomorrow at the latest, after being conferenced in Rome," Father Dave said, trying to calm the family.

"What about school? What about our lives?" Cate said with just a little agitation, and she was right.

"Mom and I will speak to the superintendent… the three of you may be removed from school for the foreseeable future," Jim stated clearly. No one dared to argue.

"If need be, we can arrange something through one of the Catholic schools in the Philadelphia area for you to complete the year, maybe even have you attend your classes at Drexel, or St. Joe's." Father Dave was trying to cover as many bases as he could in an attempt to placate the concerns of everyone at the table.

"Isn't Villanova a Catholic school?" Randy asked. He had applied to attend Villanova after graduating.

"Yes, it is… I'll see what I can do," Father Dave replied.

"Okay." Carol was making a list. "That covers school. Jim, what about work? Can you take some family leave time?"

"I should be able to." Jim thought for a brief moment then stated, "Yes, I will. I've been there long enough."

"Mom? What about you?" Cate had shed her agitation and was now genuinely concerned.

"I'll be okay." Carol tried to reassure her daughter.

"What's going on? Anything that I should know about?" Father Dave had to know everything if he was going to protect them.

"Dave, Carol's pregnant," Jim stated.

"Oh my god! Way to go!" Father Dave's somber, concerned features immediately changed into a blossom of joy and elation. "How far along are you?"

"Thirteen weeks," a blushing Carol stated.

"Okay, well, we can provide any medical assistance you may need. We can even relocate you, should that become necessary," Father Dave assured her.

"No, absolutely not." Carol was emphatic.

"All right. Well, we'll cross that bridge when we get to it. Ah… there is one last thing, and Randy alluded to it earlier," Father Dave continued.

"What? What did I say?" Randy looked confused.

"Yes, Randy, I did see *Contact*, and I do remember the harassment that the Jodi Foster scientist received. I think before word of this gets out to anybody… and I do mean anybody"—Father Dave was looking directly at the three Ludyte children—"we should relocate all of you to the provincial residence in Philadelphia. Like an embassy, the provincial residence is legally considered the sovereignty of the Vatican. No one, including the United States, can touch you while you stay there."

"For as long as we stay there." Cate was not pleased with being cut off from her so-called life, but she knew that in the long run, being the favorite sibling of the boy who changed the world was going to be a very exciting thing.

"Okay, Carol, anything else on that list that we need to cover?" Jim asked, interrupting his daughter.

"Not really. We can simply tell neighbors, friends, and family that we are taking an impromptu extended vacation to celebrate the coming of a little Ludyte," Carol mused.

"That'll work. Okay, Tim, I'd like to talk to you and your dad in the study," Father Dave said as he pushed back from the table. "Everyone else… I hate to do this to you, but go pack. We leave ASAP. I will have the local seminary assign several priests to stay here to provide security for your house and belongings. Also, I will have your mail rerouted to Philadelphia. Oh, and the church is going to be helpful with maintaining your financial standard of living, for the time being. Your household bills will be paid. All in an effort to project an image of normalcy."

"Thank God." Both Jim and Carol were relieved to hear that one.

Father Dave, led by Jim and Tim, excused himself and went to the study. As he did so, he could overhear Carol tell both Randy and Cate to only pack enough for the next few days. If they had to, they would have the church retrieve additional belongings.

Father Dave closed the door to the study and turned to face father and son. He stared at them for a moment.

Jim spoke up first. "Looks like you're going to save this family… again."

Father Dave slapped him on the shoulder and said, "C'mon, we have to get this stuff together."

CHAPTER 49

Venture Lab, Pasadena, California
Thursday, January 22, 2015
4:12 a.m., EST; 1:12 a.m., PST

"COULD THE MAGNETIC field reorientations be a code and not just a carrier?" Evan asked.

"How?" Julie was committed to figuring this out.

"What if each reorientation point corresponded with a symbol in a code? That would explain the why part of the reorientation question," Evan mused.

"Okay, but what code?" Julie asked.

"*Venture 1*—like *Venture 2* and the *Voyager* twins—was programmed in FORTRAN," Evan answered.

"I seriously doubt that an alien agency is going to know FORTRAN, let alone any other Earth language," Julie said with just a hint of sarcasm.

"Well, then what? Is machine code simple enough to break down into a series of reorientation symbols?" Evan put forth.

"How about going even more basic. What about binary? *Venture*, like *Sirocco*, would interpret a binary signal coming from anywhere as one coming from Earth. It would attempt to interpret, and compile, the code. If it couldn't, it would signal for a resend of the program."

Just like her little rover crossing the plains of Mars, Julie was starting to make some progress on the problem.

"We have to look at the telemetry," Evan said as the two scientists did an about-face in the empty hallway and headed back to the

Sirocco lab. "Can you show me the data that you interpret as indicating the reorientation?"

Julie checked the systems for *Sirocco* and made sure that it was safe and secure before joining Evan at the conference table. Shuffling through several files on her laptop—not to mention the surrounding piles of papers and printouts—she finally found what she was looking for.

"Here it is," Julie finally stated.

Pulling a chair in behind her at the table, Evan began his own mental analysis of the information. To begin with, he had to remind himself what he was actually looking at. Magnetic field data could be represented in any one of a variety of units: gauss, teslas, amperes per meter, webers, and so forth. The *Venture* projects used teslas. The MAGROL data showed a concentration strength of 3.25×10^{-8} teslas. Not much there, but that was not the information he was looking for.

"C'mon, Evan, what happens to the field strength when the polarization is reversed?" he asked himself. Then he answered himself, and chuckled at the notion that an insane person answers his own questions. But weren't they both a little insane for even considering all of this?

Refocusing on the data, Evan could almost reach out and grasp what he was looking for. "The field strength stays the same. Then what?"

Evan jumped into the depths of contemplation. *Wait, if the strength of the field is 0.0000000325 teslas, then... wait. The attractive and repulsive forces are the same, only the orientation reverses. One is attractive, and one is repulsive.*

"How many data points do we have here?" Evan was on to something.

"I'm not sure, many. But I don't think it's enough to interpret a code," Julie answered.

"I'm not looking to interpret a code. I just want to verify that the polarizations are oscillating between positive and negative, and I don't really think it's a repolarization. I think it's more of a redirection from attractive to repulsive forces, like flipping the current back and forth on an electric magnet," Evan explained.

Now Julie saw where Evan was going, and he said she was brilliant. Continuing, this time Julie wasn't sure if he was talking to her or to himself. "The first- and second-shift technicians were supposed to record several pieces of data. Otherwise, we would have a hard time sorting it all out from the direct download telemetry. At the beginning of each shift and at the end of each shift, the technicians should have recorded not only the transmission power levels but the magnetic field strengths as well."

"How are you going to be able to tell if it's an attractive force or a repulsive force? The *Sirocco* has magnetometers, but even with those newer ones, we can't recognize the difference."

"Hmmm, let me think." Evan was in his element now. He had a problem, and he knew the answer. He just needed the solution to get him there. This was the environment in which he thrived.

"What if...? No, that won't work."

Now Julie was sure Evan was speaking to himself.

"Hold on..."

She just let him roll with it.

"If the beam is using *Venture* as one of the poles of the transmission, then the actual linear force on the probe should change as the beam alternates between positive and negative. If so, then there should be a corresponding change in *Venture*'s velocity."

"A nudge, basically," Julie clarified. *Keep going, Evan, keep going,* Julie thought.

"Yes, a nudge just might be noticeable in the spacecraft's velocity. If it is forceful enough," Evan stated.

"However, one problem with that is the beam is not on the same vector that *Venture* is." Julie hated to throw a bucket of cold water on his fire, but she was right.

"How do we know that?" Evan asked.

"From the MAGROL. When you had *Venture* perform the MAGROL, the field fluctuated. Very slightly, remember?"

Of course, Evan remembered.

Julie continued, not even noticing the nod of his head, "If the beam was directly at *Venture*, on the same vector that it's traveling, then the rotation of the magnetometers would have produced fluctuations that were symmetrical, and they didn't. Similar to focusing a beam of light with a magnifying glass. Hit the glass straight on, perpendicular to the optical focal point, and the light beam is symmetrically converted. Evidenced by the pinpoint of light emerging from the glass. Hit the glass at an angle and the light is dispersed, or asymmetrical."

Evan grabbed the papers, looking for the MAGROL data. Finding it, he started comparing values. With a look of defeat, he dropped the pages back onto the pile and turned to Julie. "You're right. The values are not symmetrical. The beam is hitting *Venture* from an oblique angle."

Julie took the now-empty cup of coffee Evan was using and went to refill it. Something didn't fit, though, with their analysis. So what if the beam was engaging *Venture* at an angle? They should still be able to detect whether or not *Venture* was being affected.

"That's it!" Julie had it.

Leaving the cup on the counter, she hurried back to Evan. "Has *Venture* had to undergo any course deviations?" she asked.

"What?" Evan asked.

"Has *Venture* had to undergo any course deviations?" Julie asked.

"I don't know. Why?" a puzzled Evan replied.

"If it has, then we might be able to match the course deviations with the beam oscillations and get an idea of the beam's magnitude."

She was pleased with herself. It was a long shot, but if it held, they would have another piece to the puzzle.

Quickly turning and heading for the door, Evan said, "I'll be right back. I need to check the telemetry logs." *And make a phone call.*

Evan kept that last part to himself.

CHAPTER 50

The One

The Book of The One
Book of Propagation, **block 8, level 13.**

> *13: And the benefits of communion with The One shall be spread throughout the heavens, to the extreme extent of the influence of The One.*

The Book of The One
Acts of Salvation, **block 3, level 20.**

> *20: And The One will overtake the course of all misguided civilizations and lead them to a future of unity and peace through the blessings of communal completeness.*

CHAPTER 51

The Terraces, Philadelphia, Pennsylvania

THE PROVINCIAL'S RESIDENCE sat on nearly nine acres of prime real estate located on the campus of St. Joseph's Jesuit University, at the corner of City Avenue and Cardinal Avenue, in Philadelphia. The residence was upgraded significantly after the various global terror attacks of the early 2000s.

Today, the home was more of a compound than a residence. The location was comprised of the provincial's residence, which included a three-story main building and two additional outbuildings, totaling 23,350 square feet. There were two gated entranceways: one off City Avenue, and the other off Cardinal Avenue, both with retractable tire trundles and concrete barriers. Surrounded by a tall iron fence, the dwelling known as the Terraces, at 5700 City Avenue, had been home to Philadelphia's archbishops since 1935. The property included an indoor/outdoor swimming pool, a gardener's cottage, and a six-car garage. During Cardinal John Krol's era in the 1970s and '80s, it also featured a par-three golf hole and putting green.

The residence, which faced City Avenue, not only was situated behind an imposing iron fence but several hardwood and pine trees, allowing for limited visibility of the actual mansion. Constructed in an L shape, the internal yard was surrounded by an impenetrable growth of hedges and trees. Leading onto the property was a paved loop driveway, with a smaller looped primary driveway leading to the official residence entranceway. Covering several windows, presumably those of the actual living quarters, were quarter- to half-inch-thick steel bars fashioned in an ornate grate pattern.

One of the largest private homes in Philadelphia, the stately three-story main dwelling of nearly thirteen thousand square feet sits on landscaped acreage that sweeps from City Avenue to Overbrook Avenue, at the rear of the property. According to public records, the primary construction of the residence was both natural rock and reinforced concrete block. Each block weighed over thirty-five pounds and provided nearly eight hundred cubic inches of six-thousand-pound compression protection. Ideal for low maintenance of both above and below grade. The internal living quarters were protected by half-inch rebar reinforced concrete, laid in one continuous pour.

There is a full-time contingent of security personnel, as well as remote passive protection provided by an undisclosed security agency. The passive security measures include building entrance detection, motion detection of the surrounding yards, and electronic interference protection of the entire estate. The main entrance is governed by a walk-through metal detector, as well as handheld wand detectors, when necessary. All visitors to the residence must enter by way of the front main entrance and submit themselves to a personal search. Armed security guards, accompanied by sniffer dogs, patrol the grounds and all non-private interior spaces in a continuous random fashion. A no-fly zone extending to three thousand feet above the estate could be enforced by the efforts of McGuire AFB, located in New Jersey, as well as forces from Pennsylvania, New Jersey, and Delaware Air National Guard divisions. The no-fly zone could be initiated by a single message from either the provincial or his designee at a moment's notice.

The security features of the residence are enhanced by additional measures that are not easily observed. The utility supply to the residence is comprised of an onsite six-hundred-foot-deep solely dedicated freshwater well that pumped water to a contained filtration and purification system. Electrically, the Terraces are connected to the primary Philadelphia power grid; however, in the event of either a grid failure or an internal power loss, the electrical supply can be supplemented by a pair of 1,000-kW generators, specially built by Generac. Each generator can be tuned to respond as quickly as seven seconds after primary power loss. Feeding the massive generators are several Generac UL-142 model double-walled fuel containment tanks storing enough diesel fuel to run continuously, at full load, for thirty days.

A boosted fiber-optic telephone system is provided by the local telephone network; however, a continuously manned system provides human reception, and screening, of all incoming telephone calls. Not part of the locally provided com service is an encrypted emergency microwave transmitted line that connects directly to the Vatican. Standard Internet service is provided by an undisclosed local ISP company, with access by way of a dedicated T5 line. The communications center, located deep within the Terraces, utilizes an OC4 configuration (short for Optical Carrier level 4), which provides access speeds of roughly one hundred T3 lines. Several cascading firewalls protect the Terrace's Internet service, as well as a 24/7 human monitor. Virus (and intrusion) protection is state of the art, the details of which are not available.

What is known is that the entire computer system, both internally and web-accessed, is protected by a Russian-doll configuration of protective shells, each one governed by successful completion of the previous shell, and by either biometric or nine-character password-level security, depending upon the depth of the shell. It is an unsubstantiated rumor that the password changes according to a variant of a World War II Enigma encryption machine. Passwords are created at the Vatican Security Police Internet Division, Vatican City, and transmitted via secured microwave system to various provincial locations around the world. Once a destination receives the encrypted password, it must apply the correct key in order to read and apply the password. Passwords are changed on a random basis, with few exceptions. A password can be reset upon the request of a provincial or the Holy Father.

The various biometric safeguards utilized throughout the residence are configured to release upon the successful entrance of a viable sample. The system is capable of immediately detecting the viability of a biometric sample. Should the sample not be viable, the system would collapse; and after ninety seconds, unless the reset command is validated by the computer core (located in a climate-controlled room well beneath the swimming pool), the system is purged. Physical access to the core room is by a simple entry lock. Presumably, if one could make it to the door of the core room, then one may have access to it.

Food preparations are offered by a fully staffed in-house kitchen and wait service. All employees are prescreened by the Vatican Security Police. Supplies are provided by local farms.

Located seven stories below the City Avenue wing of the residence is an emergency bunker capable of sustaining a population of seventeen adults for twenty-one days, extendable to forty-two days with the implementation of strict rationing. Honed out of the deep bedrock of the Delaware Basin, the bunker is initially protected by a fifteen-ton, triple-pinned, laminated stainless steel door, with sixteen locking four-inch-diameter case-hardened steel bars that extend into the door's steel frame. Communication utilities, along with electrical and water/sewage utilities can be isolated from the main aboveground facility. In the event of a failure of the primary Philadelphia power grid, the bunker can draw its power needs directly from a Hydrogenics HyPM™ XR fuel cell system, capable of producing 627 kW of AC emergency power.

The computing facilities contained within the bunker have nearly the same capabilities as those above ground. Communications are supported by a buried OC4 line connected to a secondary microwave transmitter located at a secured non-Philadelphia site several miles away. The consumables store is well stocked and contains a twenty-one-day supply of emergency rations and freeze-dried provisions.

Additionally, the bunker contains a basic medical facility, equipped to provide first aid as well as simple surgical and diagnostic assistance. There is a supply of essential medications, including a considerable supply of potassium iodine tablets. Furthermore, the underground complex is hardened against electromagnetic pulse interference and floats on an array of earthquake-absorption springs. Lastly, it is equipped with remote sensing capabilities to test aboveground conditions for chemical, biological, and radioactive contaminants. In the event of an airborne attack, the bunker can be hermetically sealed with a positive pressure of 20 millibars. Entry to the bunker, under pressurized conditions, is rerouted through a double-chambered airlock system. Non-pressurized access to the bunker is by way of the primary fifteen-ton door.

To call the bunker a fortress within a fortress is an accurate euphemism.

Placed at the provincial's personal access is a fleet of five outwardly nondescript armored cars, constructed by a research and development division of General Motors. The only externally visible features singling out the cars are their tinted windows, which are one-way darkened to 32 percent. Parenthetically, a similar window design was employed by the designers of the federal building in Philadelphia.

Each car is equipped with GPS location and mapping systems, as well as a secure 5G mobile-wireless network. Additionally, there is an encrypted satellite telephone, along with an interactive video system so the provincial may conduct secure video conferencing.

A double-walled, armor-plated fuel cell—encased in a specialized foam to protect it from rupture in the event of collision or small-arms fire—feeds a fuel-injected V8 that averages nearly twelve miles to the gallon and is capable of an undisclosed top speed in excess of 100 miles per hour.

Furthermore, there is an onboard Halon fire-suppression system, along with a separate oxygen supply, stored in the trunk, routed by way of steel-reinforced tubing to two interior ports: one located under the front passenger seat and one under the rearmost seat of the passenger compartment. Included among the various emergency medical supplies are several units of the provincial's blood type, to be used in the event the motorcade's ambulance is intercepted.

The car is heavy, to say the least. The thick armor-plated doors are so substantial that it is nearly impossible for one person to open them from within without the aid of the onboard egress system. In the event of a loss of all internal power, each side door, as well as an emergency hatch in the roof, can be mechanically ejected with the use of explosive charges. A similar system was used in the space program to eject the hatch doors on early capsule designs.

The interior can be cut off from the outside environment and sealed in case of chemical attack. That is not to say that the windows are incapable of being lowered—a requirement of the current provincial. However, upon detection of any number of hazardous conditions outside the vehicle, the windows will automatically sound an alarm and then, eight seconds later, close and seal. It rides on special Kevlar-reinforced Goodyear run-flat tires, capable of withstanding a variety of degrading attacks, including punctures, chemical corrosives, and radioactive disintegration. Moreover, the tires are equipped with retractable small-grade spikes that automatically deploy when there is a low coefficient of static friction detected by the onboard computer system. There are night-vision cameras mounted inside the grill. Their images can be projected onto the windshield in a heads-up configuration, should the driver require it.

Any designated agent assigned to drive the provincial has to take an intense two-week-long defensive-driving class provided by the US Secret Service Academy in Beltsville, Maryland. The practices of evasive maneuvering, high-speed cornering, and precision driving, as well as basic medical training, are covered.

"It actually handles quite well, considering how much it weighs," one driver said.

There are no rocket launchers, grenades, or built-in offensive weapons of any kind. However, stored within the trunk is a wide array of defensive devices.

There was a total of three fully equipped vehicles, along with one-scaled down version, and one unmarked ambulance to provide support, and distraction, in the provincial's carpool. Each vehicle is eighteen feet in length and features military-grade armor (a laminated composite of steel, aluminum, titanium, and ceramic plate) surrounded by replaceable Kevlar sheets on the doors and quarter panels. In an effort to conserve weight, the windows are double-paned, laminated sheets of tempered glass, accounting for a total thickness of only one inch. The protective ability of the windows comes from the positive pressure maintained between the two sheets of glass. Sealed champagne bottles exhibit a similar shatter resistance, as evidenced by the many viral videos demonstrating that so long as the seal is maintained, a champagne bottle can be used to hammer nails.

The chassis is of a reinforced frame construction, with added shielding to withstand the detonation of an improvised explosive device directly under the passenger compartment. Lastly (and some would say "sadly"), there is no passenger-side ejection seat, but there are air bags.

CHAPTER 52

Ludyte Home, Springtown, Pennsylvania
Thursday, January 22, 2015
4:12 a.m., EST; 1:12 a.m., PST

IT WAS VERY early in the morning when the phone rang in the Ludyte home.

"Timothy James Ludyte, it's for you," Carol called out in a loud voice.

Three names. Tim knew he was in trouble now. *God, please let it be important enough to save my life.*

"Mmm… yeah… what do you want?" Tim asked through the fog of sleep. "I mean… hello?"

"Tim, I'm sorry for bothering you so early in the morning. This is Dr. Wills."

Tim straightened right up. Now he was awake! "Oh, I'm sorry. Yes, good morning. How may I help you, Dr. Willis—I mean Wills, Dr. Wills."

Evan chuckled. If only Tim knew how much he really needed that. "You see, Tim, I am actually quite embarrassed, but we seem to have misplaced some information from *Venture 1*, and I was wondering—actually, hoping is more like it—that maybe you might have a copy."

"What are you looking for?" Tim asked, rubbing the sleep away from his eyes.

"Well, it's a simple piece of information. You may not have even gotten to it, and if you did, you may not know what you're looking at," Evan remarked. "We need the downlink power level telemetry. Have you come across it yet?"

"I haven't seen it yet. There are several full boxes. I'll search for it today, after school. If I find it, I'll give you a call right away," Tim answered.

"You sure you couldn't go check right now? I can wait. It's very important." Evan thought he'd press his luck a little.

"I can't keep the phone tied up. But, should I find the data, I will call you back immediately," Tim stated.

Needing to keep Tim from growing too suspicious, and needing his help, Evan took a deep silent breath and exhaled slowly, cleansing his in-the-moment mind. "That's great, Tim. I'm really sorry for disturbing you and your family. Sometimes, working third shift, I tend to forget that the real world functions on a more normal time schedule. Tell you what. Take your time looking for it. When you find it, just give me a quick call."

"No problem, Dr. Wills. No problem at all." Tim hung up and turned to lean back against the hallway wall. "Big problem, Dr. Wills. A very big problem." Tim slid down the wall as he spoke quietly to himself.

Tim's mother emerged from the bathroom and saw her son sitting on the floor, staring. Sliding down the wall opposite him, she simply sat there. They sat for what seemed like an eternity, gazing at each other. Finally, Tim gave a head shake as he refocused on his mom and asked a completely unexpected question. "So, if it's a girl, what are you going to name it?"

"What?" She was taken off guard with that one, considering everything that had been going on lately.

"If junior's a girl, what are you going to name it?" Tim asked again.

"Ah... I don't know. We haven't talked about that yet," Carol stated.

"I suggest *Willowmeana*." Tim smiled as he said that.

"Willowmeana?" She smiled. "Really?"

"Yes. That or maybe *Lucinda*." Tim was almost laughing now.

"Okay, I'll bite. Why?" Now her curiosity was up.

"Well, if you name her Willowmeana, then she can be called Willow… I like that. If you call her Lucinda, then she would be Lucy Ludyte, or Lu-Lu." Tim smiled.

"Great, so you want us to name her after a tree. Thanks, Tim." Tim's mom was laughing too.

As they were discussing what to call little "to-be-named-later," Tim's brother came and sat on the floor next to him. "If I had to name it… I mean her… I'd pick *Katherine*."

"Why? We already have a Cate," their mom asked, confused.

"After Katherine Hemmingway—she was absolutely gorgeous." Randy was right, and the three of them nodded in agreement.

"And classy," Tim added.

"Oh yes, very classy." Apparently, Katherine Hemmingway was on Randy's list of "girls he'd love to date." Tim just smiled.

Rubbing her eyes to wake up, Cate padded down the hallway still in her Elmo nightshirt. As she sat next to her mom and rested her head tenderly on her shoulder, she asked, "What's going on?"

"We're discussing what to name the baby," her mom calmly told her.

"Christopher Evan Ludyte," Cate said, as if the decision was a no-brainer.

"Wait, no! We are not naming *her* Christopher Evan Ludyte." Tim chuckled.

"Why not? And who said it's a girl?" Cate demanded to know.

"Well, first, it has to be a girl… it's the law of nature," Tim said matter-of-factly.

"Oh, this is going to be good. Go on." Carol couldn't wait to hear this one.

"Everyone knows that birth gender—" Tim started to say, only to be interrupted.

"Sex," Mom corrected him sternly.

"What?" Tim stopped and asked.

"It's not gender, it's sex," Mom elaborated.

"Really? You sure?" Randy asked.

"Pretty sure," Carol replied.

"Whatever... where was I?" Tim stated as he shook his head.

Randy leaned over and said, "Everyone knows that sex..." He looked at his mom as he said that, who simply nodded an approval.

"Oh right... Everyone knows that birth sex follows a sequence: boy-girl-boy-girl." As Tim identified the order, he pointed to his brother, then his sister, then himself, and last to his mom's stomach.

As if on cue, they started to laugh. Randy laughed so hard he fell over. That was all that was needed to wake their father and Father Dave. Both men came stumbling out of their respective rooms.

"Is everything okay?" Jim asked.

"Yes, everything is absolutely perfect," Carol announced. She really needed that moment, no matter how brief. To have a moment of bonding with just her children gave her the strength to start what promised to be a long day.

Father Dave just stood there, scratching his head... literally. His hair a mess, his face unshaven—he looked like he hadn't slept well. And who could blame him? He was the point man in what was going to be the event of all events. And unknown to Father Dave—or anyone else—it was going to truly begin in just a few hours.

CHAPTER 53

Venture Lab, Pasadena, California
Thursday, January 22, 2015
4:29 a.m., EST; 1:29 a.m., PST

WHAT NOW? EVAN wasn't sure what to do next. He needed that data, but he also needed to keep a lid on all this—as long as possible. Grabbing the folder that contained the most recent telemetry logs, Evan turned for the door, and the *Sirocco* lab, when an unscheduled downlink from *Venture* came through.

Most of the time, when an unscheduled downlink is received by the shared seventy-meter reception antenna, an alarm is tripped. Unscheduled downlinks happen so infrequently that an alarm is typically a shock to everyone on duty at the time; and this time, Evan was the only one in the lab, for the moment.

"Damn," Evan whispered under his breath as he turned and looked at the little blue light blinking on one of the solid-state monitoring boards. Even as he shut off the annoying *chirp-chirp* that the alarm sounded, he knew what this meant. There were protocols in place for unscheduled downlinks, and these protocols were automatic. Evan could not have stopped the alert going out even if he tried. The system was configured in such a way that if something like this happened, a notification, most likely by landline telephone, would be automatically sent out to the ranking project leader—in this case, Dr. Patricia Katz.

It was said that Dr. Katz was formed out of the now-broken molds of the old school. She was around when the *Voyagers* were first conceived as part of the *Mariner* program—*Mariners 11* and *12*. Then she watched the *Mariner* program come to an ignominious end with *Mariner 10*, thus leaving *Mariners 11* and *12* to suffer yet another name change—this time, the twins would be labeled

Mariner Jupiter-Saturn. Eventually, the project renaming settled down, and Dr. Katz found herself a part of the newly announced *Voyager* program. And, well, the rest is legend. She is eccentric, to the greatest extent of the definition. Rumor is that she even knew where all the bodies were buried… on Mars. She could be that dangerous, if she chose to be. Not a woman to be feared, no. But Dr. Katz was a woman to be respected, which could be worse than being feared.

Evan knew what was going to happen next. At any moment, the phone would ring, and Dr. Katz would demand an explanation as to why she was awakened at such an ungodly hour. He could simply tell her that the unscheduled downlink was the result of yet another failing system on *Venture*, due to its dwindling power supply; and she'd probably buy that, until she'd come to the office in the morning and check the computer logs herself. No, he better be straightforward with her—or as much as he could be—and still maintain his credibility.

Quickly running over to the *Sirocco* lab, Evan bounded into the room, announcing that he had an alarm. "I've got a downlink alarm!"

"Oh shit." Now it was Julie's turn to stay calm. Knowing what this meant, she checked the latest status of *Sirocco*, looked at the Mars clock, and quickly did the mental math—*Sirocco* still had another fifty-six minutes until Martian dawn and the start of another day's prospecting. She had a little time to spare.

Evan didn't even wait for her; he quickly turned and bolted back to the *Venture* lab just as the phone started to ring. "Oh great, just great." He hadn't even had time to check the downlink to determine what tripped the alarm. Taking a deep breath, followed by a hard, dry swallow, Evan picked up the phone on the fourth ring. Julie was just entering the lab.

"*Venture* lab, Dr. Wills speaking."

"What's going on?" a very calm Dr. Katz asked. You didn't survive in this business without, at the very least, a minimal amount of people skills, even if you had the reputation of Dr. Katz.

"I'm sorry, Dr. Katz. I was across the hallway getting coffee when the alarm sounded. I haven't had time to check the telemetry."

A partial truth was better than an outright lie.

"Okay. I'm going to shower and dress. That'll take me thirty to forty-five minutes. I will call you back then. Will that be enough time for you to get a handle on things?" Dr. Katz asked.

What was he going to say other than "Yes, thank you, Dr. Katz. I'll check and talk to you in forty-five minutes."

"Good." The phone clicked dead.

"Okay, we have forty-five minutes to figure out what happened," Evan stated, more to himself than anyone in particular.

What to do first? Well, according to SOP, in the event of an alarm, he needed to back-check the offsets, verify signal stability, and check the telemetry. The actual downlink from *Venture 1* was weak, on the order of 0.1 billion-billionth of a watt, and yet the seventy-meter dish used for communicating with it was still able to detect the signal.

"Julie, check the signal stability for me. I'm going to start on the telemetry."

Julie sat down in front of a downlink monitor, and after Evan gave her the necessary password, she began running diagnostics on the X-band downlink system. Evan was scrolling through screen after screen of raw telemetry, looking for anything that might jump out and catch his attention.

"Diagnostics running, so far nothing," Julie announced.

"Okay… leave that and come double-check this telemetry with me," Evan commanded.

Screen after screen of raw data numbers... zeros, ones... in a matrix of information. Some of the information was actually represented in base-ten numbers and not in binary code. Nothing appeared off, though. Everything appeared to be as it should, especially when cross-referenced with previous data.

Pushing away from his computer, Evan whipped off his glasses. "Damn, what happened?"

Julie was still glued to her computer, checking. Dr. Wagner had a fast mind when it came to pattern recognition.

"Julie?" Evan called over to her.

Nothing.

"Julie!"

Still nothing.

"Dr. Wagner!"

Julie slowly looked up from the screen that had her so engrossed, her face devoid of all color, her eyes growing into an astonishing look as she turned to face Evan.

"What?"

Now Evan was concerned—truly concerned. "Julie, what's going on?"

Nothing, just a blank two-thousand-yard stare that pierced right through him. Evan gently pushed her aside and looked at the screen she was reviewing. It was a screen that compared combined data from the entire electromagnetic spectrum, data that they had never even thought to check before. He saw nothing. Wait... cross-checking previous data.

"I see nothing, Jules."

Dr. Wagner turned back to the screen, her fingers dancing on the keyboard as if she were playing a Grand Steinway. She finally pressed the reconfigured F1 key and executed a simple compare-and-contrast program.

She pointed at the data as it flew down the screen. Then she pressed the space bar, halting the cascading information, and looked up at a completely bewildered Dr. Wills. And calmly and quietly, and quite fearfully, she said, "I think we're under attack."

CHAPTER 54

Philadelphia International Airport, Philadelphia, Pennsylvania
Thursday, January 22, 2015
6:08 a.m., EST; 3:08 a.m., PST

CARDINAL ZIEST HAD arrived in Philadelphia shortly after 6:00 a.m., having flown straight back from Vatican City. He was not alone. Accompanying him was a contingent of Gendarmerie Corps of the Vatican City State and, more impressively, what appeared to be a squadron of Pontifical Swiss Guard.

The Pontifical Swiss Guard, commonly known as the Swiss Guard, is a dedicated, and separate, branch of the Swiss Defense Force, has been in service to the Holy See since 1506. Every member of the guard is devoutly catholic, an exceedingly obedient and skilled soldier, and male. As the oldest active-duty military unit presently in existence, the Swiss Guard are responsible for the personal protection of the pope and the Apostolic Palace, which includes St. Peter's Basilica, the various buildings within the Vatican, and Castle Gandolfo. However security of the Vatican City State is the responsibility of the Gendarmerie Corps. Enter Vatican City and you fall under the jurisdiction of the Gendarmerie Corps; enter St. Peter's Basilica, or any of the pontifical buildings, and you fall under the very close scrutiny of the Swiss Guard.

The seventeenth-century uniforms and pole weapons that are most commonly seen on television are part of the pomp and pageantry that is the Vatican. However, underneath the flashy costumes are well-equipped, well-armored commandos, each with a papal license to kill—if necessary. The papacy has at its complete disposal one of the best-trained, best-equipped, most dedicated fighting forces the world has never fully known about, or understood for that matter. To the common people of the world—

and the Vatican seems to have little desire to dissuade this view—the Swiss Guard appear to be little more than well-costumed actors, placed around the Vatican to enhance the ambiance. Such a view cannot be further from the truth. After the May 13, 1981 assassination attempt on Pope John Paul II, the Swiss Guard underwent a paradigm shift, increasing its focus on non-ceremonial duties and terror suppression. They are a force to be reckoned with, and the world's militaries know it.

As the caravan of provincial vehicles approached the Terraces, Cardinal Ziest's private secretary placed a telephone call from the car. The call, placed in the open, on unsecured lines, was to Father Davidson's cell phone and contained one simple message: "It is time to come home."

Back at the Ludyte home, some sixty or seventy miles north of Philadelphia, Father Davidson, having received the message, snapped closed his cell phone, and turned back to the bathroom mirror and his half-shaved face. He knew he only had a few minutes to himself, and then he had to get this family out and on its way. They were going to use the family cars, as if they were going on a vacation. Carol and Jim had already left the house and were conferring with the school superintendent. The kids were supposedly packing.

It was just then that the doorbell rang, startling Father Dave. He stuck his head out the bathroom, face full of shaving cream, just as Randy answered the door.

"Yes, may I help you?" Randy may have only been eighteen, but he cast an imposingly strong figure.

"Hello, my name is Father Goosick. Here is my identification." The young priest at the door, dressed in denim jeans and a St. Loyola rugby shirt, handed over his seminary ID.

Randy checked the photo on the ID with the man standing in front of him, and being satisfied, he stepped aside and let him in. His car, a nondescript red SUV, was parked neatly in the driveway, locked.

Father Dave emerged from the bathroom, still in sweatpants and T-shirt. "You're from the seminary?"

"Yes, and you would be...?"

One thing he had to hand to Father Goosick was that he was suspicious, and for this assignment, that was a very good characteristic.

"I'm Father Davidson. You may call me Dave, as we want to keep as low a profile as possible," Father Dave stated.

"That's why I came in civvies. My name is Richard, or just Rich."

The two priests shook hands. Turning to go back down the hallway, Father Dave asked Randy to attend to Father Rich while he finished dressing.

"Can I get you anything? Something to drink?" Randy asked.

"No, I'm fine. I left my overnight bag in the truck. I'll get it later, but where would you like me to sleep?" Father Rich asked politely.

"You can have my room. My brother, Tim, is somewhat—how shall I say it? Well, he's fifteen." Randy noticed that the young priest couldn't be more than four or five years older than himself, so he thought his room would be more fitting. "Feel free to make yourself at home. I cleaned out the top drawer of the dresser for you, and there should be room in the closet," Randy said, as he escorted Father Rich to his bedroom.

Sitting on the side table was the current *Sports Illustrated*—the swimsuit issue. Father Rich picked it up and, feeling Randy's embarrassment, started flipping through it.

"Oh, I'm sorry," Randy said sheepishly.

"Hey, it's all right. My issue didn't come in the mail yet." Father Rich smiled and put the magazine back down on the nightstand. He would check it out later, in private.

"Well, this is it. The TV has cable, and the DVD player works, so... feel free." Randy slowly turned around in his room, waving at its various comforts.

Father Rich seemed happy with the accommodations. This was an assignment, after all—not a vacation. He had been told to relocate to the Ludyte house and reside there until notified, maintaining the appearance that he was a relative who was house-sitting while the family took a much-needed vacation.

Father Rich followed Randy back into the hallway and toward the kitchen. Randy was trying to give him as much of a tour as he could when Cate walked in from the family room. "Hi."

"Hi," Father Rich responded.

"Cate, this is Father Rich. He's going to stay here while we're away, right?" Randy said to Cate while, at the same time, asking Father Rich, who simply nodded and extended his hand to Cate.

"I'm pleased to meet you, Cate." Father Rich smiled.

"Oh... ah... me too." *Damn, he's cute*. Cate had to remember that she was fawning over a priest.

"Hi," Tim said as he closed the door to the study.

"Hey," Father Rich said as he extended his hand to Tim. He had now met the family, except for the parents.

"This is Father Rich," Randy said as the two shook hands.

Cate, turning away from the young priest toward Tim, said under her breath, "Father Rich. More like Father What-a-Waste, if you asked me." She gave a disappointed little smile and then went back to her room.

Father Rich must have heard her because he simply shrugged, turned to Randy, and quietly said, "I seem to get that a lot."

The two shared a laugh as they leaned against the counter, waiting for Father Dave to return.

In the midst of some small talk, mostly about the usual things young men discuss—sports, girls, and back to sports—Father Dave returned.

Dressed in casual clothes that he had to borrow from Randy's dad, Father Dave briefed Father Rich on the situation without cluing him in on the budding *new reality*. Father Dave could immediately understand why the seminary rector chose Rich Goosick for this assignment. Besides having the looks to easily pass as a member of the family, Father Rich was smart, appeared to be clever, and asked few questions. He was perfect for what was coming.

"Father Rich, would you come with me for a moment, please? Church business." Father Dave escorted Father Rich into the man cave.

"Yes, sir?" Father Rich asked once they were sequestered.

"What I am going to ask you is a most difficult question, yet I feel the query is necessary, nonetheless," Father Dave began.

Sensing the tension in his superior's voice, Father Rich simply replied, "Go on."

"What I told you in there was only the tip of what may turn out to be an enormous iceberg, and you've just agreed to help steer the *Titanic*," Father Dave stated.

"From the way the rector spoke, I assumed as much," Father Rich replied.

"Then you may better understand my question. Are you presently armed?" Father Dave asked.

"I am, Father," Father Rich stated and pulled up his sweatshirt to reveal a Springfield Armory XD Mod.2 Sub-Compact .40-caliber handgun snuggly stowed in a side holster. "And I'm even licensed to carry."

"Good, very good. And are you prepared to use it?" Father Dave asked.

"If I were not, I would not be carrying it, would I?" Father Rich responded.

"A most excellent answer. Then let's return to the kitchen. The church's business is now understood," Father Dave stated and, putting an arm around the young priest, guided him toward the kitchen door.

"He's not going to stay here 24-7, is he? I mean, he'll get bored. I'd get bored, and I live here," Tim asked.

Father Rich answered casually, as if he had rehearsed the answer. "No, I won't be alone. Sister Marsha Treden will be coming to stay with me. She is a novitiate at the convent of Our Blessed Lady. If need be, the two of us are willing to pass ourselves off as a married couple… with me playing the part of your out-of-town cousin. Father Dave had requested two members of the clergy who would be willing to undertake what could turn out to be a lengthy, difficult assignment, protecting a family. Sister Marsha and I volunteered from a very short list of possible that the rector had compiled. I assure you, we'll be okay."

"When should Sister Marsha get here?" asked Father Dave.

"She should be arriving later this afternoon. Is there a bedroom that she can use?" Father Rich asked.

"Yeah, I don't think Mom and Dad will mind." Randy pointed down the hallway on the opposite side of the house.

"Perfect. Then I'll just go get my bag and settle in." Father Rich excused himself and went out the front door to his waiting truck.

"Tim, Randy, are the two of you packed?" Father Dave asked, although he already felt he knew the answer.

"Got it covered," Randy answered for the both of them.

"Great. I'm going to check on Caitlin. I suggest we all just relax until your parents get home," Father Dave said. *So far, so good.*

Randy went to the family room and flipped on the television just as a news break was ending. He caught the last of a report of something happening in Philadelphia that involved the cardinal and an unscheduled trip to Rome. Randy jumped to his feet and called for Father Dave, who came quickly into the family room.

"To recap: Cardinal Ziest's return from the Vatican today was unscheduled. Reports have it that he was recalled to Rome for an emergency meeting with His Holiness, Pope Matthew. Details of the trip remain confidential at this time, but it is known that the cardinal returned in the company of several plainclothes individuals as well as a number of large sealed containers that were being handled with great care. The cardinal's party bypassed the normal US customs checkpoint and entered several waiting vehicles..."

Father Dave picked up the house landline and immediately called the provincial residence in Philadelphia. After a quiet conversation, he hung up the phone and called for everyone, including Father Rich, to join him in the family room.

Father Dave took a deep breath and let out a long sigh as everyone filed in and found a place to sit. No one said anything for quite some time.

Then Father Dave started. "Okay, here's what's going on. Apparently, the Vatican is greatly concerned about safety in regards to this issue. They have dispatched a contingent of security personnel to Philadelphia. They would be the plainclothes individuals we saw on the news just now."

"Security personnel? You're talking about the Swiss Guard?" Randy interrupted.

"Yes, that would be correct, along with members of the Vatican Police Department," Father Dave answered. He then continued, "Because of the presence of such a force here in Philadelphia, His Holiness has composed two letters, both with the papal seal. One letter is to the US secretary of state, and the other is to the UN

Vatican ambassador. Both letters arrived with the cardinal today and were immediately dispatched by courier, which may explain why the local news is all over this.

"The letter to the UN is not important at this time. However, the letter to the State Department is of concern. The cardinal assured me that the letter contains a formal notification that the Vatican has placed Swiss Guards on American soil, and that this force is here solely for the protection of specific members of the church. No details identifying who those members are, where they live, or why the Vatican believes they need protecting, have been included in the communiqué." Father Dave paused for a breath.

"What? Why? I thought you said you were going to handle all the details." Tim's voice was understandably unsteady.

"I am told that the cardinal has a third letter that he has been instructed to hand directly to me. He does not know the contents of this third letter, and it too has been closed with the papal seal. I can only guess that it contains instructions and possibly an explanation of what is happening," Father Dave explained.

"All right, so how does this really change anything?" Randy asked.

"What this does is give a reason to not only the federal government but, more ominously, to the news crews to be on the watch for anything unusual. That means that should one, or two, unidentifiable cars suddenly gain quick and easy access to the Terraces, well… you can imagine how that would play out in the news. Add to that the sudden and unexplained disappearance of the Ludyte family… well…"

Father Dave was trying to keep a handle on current events when Father Rich quite unexpectedly offered a suggestion.

"If I may—and I'm not asking for any details beyond that which I need to know—I suggest that we leave right now."

"We?" Cate was confused.

"Yes, we. If timed correctly, we should be able to whisk you out of here, and to Philadelphia, with a minimal amount of attention being paid," Father Rich stated.

"How?" This time, it was Father Dave asking the questions.

Father Rich explained his idea. "I have a truck. Caitlin and I will simply go for a drive. Tim can come along. We should leave soon though. Then, later, when Sister Marsha arrives, Randy, you and Sister Marsha go for another drive, like it were a date."

"Mary's not going to like that." Tim prodded his big brother, earning him a glare in return.

"Sister Marsha's only twenty-one and could easily pass as your girlfriend," Father Rich continued. "To sell the illusion even more, take her someplace where you would be seen. Take her for ice cream or something. Then, later this evening, head for Philadelphia instead of coming home."

Father Dave was impressed with the speed and ease with which Father Rich grasped the emergent nature of the situation.

"Okay, that could work… split the group up and take different routes. I like it."

Randy was nervous, but he understood.

Father Rich went on. "Then, Father Dave, you wait here for the parents to return. After they do, obviously, brief them on the most relevant events, and tell them that the three of you will leave after I return from Philadelphia."

"Jim and Carol aren't going to like splitting up the family, but they'll just have to understand," Father Dave said.

"Okay, then it's agreed. We'll head to Philadelphia in separate vehicles, and at different times." Father Dave was trying to summarize the plan when Cate sheepishly raised her hand.

"Yes, Cate, did we miss something?" Father Dave asked.

"Ah… we're all still going to be driving up to the cardinal's house in plain view of everyone," Cate pointed out.

"She's right. Damn." Father Dave was running his hands through his hair, messing up his neat high-and-tight set.

"I got that covered too." Father Rich was definitely earning everyone's trust, and quickly. "Use the underground access to the bunker. You should be able to gain entrance to the residence through that."

"Brilliant!" Father Dave was patting down his pants, looking for his cell phone; he needed to retrieve a number from its memory.

"But I don't know how to get you to the line station that accesses the Ecclesial Spur." Father Rich slumped after saying that, as if he had just let everyone down.

"I do." Father Dave found his cell and was scrolling through its memory. Finding the number he needed, he pressed the DIAL button and turned to walk into the kitchen. The rest of the group in the family room simply looked at each other as they all overheard Father Dave say, "John? Dave Davidson. Hey, I hate to do this to you, but I need a favor."

Then the conversation became unintelligible.

CHAPTER 55

Venture Lab, Pasadena, California
Thursday, January 22, 2015
9:16 a.m., EST; 6:16 a.m., PST

"UNDER WHAT? AN attack? Don't be absurd," Evan stated dismissively. The day shift was coming onboard, and he had a DLA (downlink alarm) to deal with. He certainly didn't need this.

"Well, not us… yet… but *Venture* certainly may be. Poor thing," Julie said with the emotion one would pour out for a homeless puppy.

Just then, the phone rang.

"Shit!" Evan looked up at the wall clock. Forty-five minutes: Dr. Katz was nothing if not punctual. Picking up the phone on the second ring and trying his best to swallow his nerves, Evan eventually said, "*Venture* Lab, Dr. Wills speaking."

"Evan, what do you have for me?" Dr. Katz calmly asked, reestablishing her professional status.

"Ah… I-I'm… that is we…" Evan was falling all over his own tongue. He was having a difficult time maintaining his concentration on the present DLA.

"Evan, take a deep breath." Dr. Katz paused. "Okay, now what the hell is going on?"

"I'm sorry. The downlink from *Venture 1* is indicating a minor anomaly that the filters kicked back as being… anomalous."

Evan was kicking himself for that one. Julie smiled slightly.

"Okay. Now listen to me carefully. I will be there in thirty-five minutes. Be prepared to make a sitrep of the alarm at that time. And call Fudd. Tell him that I said he should be there. You got that?" Dr. Katz said with the calm force of a person who knew she was in charge—and she was. "Oh, and lock the lab. I don't want day shift getting their panties in a wad just yet."

"Got it—sitrep in forty-five," Evan repeated.

"Thirty-five," Dr. Katz corrected.

"Thirty-five. Right. Sitrep in thirty-five, call Fudd, and lock the lab," Evan repeated to Dr. Katz, who simply hung up the phone.

"Ah, Evan, I know I should know this, but… who is Fudd?" Julie asked. "And lock the lab? Why?"

Evan, while gathering some printouts from a pile on the table, proceeded to explain to Julie that Fudd is, in fact, Elmer Finkleburger, the assistant administrator for Deep Space Exploration. He isn't a terribly bright person, but he is the one who signs the paychecks. Evan went on to tell Julie how Dr. Finkleburger—whose PhD is in business management and, therefore, discounted by the scientific doctors in the building—got the nickname Fudd. It was a reference to Elmer Fudd, the bumbling hunter in the classic Bugs Bunny cartoons produced by the Looney Tunes division of Warner Brothers. As to why Dr. Katz wanted him at the sitrep was anyone's guess.

"Oh." Julie was just trying to absorb the moment. "Well, the sun is rising on Mars soon. I better go take care of things there, and then I'll help you prepare."

"You still have to explain to me the whole *Venture's* under attack thing," Evan reminded her.

"I will, when I get a chance. Give me…" She looked at the clock, thought for a moment, and then said over her shoulder as she headed for the door, "Give me twenty minutes."

"Okay. Hey, Julie… thanks."

Evan was standing in a pile of problems, and he knew at that moment the only friend he could depend upon was Julie. She just smiled and disappeared out the door.

What now? Get a hold of yourself and the situation, Evan. First, find Fudd's number and invite him to the sitrep that will be held in... He looked at his watch. *In thirty minutes.*

* * *

Better than her word, Julie returned in fifteen minutes. Apparently, her shift relief was early, and thanks to the *Venture* lab being in a lockdown configuration—which generated a tremendous amount of speculation—she was able to skip out on having to give the usually detailed debrief of *Sirocco's* dusty night on the inhospitable Martian desert. She had returned to the *Venture* lab just in time to help Evan assemble the last of the slides he had compiled to explain why the alarm may have been triggered.

"Do you want to mention the magnetic beam?" Julie asked innocently.

One thing Evan had learned was to give Dr. Katz only the information she asked for and little else—if he wanted to keep his job, that is. "Not yet. I'd still like to hear your attack explanation first."

"Okay." Julie understood. As they ordered the last few slides, all she wanted to do was pull up the comparison data and reexamine it, but now was not the time.

They had a slide showing the downlink power levels... from a while ago?

"Ah, Evan, where is the most recent information—you know, the info since the magnetic beam was detected?"

"I don't have it," Evan stated.

"What?" Julie asked.

"Yep, can't seem to find it. All I have is the info from about a week prior to the beam and the data you were working with an hour ago. That's it," Evan explained.

"Great, now what? What if she asks for it?" Julie asked.

"We'll just have to hope that she doesn't," Evan commented as a wave of nerve-induced nausea swept over him.

"Okay." Julie bent back over the printouts. "But you know she will."

Julie was right, but he had no time to worry about that at the moment. The day shift was trying to get in, and the lockout only fueled their rumor-fed gossip network. Evan and Julie were engrossed in printouts and slides, one or the other occasionally looking up at the wall clock. Time was up.

"Hey, maybe she'll be late?" Julie said, overly optimistic.

Using her own codes to deactivate the lockout, Dr. Katz—coffee in one hand, bagel in the other, briefcase/purse slung over her shoulder—walked in. Her glasses hung around her neck like a piece of functional jewelry, while a scarf draped down around her shoulders like a mantle of office. She looked every bit the aged college professor everyone has had one too many times.

Falling into a chair at the side of the table (Dr. Katz didn't like to sit at the head of tables), she set her cup down and asked, "Okay… where's Fudd?"

At that, in walked Dr. Finkleburger, accompanied by four other VIPs. He probably heard her, but it was rumored that even he was afraid of Dr. Katz. So if he did, he would never say anything—especially in front of her minions.

"My apologies. I was on an important call," Dr. Finkleburger offered and then gave a somber, apologetic glance to Dr. Katz.

In short order, the conference table was surrounded by several ranking *Venture* project members, including Dr. Wasserman, team coordinator; Dr. Hitz, day shift primary monitor; Dr. Guth, telemetry data something or other (Evan never could remember); and Dr. Bahr, a senior project manager, though not as senior as Dr. Katz. And of course, Dr. Katz.

Dr. Finkleburger took the seat at the head of the table, believing it was left vacant for him. However, the truth was that it was left vacant because no one wanted it.

Good for Fudd.

Evan introduced himself. Even though everyone knew everyone else, there was a protocol to follow. Julie turned on the projector for the slides. She would act as his assistant for the duration of the meeting. Finally, after thanking everyone and apologizing for the emergent nature of the briefing, he began.

"According to the logs, at 1:27 this morning, the seventy- meter station received an unscheduled, unexpected downlink from *Venture 1*. The automated systems fed the data burst directly into the downlink filters and detected an anomaly."

"What sort of anomaly?" Dr. Guth asked.

"We're still looking at the nature of the anomaly at the moment. However, what I can tell you is that the anomaly appears to be uncharacteristic of the known system failures that we have already cataloged and attributed to the power decay," Evan clarified.

Julie shuffled slide after slide onto the projector, trying to stay with Evan as he went on about the power-consumption figures and the various systems that had to be shut down over time.

Several minutes later, and after a dissatisfied stare from Dr. Katz, Evan said, "The data indicates that something may have occurred to *Venture's* plutonium core. As you all know, the core is slowly decaying and turning into Uranium. Well…"

Oh god, where is he going with this? Julie thought.

"The decay may have… slowed." Evan nearly whispered that last word.

Silence. Pure, terrifying silence filled the lab. Everyone knew that what he had just proposed was impossible.

"And that would cause an alarm?" Fudd asked.

Well, almost everyone.

"No. No, actually it wouldn't… I-I mean it shouldn't." Evan stuttered. "The system is not configured to deal with a change in the laws of thermodynamics."

"Then what caused the alarm that got us all sitting here in the first place?" Fudd must not have had his coffee this morning, for that question had just a bit of venom in it.

"A downlink alarm can be tripped for any number of reasons, from a primary system failure to an unexpected power surge in the transmission. The system filters out known expected anomalies and trips when it doesn't know what to do," Dr. Katz chimed in.

Obviously, she couldn't help putting Fudd in his place—signing checks.

"Proceed, Dr. Wills," Dr. Katz said.

"Yes, thank you," Evan stated. "We haven't yet been able to pinpoint exactly what caused the trip. However, early indications are that there has been an unforeseen power variation in the transmission."

"What could cause this variation?" Dr. Bahr, who already knew the answer to his question, asked it for the benefit of everyone else—except for Patricia Katz, who knew pretty much everything.

"Several things. The most obvious being a mechanical malfunction, an unforeseen change in the decay rate of the core, or even a magnetic field shift. The truth of the matter is we don't know what's going on out there at this time."

Evan was grasping for help, and unfortunately, Julie had none to give... just slides.

"Okay," Dr. Katz interrupted. "Allow me to try to sum this up. What we have here is an old, slow system in *Venture,* with a dying core that may, or may not, have undergone some kind of... can we say heart attack?"

"Yes, that would be as good a summation as any." Evan took a big breath of relief.

"When can we expect a progress report on its condition?" Dr. Bahr was looking back and forth from Evan to Katz and back to Evan.

"Dr. Wills?" Dr. Katz waved a hand at Evan.

"I'm sorry." Evan roused himself from a brief moment's contemplation and continued, "With any luck, we should be able to ascertain *Venture*'s most current condition within the next thirty-six to forty-eight hours."

"Why so long?" Fudd—again with the truly stupid questions.

This time, Dr. Bahr jumped in. "Because, Elmer, the thing is 140 SAU—that's over thirteen billion miles—away. On a universal scale, that's nothing. For us, though, it is substantial."

"Oh. I see," Fudd said. "But I still don't fully understand why we had to lock down the lab and have this meeting."

The annoyance in Dr. Katz's response was thick. "Because I said so."

With the slightest of flinches, Fudd then asked one last question, "Can we, at least, unlock the lab?"

Dr. Katz nodded.

The conversation then moved on to other possible problems with *Venture,* and soon the sitrep turned into an impromptu vehicle briefing, with every technician and functionary in the room vying for attention from the senior team leaders. After twenty-five or thirty minutes, the conversation most assuredly had moved away from the tripped alarm.

Evan motioned Julie aside. "Well?"

"I don't know, Evan. You almost let it slip out with that talk about the magnetic field and the power levels. We have to be sure before we press the button on that one," Julie affirmed.

Julie was right, of course. If indeed the alarm trip was because of some form of aggressive act being played out with *Venture*, then forget pressing the button. It would be time to throw their bodies against it and then run like hell.

As the conference broke up and the day shift began their routines, Dr. Finkleburger went in search of Dr. Katz.

"Dr. Katz!" Finkleburger called over several people blocking his way. "A word, Pat, please."

Meeting at the back of the lab in semiprivate, Dr. Katz asked, "Yes, Elmer. How may I help you?"

"Pat, I need to discuss something of critical importance with you," Dr. Finkleburger stated.

"Okay. Can it wait until we get a better handle on *Venture*?" Dr. Katz asked.

"I'm afraid not. It has to do with *Venture* and a letter received by the State Department," Dr. Finkleburger stated.

"My office then," Dr. Katz directed as she walked out of the lab and headed straight to her private office across the hallway.

CHAPTER 56

Ludyte Home, Springtown, Pennsylvania
Thursday, January 22, 2015
10:05 a.m., EST; 7:05 a.m., PST

HAVING FINISHED HIS brief cell phone call from the kitchen, Father Dave rejoined the kids back in the family room. *God, I'm getting too old for this shit*, he thought.

He outwardly said, "We're all set. Father Rich, Cate, and you, Tim, are to make your way to the Colmar SEPTA station. Where you'll be met by a white-capped SEPTA police officer by the name of John Gorski. Make sure he shows you his ID. He knows to do that. He'll escort you through several stations and eventually onto the Ecclesial Spur, as they seem to call it. Follow his directions. He's a good guy."

"Who's John Gorski?" *Good question*, Tim thought.

"I haven't always been a priest. Let's just say that John and I go a long way back… like your dad and me." Father Dave looked at Tim and winked.

"Him too?" Tim asked, bewildering most everyone in the room.

"No, not the same as your dad, but close. Let's just say that marines never leave a man behind… in any circumstance," Father Dave said. He then pulled Father Rich and Cate aside for a little private chat.

Tim knew better than to push the topic any further and grabbed Randy by the arm and led him into the study. He needed help with some boxes.

***

"Okay, you two," Father Dave said as he pointed at Father Rich and Cate. "You will follow John's directions as if they came from me. Got it?"

Both Father Rich and Cate looked at each other, nodded, and listened as Father Dave went into detail about the rendezvous with John, the route they would take, the story they would give John about why they needed to get to the Spur—everything he could think of. This was going to be a tricky maneuver (and one that he hadn't planned on), so he was winging it and trusting in God and the brotherhood of the corps.

The time to depart for Philadelphia came quickly, and Carol and Jim weren't home yet. Not able to wait any longer, Father Rich grabbed his keys and called for Cate and Tim. Hopefully, they would make it to the Colmar station without any difficulty.

Caitlin sat in the front seat, and Tim took the seat directly behind her. She was more than a little confused as to why Father Dave felt the need to cloak-and-dagger them away like this, especially if no one knew about either the discovery or their involvement. Although, Cate did have the feeling that something was amiss. Call it intuition.

As they backed out of the driveway and started down the road, they passed a news van. That seemed more than a little strange, considering Springtown was a sleepy little town with barely seven hundred people in it. No matter—perhaps the news crew was reporting on some unrelated event. In an attempt to distract everyone away from the van and what was going on, Father Rich turned on the radio. He forgot that he had it tuned to the Philadelphia twenty-four-hour news station and wasn't quick enough to change the station before they heard part of a report.

"In a related story, the National News Network is reporting that the discovery, confirmed by a Vatican letter to the State Department, was first uncovered by a local Pennsylvania student. Due to his age, his name is being withheld at this time. However, it is believed that he attends Bingen High School, located in northern Bucks County."

Father Rich reached for his cell phone and handed it to Caitlin. "Here, call Father Dave and tell him what we just heard."

***

Just as Carol and Jim walked into the house, Father Dave's cell phone started to play the Marine Corps Hymn... someone was calling and not texting. Father Dave looked at the phone, saw a number that he didn't readily identify, and pressed the button to send the call to voice mail.

***

"Damn! I got his voice mail." Cate was beside herself.

"All right, let's just stick to the plan and get out of here as safely as we can. With any luck, we won't be noticed."

Father Rich was right; nothing had changed.

***

"Jim, Carol, sit down. We need to talk." Father Dave motioned them to the kitchen table.

Randy got up from the table as his parents sat down. He excused himself and went to the family room. Maybe some TV would soothe him.

"What's going on? Where are the kids? And what's that news van doing roaming the neighborhood?" Carol asked, trying very hard to keep her panic in check.

"What?" Father Dave got up and bolted for the front door. "Damn, I was afraid of this."

Just then, Randy came in from the family room with a look of protective anger on his face. "We're on TV."

"No, that can't be." Father Dave was quickly losing control of the situation. *How did the news find out about this? How did the news connect it to the Ludytes? How did the news track them down so quickly? What the hell was going on?* These were just a few of the many questions streaming through Father Dave's migraine-riddled mind.

"According to the TV, someone at Bingen High School telephoned in a news tip about the discovery," Randy reported. He then turned back to the family room to continue his monitoring of the news.

"Okay, will someone please tell us what the hell is going on? Where are the kids!" Jim was now getting flushed. This was spinning out of control.

In as much of a soothing, calm voice as he could manage, Father Dave sat at the table with Carol and Jim. He explained to them the events of the past several hours. "It all started when we saw on the news that Cardinal Ziest had returned from the Vatican unexpectedly, and with what the news called 'suspicious companions'."

"How did the news find out?" Jim asked.

"I'm not really sure. Perhaps it was just a matter of being in the wrong place at the wrong time, or the right place—whichever way you want to look at it. But, at any rate, once the news reported that the cardinal had returned, I arranged for the kids to head for Philadelphia. Father Rich Goosick is driving Caitlin and Tim there right now," Father Dave explained.

"Who is Father Goosick?" Carol was okay. So far.

"He's the curate who will be house-sitting for you while you're in… exile. The rector sent him over at my request, remember?" Father Dave was trying to be comforting.

Jim nodded and reached a hand across the table to Carol. She was shaking ever so slightly.

"Go on, please," Carol said.

"Okay, they're headed for the Colmar SEPTA station, where they will be met by an old Marine Corps friend of mine, John Gorski. I'm not sure if you ever met the 'Gork,' Jim. He's a good man—I trust him with my life," Father Dave said with the absolute assuredness of a decorated marine, which he was.

Jim simply nodded. He needed no additional information about this Gorski person.

Father Dave continued, "Anyway, Gork will escort them to the Ecclesial Spur, where they will be met by security personnel from the Terraces. From there, it's a simple train ride directly to the provincial's residence. No driving up the driveway. No being seen by cameras."

Carol felt some of the edge wan from her spine. Okay, now what was next?

"Later this afternoon, Sister Marsha Treden should arrive. She'll escort Randy to the same train station and get him safely to Gorski. Then, later tonight, the three of us will make our own way there. We all felt that it would be best to separate and meet up again in the safety of the Terraces," Father Dave stated.

He was right; this way, the entire family wouldn't be caught out as a group.

"Wait, Dave, what did Tim do with the data... the proof... all the printouts?" Jim felt the huge lump in his throat return.

"No problem. Last night, Tim and I scanned much of the information onto my laptop. I then burned several CD copies. Before they left, I asked Father Goosick to mail two envelopes, each containing a CD copy. One is going to my mailbox in Arizona. The other is going to my sister in Minnesota. I have a CD copy with me, and the laptop. Tim has the actual paper documents with him, condensed into two boxes."

Father Dave felt the information was safe and secure. Jim nodded his agreement.

Breathing a little better, both parents sat and discussed the finer details of their escape with Father Dave. The afternoon was growing old when the front doorbell rang. Thinking that it was Sister Marsha, Father Dave answered it, only to find a mousy kid about Tim's age.

"Ah, is Tim home?" Harvey Wallingsford asked. He looked just a little scared.

Looking up and down the street and seeing nothing, Father Dave motioned for the young man to quickly enter the house. Carol heard Harvey's voice and quickly came out of the kitchen to greet the young man.

"Ah, Mrs. L, what's going on? There were people, newspeople, at school today asking all kinds of questions," Harvey stated.

"What kind of questions?" Tim's father asked as he placed his arm around Harvey and walked him into the kitchen.

"I'm not sure. I didn't hang around," Harvey stated. "Does this have something to do with Tim's senior project?"

"What do you know about that?" Father Dave asked.

Harvey turned to the very large marine/priest and said, "I helped him set up some worksheets. He had a whole lot of numbers that he wanted to look at."

"Are these the worksheets?"

Harvey nodded at the printouts Father Dave held up.

"Harvey, look, Tim found something in those numbers that was… well… really cool… and there are going to be a lot of people who will want to know about it. People who are not necessarily friendly."

Jim waved a hand at Father Dave to make him stop patronizing the kid. Then he turned to Harvey and said, "Harvey, Tim found evidence of extraterrestrial life."

"What? Really?" Harvey couldn't believe his ears. "You're telling me that Tim found… wait. Did he find the Predator or ET? Or did he find GORT?" Then quietly Harvey said, "The Predator would be cool. Imagine the Predator versus GORT?"

"We sent him to a place in Philadelphia where he'll be safe. Later, we're all going to join him there."

Father Dave had no idea what Jim was doing by telling this kid the truth.

"Oh, okay. Well, when Tim gets home, tell him that I stopped by to see if he was okay." Harvey was trying to contain himself. Trying and failing.

As Harvey turned to head for the front door, the doorbell rang again. Opening the front door, Harvey came face-to-face with an extremely attractive young blond lady.

Great, another girlfriend of Randy's, Harvey thought. Then he said, "Oh, hi! I don't live here." Harvey wasn't even trying to hide his laughter now as he squeezed by the young lady and through the doorway.

Welcoming the newcomer, Father Dave shut the door behind her and asked, "Sister Marsha?"

"Yes. Father Davidson? I'm really confused. I was told to dress appropriately for my age, and to wear makeup. What's going on?"

Poor Sister Marsha. Only a year in the service of our Lord, and already, she was being pressed into some tricky stuff.

CHAPTER 57

San Fernando Valley, California
Thursday, January 22, 2015
4:25 p.m., EST; 1:25 p.m., PST

EVAN AND JULIE agreed to meet later at her house out in the valley after they both went home to freshen up and maybe catch some sleep.

Yeah, wishful thinking, sleep. Evan tried, but sleep was not coming, and soon he found himself driving out to the San Fernando Valley and to Julie's.

As Evan merged onto the 134, heading north to Julie's, he started thinking about how history had never been kind to those who ushered in a new era of mankind. Columbus came to mind. The guy died poor, and no one really knew where he was buried. Evan did not want that future. He just wanted to live his life, maybe marry and raise a family… maybe not. He certainly didn't want to be on the leading edge of the biggest event in the history of… well, history.

For the next hour, all he could think about was what would happen if, indeed, they were correct, and *Venture* was being influenced by some unknown alien intelligence. What would that mean to everyone?

The incredible fame and attention such a discovery would bring.

The incredible horror and fear such a discovery would bring.

One thing was certain though. Whatever it would bring, it would be a goddamn mess.

Startled out of his daze by the ringing of his hands-free device, Evan pressed the CONNECT button. "Hello."

It was Julie, and she sounded out of breath. "Evan, thank God… where the hell are you?"

"On the one thirty-four. What's wrong?" Evan asked.

"Are you heading here?" Julie pressed.

"Yes, why? What's going on?" Evan was getting nervous.

"I guess you haven't seen the news, have you?" Julie was trying her best to stay calm.

"No. What happened?" Evan was getting that prickly feeling creeping up his back—the one that foretold of impending trouble.

"It's out. It's all over the news. Some kid in Pennsylvania got a hold of *Venture*'s telemetry and discovered some kind of alien signature in it. Dear god. Evan… it's out!" Julie exclaimed.

"Did you say a kid in Pennsylvania?" Evan asked.

"Yeah, why?" Julie answered.

"Did they give his name?" Evan knew who it was; he just wanted to know if the world did too.

"No, the newspeople are holding the name because of his age… that and they can't seem to find him," Julie replied.

"Okay, I should be there shortly. Keep watching, and take notes." Evan pressed a button, dropping the call.

So it's out. How did Tim—and who else could it be—find an alien signature in the telemetry? Julie and I have been through every part of the teleme—

Evan froze in mid-thought. "Oh shit!" Evan yelled at his steering wheel. The power level data—the telemetry that Evan couldn't seem to find. Tim had it, and he looked at it. But he couldn't possibly know what he was looking at. He had to have gotten help. The potential of this shit storm was getting worse the more he thought about it.

CHAPTER 58

Ludyte Home, Springtown, Pennsylvania
Thursday, January 22, 2015
4:39 p.m., EST; 1:39 p.m. PST

AFTER THEY BROUGHT Sister Marsha up to speed with her role in the plan, she quickly dumped her bag in the master bedroom and went in search of Randy. If the two of them were going to pretend to be on a date, it might be nice if they actually met first.

Sister Marsha and Randy talked in his room, breaking one of the Ludyte family rules about not having the opposite gender in one of their bedrooms. Both parents knew Sister Marsha was safe and that their son—if nothing else—was a gentleman.

While the kids talked, Carol threw some clothes for herself and Jim in a bag. Jim took care of packing the bathroom stuff and medicine. Father Dave watched the news, hoping for a window in the coverage that they might be able to exploit.

"Okay, we're ready."

It was Randy and Sister Marsha. To keep appearances consistent with the story that they were on a date, Randy agreed to take his car, and then Sister Marsha would drive it home and hide it in the garage. The family car (Carol's car) would be gone by that time, and Jim's car (the '68) would be in the second bay of the two-car shed.

"Great, you guys know what to do? Where to go?" Father Dave was nervous again.

"Yes, I think so." Sister Marsha was surprisingly calm. For the moment.

Carol came down the hallway from the master bedroom carrying an overnight bag. Her husband was right behind her with a bag of his own. "You kids ready?" he asked.

"Yep—we're going to the Driftwood first." Randy turned to Father Dave and quickly explained that the Driftwood was a local dive where the high school kids liked to hang out. "We'll grab a quick bite and then tell everyone that we have tickets for a concert and that we have to run."

"Okay, that should do it. Be careful." Randy's father was confident that his oldest could handle things; and not only that, there was Sister Marsha. *They'll be fine. That's it, Jim. Keep telling yourself that.*

As the kids headed for the door, Father Dave checked for anything out of the ordinary. So far, nothing. "Okay... be careful." Father Dave raised his hand and gave a quick blessing, just as he had to Cate and Tim.

Randy couldn't help but wonder to himself, *Be careful? That's strange. If I wasn't already going to be careful, then them telling me to be careful wouldn't make me be careful.*

Father Dave closed the door behind the couple, and Carol watched from a window as Randy pulled out of the driveway. As the car vanished down the road, she turned back to see the two men head toward the garage. "Hey?" she called after them, but it was too late. They had closed the door to the man cave... so she thought she'd make some sandwiches. She certainly did not want to watch TV.

"Dave, now that the kids are gone and Carol can't hear us... level with me," Jim pleaded.

"Jim, I've been straight with you from the beginning," Father Dave stated.

"Oh, don't give me that bullshit. What do you really think?" Jim was understandably angry and scared.

"Okay, my gut feeling is that someone leaked the information, probably from either the State Department or the UN. I don't know which. What matters now is where we go from here," Father Dave explained.

Just then, Carol opened the door and did something she rarely did. She entered the man cave. "Guys… I need to talk to you about something."

Both Dave and Jim swiveled in the chairs they were in and beckoned her to sit.

"Earlier, Tim got a telephone call."

"From whom?" Jim asked.

"I don't know, but the person was very insistent that Tim search through the stuff he got from that scientist in California. Something about power levels and data… I only overheard a little of the conversation," Carol explained.

"What did Tim say?" Father Dave asked.

"Only that he would look through the information and call him back. Then all hell broke loose, and… well, I don't think Tim did anything else," Carol surmised.

"Well, that could answer one question—how did the leak occur?" Even as Father Dave said he wasn't sure of his conclusion about the leak—no matter, because the information was out. And like a bullet fired from a gun, once the trigger was pulled, there was no pulling the bullet back.

"Well, I just thought I should tell you. Hey, I made some sandwiches. C'mon, let's eat something," Carol insisted.

"Thanks, we'll be right there."

Carol knew that was Jim's way of saying that he needed a few more minutes with Dave. She got up and went back to the kitchen.

"This doesn't change anything, Jim. We still have to get to the residence—tonight," Father Dave clarified.

"I know. But if it was that scientist in California who called looking for the information, then that means Tim has the original copy, which raises the stakes considerably," Jim concluded.

"I know," Father Dave said. He got up and patted Jim on the shoulder as the two men went into the kitchen.

CHAPTER 59

SEPTA Station, Colmar, Pennsylvania
Thursday, January 22, 2015
6:19 p.m., EST; 3:19 p.m., PST

THE COLMAR STATION was a typical suburban subway stop on the SEPTA line, designed to shuttle commuters into, and out of, Philadelphia. During the day, it saw more tourism and shopping traffic than commuters.

Father Rich parked, grabbed one of Tim's boxes, and as he emerged from his SUV, he quickly scanned the area for problems. Caitlin took her day bag, along with Tim's, and casually stepped out of the passenger side. Already on his feet, Tim hiked up the other box that he had packed, and he waited for Father Rich to take the lead. Together, the three of them slowly made their way into the station. Finding a bench in the middle of the station (for Father Rich believed in HIPS, or hiding in plain sight), the kids sat down as he stood, scanning the crowd.

"Remember this place, Cate? Sometimes Dad would bring us this way to see Phillies games," Tim asked his older sister, trying to ground her.

"Yeah…" Cate tried to smile but was too busy looking over her shoulder.

"You like the Phils?" Father Rich asked.

"Yes, sir. We bleed Phillies' red." Tim was proud of his team—for some unknown reason.

"Well, when you want a real team, look me up," Father Rich said as he continued to scan the crowd.

"Why? Who do you like?" Tim was getting defensive.

"Me? I don't really have time to watch baseball, but my uncle works for the Boston Red Sox. He's their head clubhouse attendant," Father Rich explained.

"No way!" Tim said excitedly. "You're my new best friend."

Father Rich laughed, saying, "When this is all over, I'll see if I can get you a tour of Fenway."

Just as he finished his promise, a short, stocky man approached them. He was dressed in the uniform Father Dave identified as that of a transit police officer. "Are you Father Goosick?" he asked.

"Yes, sir," Father Rich replied.

"And these would be the Ludytes?" The police officer nodded toward the kids sitting on the bench with two cardboard boxes between them.

"Yes, sir… and you would be?" Father Rich demanded, standing in front of his charges.

The police officer reached into his shirt pocket, withdrew his photo identification, and handed it to Father Rich. "I'm John Gorski. Sergeant… I mean Father Davidson asked me to meet you."

Father Rich looked at the ID carefully then handed it back to the officer. Turning to the kids, Father Rich said, "Well, guys… this is it. My part is done, for now."

Tim got up and extended his hand to the young priest, who shook it strongly. Then turning to Cate, Father Rich extended a tender hand to help her to her feet. She looked at him and threw her arms around him, catching him by surprise.

"I'll see you again. Remember, I'm staying at your house," Father Rich said.

Father Rich helped them gather their bags and the two boxes and walked with them as they followed Officer Gorski through the station. As they neared the far end of the station where the trains were boarding, Gorski turned, shook the young priest's hand, and said, "I got it from here."

Father Rich silently gave them a blessing and turned to head back to his truck and to the Ludyte home.

"The Ecclesial Spur doesn't connect with this station, so we have to take a train into the city first. Just follow me. I'll get you where you have to go," Officer Gorski explained.

"Okay," Cate and Tim said in unison as they followed the police officer to the second train's lead car.

"How do you know Father Dave?" Tim was trying to relax by making small talk.

John Gorski understood, and as he herded the two kids into a seat, he proceeded to explain that he was in the marines with a then Sergeant Davidson, and that the two of them had been through a lot together. Tim felt himself relax, slightly, as the proud marine relived corps stories of old.

The train car shuddered slightly as the doors closed with a loud spine-chilling, scraping sound. These old trains were noisy and uncomfortable, but they had an old charm to them. Before Tim knew it, the train was taking them away, into a tunnel and into the *new reality*.

CHAPTER 60

Wagner Home, San Fernando Valley, California
Thursday, January 22, 2015
6:38 p.m., EST; 3:38 p.m., PST

EVAN PULLED INTO Julie's driveway. Her husband—Tomas Wagner, MD—had left for his shift at Pepperdine University Medical Center hours earlier.

Still wearing sweatpants and a comfy nondescript shirt, Julie greeted Evan at the door. She was padding around in pink puffy slippers, carrying a big mug of coffee. Her hair was tied back in a messy bun, with wisps falling over her bespectacled eyes. She looked absolutely gorgeous… and exhausted. She led him to the kitchen table, where she had set up an impromptu workstation.

Waving at the full pot of coffee, Julie said, "You know where the mugs are." Evan raised his hand to show that he brought his own.

"So what's the latest, since we talked?" Evan said as he unslung his laptop.

Julie took a big breath, let it out slowly, and then motioned to the answering machine. It was flashing the number 17. "Seventeen calls… all of them looking for you. I've been ignoring them, telling myself that I'm asleep."

Seventeen calls? Wow! "Well, I guess the shit storm has started." Evan filled his mug and sat in front of his laptop.

"Have you been able to look at the power level telemetry?" Julie asked hopefully.

Evan just shook his head. "I don't have it."

"What? Where is it?" Julie had a feeling she knew what the answer to the question was.

"Pennsylvania. I guess what happened was that when I packed up everything for that kid and his senior project, as I was instructed to do, the power level telemetry got caught up with it," Evan surmised.

"Well, okay. But shouldn't there be a copy in the computer backup?" Julie asked.

"Remember that memo we got about two or three months ago, the one informing us to make sure we had all necessary information backed up either in paper form or on alternate storage because of the new firewalls that were being installed?" Evan stated.

Julie had no idea what he was talking about. Two or three months ago, *Sirocco* was sitting in a ditch, along with her career. "Okay."

"Well, as it turns out, the only surviving copy of the power level data is in Timothy Ludyte's hands," Evan clarified.

"Okay, then all we need do—and by *we*, I mean the administration—is deny the discovery report. If he has the only copy of the data, then we can claim it's a hoax." Julie thought she had the answer.

"Thought of that one already. What if they—and by *they*, I mean the newspeople—want to see the actual data?" Evan asked, playing devil's advocate.

"Can the data be replicated?" Julie asked hopefully.

"You mean faked?" Evan asked.

"I didn't say that, but yes," Julie stated.

"No. The printouts of the *Venture* telemetry all contain authentication signatures in the form of a magnetic residue left behind by the printer. The paper is a special ferrous impregnated paper that was developed especially for the *Venture* program. Remember, this was years before the currently used anti-counterfeit technology of watermarks," Evan explained.

"Okay, then simply ask *Venture* to send the data again. It should have it backed up in its onboard storage," Julie suggested.

"The backup on *Venture* is an eight-track tape," Evan reminded her. "Very limited storage. That's why she's on a regular data dumping schedule."

"Great. So not only don't we have the data, Mr. Pennsylvania has the original copy that can be verified. Wonderful." Julie was fading quickly. She had no idea what to do next.

Taking a big breath, Evan suggested that they look at the data they did have and verify that *Venture* was... what? *How do we check data we don't have for something we don't know, happening thirtysomething years away?* Evan thought.

Shuffling through the papers that he brought with him, Evan tried to recreate the information they used back at the lab. Then it dawned on him. "Julie, please tell me that you saved that comparison program that you wrote back at the lab."

"Yeah, got it right here." Julie's fingers again danced on the keys of her laptop, summoning forth a simple program from the machine's magnetic memory. "Here it is."

Evan slid his chair around the table to sit next to her, in front of the computer. "Okay, walk me through the *aha* moment."

"All right, we were checking the raw data, remember? I was running a diagnostic on the X-band connection when you asked me to let it run and check the raw data with you," Julie stated.

"I remember," Evan confirmed.

"I saw something that didn't look right. So I quickly set up a compare-and-contrast program just to check for variations in the data. Nothing special, just a simple statistical variation check. That's when I saw it. The program that I ran didn't kick anything back that was alarming, but the data wasn't what I expected," Julie continued.

"How? I looked at the same data and saw nothing," Evan pressed.

"The power level data that we had, albeit not the complete run, was enough to show that the core was indeed reenergizing," Julie stated.

"But that's impossible. The plutonium-238 can't be magically reenergized. Yes, theoretically, it could be, I suppose—if the alpha decay could somehow be stopped. But that would require a huge amount of energy," Evan replied.

"That's exactly what I thought, but then I remembered the magnetic beam. We never did get a chance to check and see if it was actually oscillating between positive and negative. But we do know it's there, and we know that to project such a beam would require an enormous amount of power too," Julie said.

"And so, whatever was powering the beam, you think could force a reenergization of the core." Evan was having his own *aha* moment.

"Exactly. We know of nothing that can do such things naturally, so the only cause has to be artificial. And why artificially alter *Venture* unless there was an intelligence behind the effort?" Julie was reaching, but not that far. And it did make sense.

"Okay, let's say I agree, but how did this fifteen-year-old come to the same conclusion?" Evan asked.

"Remember, he has the entire data run. We only have a small snippet. We had to puzzle it together from only a few snapshots—he has the entire picture. All he would've had to do is set up a similar compare and contrast, and he'd have it. Hell, he could probably even do it in Excel, if he was good enough. Remember, the news said that evidence of extraterrestrial life had been discovered. It didn't say anything about what the evidence was," Julie explained.

Evan sat back and rubbed his face with both hands. "Can we use what we have to prove the alien contact theory?"

"I don't know. We have a lot of old data and circumstantial conclusions. What we really need is the original power-level data," Julie stated.

"That, we don't have," Evan said with just a little exasperation.

"Exactly." Julie now sat back in her chair as well.

Evan, looking around the kitchen, said, "Did you paint since I was here last?"

Julie broke out laughing. She needed that.

Surgical Staff Lounge, Pepperdine University Medical Center, Malibu, California
Thursday, January 22, 2015
7:05 p.m., EST; 4:05 p.m., PST

"My god, Tomas! You mean to say that the news reports are true?" asked Dr. Skidowski.

Dr. Albert Skidowski was a well-respected general surgeon and mentor to Dr. Tomas Wagner.

"I couldn't believe it myself when Julie vented to me," Tomas stated.

A nearby nurse, tending to her dinner, asked, "Dr. Wagner? I'm sorry, but did you say something about aliens?"

"Yes. From what my wife said, it seems that one of our probes has made contact," Tomas clarified.

"Wow!" Robin answered, and then she refocused her attention on her meal.

"Tomas, if I may, what is the nature of the contact?" Dr. Skidowski asked.

"I'm not sure. Julie said something about power fluctuations within a downlink," Tomas revealed.

"Power fluctuations? Hmm?" Dr. Skidowski mused, rolling the information around in his head.

"Yep," Tomas said. "Apparently, something—or someone—is manipulating the power levels of the probe."

Having finished her meal, Robin rose from her seat at the neighboring table and walked across the lounge to her wall-mounted locker. "Dr. Skidowski, we have a lap chole in twenty minutes."

Looking at the clock, Dr. Skidowski responded to the nurse with "Got it, Robin. See you there."

"Sure thing," Robin answered as she closed her locker and headed for the door. Opening the door with her right hand, Robin reached into the pocket of her lab coat and withdrew a simple cell phone. Just as the door to the lounge closed behind her, Robin could be heard saying, "Honey, you are not going to believe what I just heard."

CHAPTER 61

The Driftwood Diner, Coopersburg, Pennsylvania
Thursday, January 22, 2015
7:08 p.m., EST; 4:08 p.m., PST

THE DRIFTWOOD WASN'T crowded, but it wasn't empty either. There were a few families sitting at various booths and tables. A little league team was milling around the walk-up ice cream window, and a few older couples were sitting at the ice cream bar. It looked like a usual evening at the local hangout.

Randy and Sister Marsha entered hand in hand; might as well make it look good. Shelly, the hostess/waitress, greeted them and led them to a side table. Randy knew Shelly from school and was confident that before he and Sister Marsha left, the entire senior class would know that he was there with some "new chick."

Shelly could be such a blabbermouth sometimes, Randy thought. But this was what they wanted—to be seen out together, like a normal date.

"So when was the last time you went on a date?" Randy had no idea what to talk about with a nun.

Sister Marsha smiled and said, "Last year, I think. It was before I entered the convent."

Randy thought then asked, "So why a nun?"

"I don't know… they say that when you get *the call*, you know it. I hate to sound weird, but the call came, and I answered it," Sister Marsha said in a simple, common tone.

All through their brief meal, they talked about growing up—Randy in Springtown, Sister Marsha about seventy miles farther north, in a small coal-mining town called Pardeesville. They shared moments of laughter and joy, and a few moments of sadness as well. There, over burgers and fries, they became friends.

Perhaps these two new friends were so enwrapped in their shared conversation, or perhaps they unconsciously wanted to forget the *new reality* that was emerging around them, that they completely missed the *SPECIAL REPORT* being broadcast on the diner's wall-mounted TV. But they were the only ones to miss it.

Just then, Shelly arrived with the check, which had a message written on the back. The owner of the Driftwood, a likable fellow named Steve, crossed out the amount owed and wrote on the back of the check: "Get out."

Randy saw the message and looked up at Shelly, who was staring at the television, eyes wide with a look of amazement. At that, Sister Marsha turned to the TV just in time to catch the final moments of the report.

Turning to Randy, Sister Marsha whispered, "We need to leave. Now!"

Without question, Randy grabbed his keys and hurriedly headed to the door. Sister Marsha casually covered their exit by pretending to be interested in the television. However, all pretense fell away once she realized the full extent of what was being reported.

Once they got into the car, Randy asked, "What was all that about?"

"You were on the news. The whole family was," Sister Marsha informed her charge.

"What? Why?" Randy asked.

"It seems that some scientist in California called the school, trying to locate your brother. And when he couldn't find Tim, the scientist left a message with the school that *it was imperative that Tim be found*," Sister Marsha related.

"What! I have to call Mom and Dad," Randy quickly concluded.

"Calm down and pull over. Let me drive. That way, you can make the call safely," Sister Marsha ordered.

As Randy pulled his car into the lot of a local gas station, his phone started to ring. "Hello?"

"Randy Ludyte?" an unfamiliar male voice asked.

"Who is this?" Randy's suspicions were climbing since the news report.

"I'm a friend of your brother's. Where is he? Is he okay? He wasn't in school today, and the newspeople were looking for him," the voice asked. "What's going on?"

"Who is this?" Randy pressed.

With that, Sister Marsha grabbed the phone out of Randy's hand and pressed the *END* button. Handing the phone back to Randy, she opened her door and motioned for him to slide over to the passenger seat. "If you don't know who's on the phone, and if they refuse to identify themselves, hang up. Your phone has a GPS locator chip. Now they have its ID number. They can track it and you," Sister Marsha explained.

"Then I'll shut the phone off," Randy stated.

"Doesn't matter. They can still track the chip. We have to ditch the phone someplace safe or they'll know exactly where you're going."

Sister Marsha was right, of course.

As she spun the car around and headed north on Highway 309, she said, "We're going to be a little late getting to Colmar."

"Where are we going?" Randy asked, fear slowly seeping into his voice.

"There is a cloistered convent a few miles north of here. We can leave the phone behind their walls with the Mother Superior. She'll protect it and not volunteer any information to anyone," Sister Marsha stated.

"Why not just destroy the phone?" Randy asked innocently.

"Doesn't matter. Unless we ruin the chip itself, they could still get a fix on the phone. Also, if we destroy it, they'll know that we know they're after you. By leaving it with the Mother, all they will get is that the phone and, therefore, you, are at the cloister, presumably for safety, and therefore out of reach," Sister Marsha explained.

As Sister Marsha finished her explanation, she pulled into the small tree-shielded parking lot of the Center Valley cloister. The cloister had a modest public parish associated with it and, therefore, had a parking lot to match. Surrounding the grounds of the cloister was a thick fifteen-foot-tall concrete wall. The only access to the cloister appeared to be through a side door located at the back of the sanctuary of the parish church.

Sister Marsha parked the car in the empty lot, grabbed Randy's phone, and quickly got out of the car. "Stay here," she said as she trotted to the still-open church.

After what seemed to be an eternity, Sister Marsha emerged from the church empty-handed.

Sliding back into the driver's seat, and just a little out of breath, Sister Marsha started the car and spun out of the parking lot. "The Mother will lock the phone in their safe until I return for it. It's safe now. I just hope we are too."

CHAPTER 62

Wagner Home, San Fernando Valley, California
Thursday, January 22, 2015
7:36 p.m., EST; 4:36 p.m., PST

EVAN TURNED TO Julie and said, "I called Tim Ludyte's school, looking for him. According to the contact I have there, through Dr. John Edleson… remember him?"

Julie shook her head no and motioned with her hand for Evan to keep the story moving.

"Well, it appears that Tim has been signed out of school for the foreseeable future," Evan explained. Then he continued with "I told my source that it was a matter of grave importance that I find Tim."

"Great… so you basically told them his life might be in danger? Isn't that a bit alarmist?" Julie asked.

Evan was fried. All he wanted to do was go for a walk in a forest somewhere and forget about everything for a while. "I don't know. Any forests around here?"

Julie looked at him, furled her brow, and asked, "What?"

"Forget it." Evan sighed. "Let's try to turn the evidence we do have into something a bit easier to follow."

"Okay, well. I think we should try to duplicate what the missing data could be and try to determine how this kid figured it all out," Julie suggested.

"I don't know when his data starts or when it ends. All I do know is when ours ends," Evan stated.

The two of them sat in Julie's kitchen into late afternoon, both caressing the keyboards of their laptops, trying to recreate what may have happened in Pennsylvania. Eventually, Evan looked up and announced, "I think I found it."

Julie stood, clasped her hands, and raised them over her head in a long, satisfying stretch. Evan watched, too tired to appreciate the view. Lowering her hands, she slid her chair around the table and sat next to him. "Show me."

Evan pressed F6 on his laptop, executing a similar comparison and contrast program to the one Julie wrote, and sat back. The program retrieved data from a dBase file that contained the make-believe information that he thought might be similar to the Ludyte files. It ran for several seconds, chewing on the numbers. Eventually, a crude bar graph appeared on the screen.

The two scientists sat and stared at the graph, each remembering that the graph reflected a best guess of what Ludyte had. Unfortunately, the graph showed an increase in the power levels. However, if that was all the information showed, then how did Tim jump to the conclusion that some alien intelligence was involved? He had to be getting help from someone. Someone had to be filling in the gaps for him. The information about the composition of the core was not secret and could easily be found on the Internet; however, the conclusion that an alien agency was effecting a change in the core was not an easy reach.

"How did that high school sophomore make the leap to alien involvement?" Julie asked again.

"From what I remember from my high school classes, we never even got close to discussing how you might reenergize plutonium-238," Evan told Julie without taking his eyes off the screen.

Bang. Bang. Bang.

A loud pounding on Julie's front door broke their concentration. Visibly startled, Julie silently got to her feet to answer the interruption.

Bang. Bang. Bang.

Whoever was at the front door sure was being impatient. Evan rose to his feet as well and slowly followed Julie into the hallway leading to the front entryway. Just as she reached for the handle to open the door, the handle began to rattle. Someone was trying to get in. The cold sweat that started to form on Evan's brow was now matched by the chill running down his spine.

Julie apparently moved too slowly for the force behind the banging, for as her hand made contact with the doorknob, the door, the doorframe, the door's side window, and the entire entryway splintered into a shower of hard oak, plaster, and glass. Julie was thrown to the floor by surprise, but mostly by the incredibly explosive used to gain forcible entry into her home. Evan stood in stunned horror, frozen out of fear and concern for both their lives.

Out of the cloud of settling dust debris, a hand extended down to where Julie was lying on the floor in front of what used to be her door. A kind hand extending to a terrified young woman, offering to help her to her feet. Julie reflexively grabbed the hand and, leaning on its owner's strength, pulled herself back to her feet.

"Dr. Julie Wagner?" the hand's owner asked. There was kindness and strength to the voice that commanded a truthful answer.

In an angry, shaky voice, Julie responded, "Yes, I am. Who are you?"

"Agent Schaffer. Germany Schaffer… Federal Department of Internal Security."

Evan moved up behind his still-shaky friend, providing a backstop for her to lean upon. "Federal Department of what?" was all Evan could get out.

Agent Schaffer finished it for him. "Internal Security."

"You don't say." The venom in Julie's tone started to surface as she looked at the huge gaping hole that used to be a nice entryway to her modern-styled Victorian house.

Evan offered his hand to the impressively large agent, who shook it with the tenderness and care of a person handling a kitten. "What do you want?"

"Dr. Wills?" Agent Schaffer asked. "You are Dr. Wills?"

"Uh-huh, what do you want?" Evan could feel Julie quaking next to him.

"I have been directed to escort you and Dr. Wagner to a conference," Agent Schaffer declared.

"You could have just called," Evan said plainly.

"Or at least knocked. I do have a knocker," Julie said as she looked around at the wreckage. "Or I did." Julie had no idea what she was going to tell her husband… or the insurance company.

"I did knock," Agent Schaffer stated plainly. "I was instructed to personally collect the two of you."

"But did you have to destroy my house?" Julie was near tears.

"I was told that the use of extreme prejudice was authorized." As Agent Schaffer finished that sentence, as if on cue, a shattering noise could be heard from the kitchen.

"What the fu—" Julie tried to turn and run back to her kitchen but was held in place by a black-clothed, body-armored, helmeted storm trooper who had quietly moved in next to her.

Agent Schaffer just rolled his eyes and looked down the hallway, past the stairs to the second floor, to where the noise had come from. A few brief moments later, another storm trooper emerged from the kitchen, this one carrying two laptops and a box of printouts and papers.

"What was that?" Julie was now seeping tears.

Storm Trooper Kitchen responded, "The sliding back door."

"It was unlocked. Did you try to simply slide the door open?" Julie's tears were evaporating quickly under the heat of her building fury.

"Sorry," Storm Trooper Kitchen said quietly.

"Hey, wait a minute... those are ours," Evan objected, pointing to the armload of computers and such. He had his entire life on that computer. "We own them, and the printouts. The lab we work at allows us—encourages us to take work home."

"Don't worry about it. He's just carrying them for you." Agent Schaffer stiffened his back, stepped to one side, and held out an arm in the direction of a waiting minivan that was burgundy in color and beat up with age.

"I thought you guys always drove black Suburbans?" Evan muttered as he gingerly stepped over and around the rubble.

"So does everyone else. That's why we don't anymore," Agent Schaffer responded.

From across the street Julie could see the neighbors peering through their various windows. *Curious snots*, she thought. All of a sudden, as if to complicate the situation further, a siren could be heard coming down the street. Apparently, someone had called the police.

As the police cruiser pulled up, blocking the burgundy minivan in the driveway, Agent Schaffer purposefully strode toward the police officer, making sure that his hands were in clear view. The two law enforcement officers spoke for a moment, exchanged vital identifying information, made notes in each other's little black notebooks, and then shook hands. Agent Schaffer then turned to rejoin his team and their two guests. The police officer backed the cruiser up and turned to circle the block.

One of the storm troopers slid open the side door to the minivan and offered Dr. Wagner his hand as she stepped in. Dr. Wills was left to his own manly ability to crawl into the van. Once the two scientists were buckled in and their gathered belongings from the kitchen were secured, Agent Schaffer slid his large frame into the front passenger seat. The windows were not unusually tinted, and the driver was even wearing what appeared to be a Dodgers T-shirt.

Evan thought that this Federal Department of… whatever was truly trying to appear unnoticed; and with the exception of their door-knocking etiquette, they were succeeding.

"What about my house?" Julie asked as Agent Schaffer simply turned around to face her and motioned for her to look out the side window.

There, at the front of her house, was a five-man crew, cleaning and starting the rebuild of the entryway, sidewalk, and hedges… as well as replacing the shattered back kitchen door.

"It should be reconstructed within a few hours. We're quite good at this."

As Julie and Evan gazed out the window, they could see a member of the construction crew planting a "Work done by…" sign in her front yard. They thought of everything. They even had what appeared to be permits pasted to a front window.

"Oh… okay. Well, they better do a good job, or I'm going to call… whom do I call?" Julie's half-chuckle lightened the situation a bit.

"Here's my card. You call me." Agent Schaffer handed her a business card with his name and a number on it and nothing else.

"Okay then," she said. She looked out the window and whispered, "They better do a *really* good job."

"Um, where are you taking us?" Evan half demanded and half pleaded.

"To school," Agent Schaffer stated.

Twenty minutes later, the burgundy minivan pulled up to a gated playground located next to a public elementary school. Waiting for them was a person who must have been a custodian because he was fumbling around with a very large key ring. A moment later, the gate swung open, and the van advanced onto the playground.

Agent Schaffer motioned the driver to pull up next to the backstop and shut the engine off.

He wasn't kidding. We really are at a school, Evan thought.

Getting out of the van, Agent Schaffer made a brief call on his cell and then opened the sliding door for the two scientists. "End of the line, for us," he said.

"What now?" Julie wasn't sure if she really wanted to know the answer but asked anyway.

"Now, you take… that." Agent Schaffer raised his arm and pointed at an approaching helicopter.

CHAPTER 63

Ludyte Home, Springtown, Pennsylvania
Thursday, January 22, 2015
8:24 p.m., EST; 5:24 p.m., PST

DAVE CLOSED HIS cell phone and turned to Jim. "That was Gorski. Tim and Cate are on the train and safely moving toward the residence."

"Thank God," Carol breathed.

"What about Randy?" Jim asked.

"No word yet, but I wouldn't worry. Sister Marsha will take care of him." Father Dave was starting to feel better about this plan. "We're going to linger around here until Father Rich returns, and then we're going to hit the road."

Just then, the front door burst open, barely holding on to its hinges, and in rushed a fully armed contingent of what appeared to be federal agents. At least, that's what the alphabet soup on the backs of their windbreakers implied.

Jim grabbed Carol by the arm and ran for the garage, grabbing his keys as they rushed through the kitchen. Father Dave attempted a delaying action in the family room, allowing Jim time to get out.

Carol hit the automatic garage-door button as they bolted into the man cave and toward the Shelby. Jim needed speed and maneuverability, and the Shelby had both. Earlier, when Jim and Father Dave had disappeared into the garage, this is what they were talking about—an escape plan.

Jim slid over the Shelby's hood, landing squarely on both feet, and jumped into the driver's seat; Carol vaulted over the closed passenger-side door and slid down into the seat. Thankfully, Jim had put the ragtop down, just in case. He cranked the engine to a roaring life, checking the rearview mirror to confirm no one was blocking his way. Jim slammed the transmission into reverse and screamed the Mustang out of the garage, just missing the still-opening garage door.

Amazingly, the entire driveway was clear as the invaders opted for street parking, and he was able to spin the car around and burn down the road. He had to put distance between themselves and their unwelcomed houseguests as quickly as possible. And he needed to get the Shelby on open highway in order to fully exploit her abilities.

Swerving around corners and twisting around turns, Jim handled the classic Ford like he was born with it, downshifting for power and upshifting for speed. He knew exactly what he was doing, and unless those pursuing them knew the back roads of Bucks County better than him, he and Carol should get clear. The problem was that no car could outrun a telephone call or a radio transmission for help. All he and Carol could do was pray that the route he was taking was obscure enough to permit their escape.

Back at the Ludyte home, Father Rich had just arrived to find himself being forced to take a seat on the floor next to Father Dave. The zip ties being used to restrain the two priests were starting to cut flesh, and Father Rich winced with the discomfort.

"Okay, who are the two of you, and where are those other two going?" asked a not-so-large man in a dark-blue windbreaker with the letters ICPS on the back.

"Who are you?" Father Dave echoed the question in his mind. He was not accustomed to being pushed around. Sadly, his reactionary defense to being bullied was rudeness. Rudeness and its close relative, sarcasm, might not work in this particular situation though. However, the zip ties cutting into his wrists pissed him off. Therefore, rude sarcasm was where he was at the moment. Additionally, the longer he could occupy these invaders, the greater the head start Jim and Carol would have.

"Okay, I can play the game. I'm Special Agent McDeal—International Consortium for Planetary Security, ICPS."

"Oh," Father Rich said as he looked at Father Dave.

Then, as if on cue, the two priests said in unison, "Never heard of you."

"No. I wouldn't think you have. We are—"

Right then, Father Dave decided to clear his throat in rude protest, clearly agitating the special agent.

"I'm Father Davidson, and this is Father Goosick—International Department of G-O-D." Father Dave thought Father Rich was going to pee his pants with that one the way he choked down his laughter.

"Funny, really. I'll let you get away with that one." McDeal chuckled then asked again, "Seriously, who are you?"

"We really are priests. I'm Father Goosick, and he's Father Davidson," Father Rich replied. "Would you like to make a confession?"

"We're very good at keeping secrets," Father Dave added.

With that, another agent handed McDeal the priests' IDs, along with a forty-caliber Springfield handgun.

Turning the pistol over in his hands, McDeal turned to Father Rich and said, "This is a lot of stopping power for a priest to be carrying."

"Rats. Big rats," Father Rich stated with exaggeration in his voice. "Rats in the rectory. Big mothers."

"Get a cat," McDeal stated flatly.

"We had a cat. It disappeared one night." Father Rich kept the tale going while Father Dave was having a difficult time stifling his own laughter. "Some say it was eaten."

"You don't say," McDeal commented.

"Oh my god! Let me tell you. One afternoon, during confessions, I was sitting in the box waiting for a customer when I looked down, and you know what I saw?" Father Rich was now having fun.

"Rats?" McDeal asked in reply.

"No. Rat crap!" Father Rich held on to the story as if it were true. "Big turds too. I mean, those things were like grapes. And they were fresh."

"How could you tell?" McDeal asked.

"They squished under my foot," Father Rich replied innocently.

That was it. Father Dave could no longer hold his composure and let go a big spray of laughter.

McDeal didn't seem too amused, however. Turning his questions toward the elder priest, he continued, "Says here that you're attached to the Vatican? In what capacity?"

"As a priest." Father Dave gave the slightest of head nods to Father Rich, wanting him to keep an eye on the active search being done of the house.

"To be sure." McDeal chuckled. "You seem to have a singular wit. And what of this?" McDeal held up the pistol, purposely ignoring the "rats" comment coming from the younger priest.

"We're Jesuits," Father Dave stated matter-of-factly.

Nodding as if he understood, McDeal took a deep breath. Exhaling slowly, he instructed his men to help the two priests to their feet. He then extracted a rather imposing switchblade from his pocket, snapped it open, and cut their zip-tied hands free. "I'm sorry. My men can get a bit overzealous at times. The zip ties may not have been necessary."

Rubbing his wrists, Father Dave asked the obvious, "What's going on here?"

"Father Davidson, where are they going?" McDeal asked sternly as he head-motioned toward the kitchen escape route. Apparently, cutting the zips and freeing their hands was just a gesture.

"I have no idea," Father Dave stated honestly.

"You, Father Goosick?" McDeal turned back to Father Rich. "Why are you here?"

"I came here at the request of my rector," Father Rich answered.

"And is it normal for a priest to carry a handgun?" McDeal asked.

"As I told you, we seem to have a problem with intruders," Father Rich stated flatly, all joking aside. Father Dave was impressed with the size of the pair Father Rich was sporting at that moment.

McDeal countered with another question. "Why would the rector tell you to come to this particular home?"

"I'm sure I don't even want to presume to know what's on the mind of the rector," Father Rich stated.

"What am I going to do with the two of you? I come here trying to apprehend suspected enemies of security and find two priests instead," McDeal stated. "Two Jesuits yet."

"What is that supposed to mean?" Father Dave didn't like this man, and that last comment secured his opinion.

"Come now, it is well known that the Jesuits are not your average, everyday priests," McDeal clarified.

Just then, a man approached McDeal and motioned him to one side. The two briefly exchanged words, after which McDeal returned to his detainees. "I have been reminded that I am to ask you for your courtesy and cooperation."

"Oh, I'm sure," Father Dave stated. "After all, we're not your average, everyday priests." He knew what was going on. Grief was being applied to the right pressure points. What he didn't know was who was applying what, and onto whom.

Having gone fishing with his own dad enough times as a kid, Father Dave knew that sometimes you have to bait the hook to catch what you wanted. "Look, I'm a personal friend of the family that lives here. I served in the marines with the father," Father Dave explained.

"And now you're a priest?" The question was genuine.

"A Jesuit, yes," Father Dave replied. "It's long story."

"Well, obviously, the Ludyte family is not here. They were our primaries. While I suspect many things, I must adhere to my rules of engagement." McDeal turned his back and whistled for the rest of his entrance force to retreat. "Good evening, fathers."

Just as McDeal was about to leave the house, he gently placed the handgun on a side table—not before removing the clip and placing it on a different table, however.

As a black Suburban and a black Corvette moved down Drifting Drive, away from the Ludyte home, Father Rich retrieved his sidearm and inserted the spare clip he carried in a concealed location.

"ICPS?" Father Dave asked Father Rich. "Ever hear of them?"

"Hold on." With that, Father Rich pulled out his cell phone and quickly dialed. "Hi, Aunt Sandy? Richard… I'm fine, thanks. Hey, I have a question for you. What can you tell me about the ICPS?"

Father Rich listened for a moment then elaborated. "International Consortium for Planetary Security. Uh-huh. You sure?" Father Rich asked. "Yep, got it. Thanks. I'll explain later."

Ending his call, Father Rich turned to Father Dave, informing him that according to his aunt, an attorney with the US Department of Justice, there was no federal organization known as ICPS. "She said she would check it out for me but was nearly positive that the International Consortium for Planetary Security is not a US-sanctioned organization."

Father Dave considered the news then, shaking his head, said "Rats."

***

Backtracking several times, Jim knew the back roads well. Eventually, he throttled back the horses under the hood of his baby and brought the Mustang to a more sensible speed. They were heading toward Quakertown by way of some back roads. Quakertown was not much closer to Philadelphia, but he didn't want to tip off any would-be pursuers by heading straight to the Colmar SEPTA station and the kids. He needed to put some distance between them and whoever just broke into their house and fractured their lives.

Crossing over Route 309 and heading west on Route 663 toward the town of Red Hill, Jim turned to Carol and said, "I think we're clear. Time to head to Colmar."

"Thank God." Carol was feeling sick, and she wasn't convinced that it was because of the pregnancy either.

CHAPTER 64

Valley Vista Elementary School, San Fernando, California
Thursday, January 22, 2015
8:55 p.m., EST; 5:55 p.m., PST

THE SIDE DOOR of a bulbous silver Alouette III helicopter swept open, even before the powerful craft had completely touched down. Out stepped a helmeted crewman carrying a stool, which he carefully placed at the door as he waved for the scientists to enter.

Locking arms, Evan and Julie ducked—out of reflex, since the spinning blades were obviously several feet above their heads—and carefully walked across the infield of the playground's baseball diamond to the waiting helicopter. Once inside, they were helped into their seat belts, and each was offered a headset to wear. Their laptops and other belongings found their way onto the seat opposite them, right next to a helmeted crewman, who placed a steadying arm on the pile. The storm trooper who was carrying the computers from the house deposited the stool in the cabin and slid the side door shut, banging on it twice after latching the handle.

Julie couldn't help but wave farewell to Agent Schaffer as the helicopter's rpm's revved up in anticipation of lifting its load of people and cargo. The funny thing was, Agent Germany Schaffer actually smiled and waved back. At that moment, Julie had the overpowering feeling that this would not be the last time either she, or Evan, would see Agent Schaffer of the Federal Department of Internal Security.

"Good afternoon," a recognizable voice called over their headsets.

Looking around the cabin, Evan spotted a very familiar person sitting in an opposite corner to where they were seated.

"Dr. Katz! What are you doing here?" Evan asked loudly over the engine noise.

Dr. Katz simply smiled, followed by a meager shrug of her shoulders, and returned to her contemplative look out the window.

The helicopter pilot, not waiting for altitude to be gained, spun the craft around as soon as the skids were off the ground and headed for the far-off mountains, climbing steeply as he did so.

So we're heading east, Evan thought. Trying to remember a map of this region of the basin, Evan couldn't recall anything up there that could even remotely serve as a secure conference site, except maybe—however, that site certainly wasn't secure. Sure it was remote, but remoteness does not imply security—at least not the type of security these guys seemed concerned about. He thought he'd test his speculation.

Motioning to the crewman sitting across from him, Evan made motions that he wanted to ask a question. The crewman held up the cord that connected his helmet to the onboard intercom system, pressed a little switch on the cord, and then spoke. "Yes, sir?"

Copying the crewman's actions, Evan found and toggled his switch. "Can this helicopter handle the altitude at Mount Wilson?"

"Sir, this helicopter is capable of functioning at much greater altitudes than any that would pose a challenge in this part of the country," replied the crewman.

"Oh, okay, just worrying—I mean, wondering," Evan corrected himself. "Did I mention I have a slight fear of—"

"Flying," the crewman completed Evan's statement. "No, sir."

Julie interrupted. "You're afraid of flying?"

"No, not at all. I love flying. You know, have a drink watch a movie, real flying," Evan said as he swallowed a bit of encroaching bile. "What I'm afraid of is crashing, without a drink."

At that, the pilot switched on and added, "We're headed to the Mount Wilson Observatory complex, and the crewman is very correct in that this aircraft, an Alouette III-SA316B, is capable of functioning at altitudes much higher than the fifty-seven-hundred feet of Mount Wilson. I wouldn't worry."

I wouldn't worry. Easy for him to say, Evan thought. Evan knew that a large machine beating the air with a fan should not be able to fly, regardless of what da Vinci says, yet here they were. With no drink service.

Eventually, after what seemed to be an eternity, Evan could look out the window and see the domes and support outbuildings that dotted the Mount Wilson Observatory complex. The helicopter circled the facility twice before noticeably losing altitude in preparation for a landing. Surprisingly, the Alouette landed right in a parking lot. And why not? There was no place else for it to land, and Evan was sure Julie would not agree to being lowered by a rope.

The crewman stood and helped unbuckle Dr. Wagner and then offered to help Dr. Wills, who was already unbuckled and clutching his laptop. The door, unlatched from outside, was thrown open. Standing there, awash in the rotor downflow, was a person who appeared to be a graduate student. With obvious disdain for being asked to help the scientists, the grad student merely pointed in the direction of one of the larger buildings. Content to let the new arrivals fend for themselves, he quickly excused himself and disappeared in the opposite direction.

Tilting his head in the direction of Dr. Wagner, Evan said, "Well, he was pleasant."

Julie's response was even more to the point. "Hopefully, he went to take a bath. Boy was he ripe. I could almost taste his stench, even in the rotor wash."

After entering what from the outside appeared to be a simple shed-type building, Evan and Julie, having lost track of Dr. Katz, were ushered by yet another grad student. To Julie's amusement, this one smelled less pungent than the first.

They were led down a long hallway to a reasonably large meeting room. Assembled at tables and desks of varying sizes were fifteen to twenty notable scientists, administrators, and two military officers, all waiting for them to arrive—or so it would seem.

Whispering to Evan, Julie confided, "I didn't know we would be making a presentation… I'm so not dressed for it."

Evan just shrugged, still unconvinced that he was not in some kind of trouble. As the room's attention settled on them, they found their way to the only unoccupied table—at the front of the assembly. Emptying their armloads onto the table, both Evan and Julie walked around to the side facing the would-be audience and sat in the only two chairs still available. They sat for several moments and just looked around the room, dumbfounded. Finally, one of the military types stood, an air force lieutenant general, and cleared his throat.

"First, I would like to thank everyone for coming to this rather impromptu conference. I am Lieutenant General Bill Waters, currently assigned to NORAD. I am the reason everyone is here today. We—that is the US and Canadian military—have been quietly placed on alert as a result of some rather remarkable happenings. I called you all here today because Administrator Culver named each of you personally as being important to the issue."

"Wow, this guy can sure speak a lot and yet say nothing," Julie whispered to Evan.

"The reason we're meeting here at the Mount Wilson facility is that I've been led to believe, among other things, that we'll have an unimpeded link to the VLA in New Mexico from this location."

The general looked at the weary faces of those around him and realized that he had better get to the point.

"At roughly seven a.m. eastern standard time this morning, a letter was hand-delivered to the State Department. The exact contents of that letter are classified. However, it bore the crossed keys and triregnum seal of the Vatican."

Everyone in the room immediately sat up, clearing their focus or shuffling pages upon which to take notes.

"According to the briefing I received directly from the SecDef, the contents made reference to… um… I don't know how to say this in any credible fashion, so… the contents of the letter made reference to evidence having been discovered that confirms the existence of extraterrestrial life," General Waters stated plainly.

Amid the stunned silence, there were the expected catcalls and condemnations for being roused and flown to such a boondoggle. The general merely stood silently, patient, waiting for the room to refocus. Eventually, those who were incredulous at what he said saw that he was not smiling and settled down as well. The general seized the moment to continue.

"While the letter did not identify any individuals responsible for this discovery, it did state that the data upon which the discovery is based is irrefutable, having been examined by their experts," the general revealed.

Julie and Evan exchanged glances, obviously both thinking the same thing: *What the hell?*

"General, can you tell us the nature of this evidence?" the representative from SETI, the Search for Extraterrestrial Intelligence, asked.

"And please don't say a 'burning bush'," an unidentified voice added.

"Or a message from Vega," added another.

"What I can tell you is that the evidence is in the form of downlink telemetry data from one of our deep-space probes," General Waters answered.

"Downlink telemetry? General, how did the Vatican get the downlink telemetry from one of our deep space probes?" another unidentified voice asked.

"I have people looking into that as we speak. We're still not sure how the information got away from us," said the general.

"Which space probe?" Dr. Katz, enthroned in the back, asked.

The room took a collective breath and held it, waiting for the general to respond.

"The letter does not specifically identify the craft. However, through a process of elimination—and with the help of NASA, JPL, and other organizations—we have narrowed our field of interest to one of five spacecraft."

"And those five would be?" Dr. Katz was starting to become annoyed with the way the military was able to speak a tremendous amount of words and not say anything at all.

"At the moment we are consi—" General Waters attempted to use the force of his rank to silence the question.

"The names, if you please," Dr. Katz said, interrupting.

Matching her gaze, the general flatly replied, "*Pioneer 6*, *Venture 1*, *Voyager 2*, *New Horizons*, or possibly *DAWN*."

"Thank you, General." Dr. Katz, the old warhorse, knew when to push and when to back off. She had gotten what she wanted, and so she knew enough to back off. It was the general's show after all.

Evan felt Julie's hand squeeze his left leg when she heard the second name: *Venture 1*. Coincidence? Couldn't be.

"Well, I believe we can discount *New Horizons* right off. She is being closely monitored as she approaches the Pluto-Charon system. The probability that contact has been made with her, without us knowing directly, is very remote," Dr. Benewah of the Institute for Deep Space Exploration offered.

"Thank you, Doctor. This is one of the reasons I summoned you here today—to help us get a handle not only on which probe it most likely is, but to help us understand the capabilities of that probe and the likely threat to Earth such contact could pose," said General Waters.

Julie could feel Evan want to rise out of his chair and clamped her hand harder on his leg. She leaned over and whispered, "Not yet. We're juniors here, remember? Wait and see if we get call—"

"Dr. Wills, Dr. Wagner…" It was Dr. Katz.

"Damn," Julie whispered.

"Perhaps you have some insight into this situation?" Dr. Katz asked knowingly.

Rising to his feet, Evan offered the following. "Dr. Evan Wills, telemetry monitor for the *Venture 1* interstellar space probe. I'm not exactly sure what new information I can offer."

Dr. Katz, either throwing her junior colleague a bone or a noose, pressed him. "Why don't you recap the briefing you gave early this morning?"

"What briefing?" General Waters asked.

"Very well." Evan took a deep breath and continued. "Earlier today, at 1:27 a.m., our seventy-meter receiving station obtained an unscheduled, completely unexpected downlink from *Venture 1*. The automated systems immediately filtered the data burst and discovered an anomaly. In an effort to determine the nature of the anomaly, Dr. Wagner—of the *Sirocco* Mars project—and I examined the data from an earlier MAGROL maneuver."

What? Dr. Katz was not pleased. That not-so-little piece of very important information was not included in Evan's earlier briefing.

"Why is Dr. Wagner involved? What is her contribution?" Dr. Katz, having wanted to ask that question earlier but letting it slide, now applied a little pressure.

At that, Julie stood and tried to rescue her colleague. "Dr. Julie Wagner, *Sirocco* Mars Lander team monitor. Our relay orbiter in synchronous station above *Sirocco* detected a faint magnetic field flux originating from…" She paused while she paged through the pile of notes sitting in front of her. "The magnetic signal was emanating from coordinates, adjusting for Earth, of RA 01:44:04, Dec -15° 56" 15"."

"What is the current position of the *Venture 1* spacecraft?" General Waters asked.

"RA 01:44:04, Dec -15° 56' 15" … give or take," Dr. Wills answered immediately, albeit softly.

"Okay… please continue. And this time, do not leave anything out, no matter how insignificant you may think it is." Dr. Katz was doing her best to coach these two kids along.

"Yes, ma'am," Evan replied. "It was at that time that I instituted an additional MAGROL, to determine the characteristics of the magnetic flux. The MAGROL determined—"

General Waters interrupted, "I'm sorry, but you've mentioned MAGROL several times. What exactly is a MAGROL?"

One of the *Pioneer* team members—and quite possibly the most senior scientist in the room—spoke up. "A MAGROL, General, is a maneuver that essentially rotates the spacecraft about its primary axis, recalibrating the magnetometers in the process. Dr. Wills more than likely was attempting to determine the origin of this magnetic flux. If I were at the station at that time, I would've done the same thing."

"Thank you, Dr. Griffith." General Waters was satisfied and turned back to Evan and Julie.

"Yes, thank you, Dr. Griffith." Evan was grateful for the life preserver just tossed to him, and he continued, "The suspect that the maneuver will provide enough information for us to conclude that the *Venture 1* spacecraft is caught in a…" Evan knew that what he was going to say next—what he had to say next—would not bolster his credibility.

"Dr. Wills?" Dr. Katz urged.

Clearing his quickly closing throat, Evan tried his best to stand as erect as he could and then continued full steam ahead (or something like that). "We believe the spacecraft is caught in a focused magnetic beam of indeterminate origin." There, he said it, out loud and in public.

To Evan's surprise, the room became stone silent.

Then after what seemed like forever, a voice from the back, a graduate student most likely, called out, "Bullshit!"

The room erupted into chaotic conversations. Evan had no idea what to think.

General Waters stood and raised his hand, demanding order. "I think, given this new piece of information, that a thirty-minute recess is in order. For the sake of everyone in this room—and you may consider this a personal request as well—I would appreciate it if private, topical conversations during your break be kept at a minimum. Additionally, I would like to remind you that cell phone or landline communication off the mountain has been temporarily terminated. Thirty minutes, people. Be prompt."

CHAPTER 65

SEPTA Station, Colmar, Pennsylvania
Thursday, January 22, 2015
9:32 p.m., EST; 6:32 p.m., PST

WHILE THE MOUNT Wilson conference labored on, on the other end of the continent, "team 2" was arriving at the Colmar Station of the Septa rail line. The station was crowded with sports fans. Randy and Sister Marsha arrived as the trains were loading to speed fanatical Sixers fans to what most likely would be another heart-wrenching loss. Sister Marsha held on to Randy's hand for dear life. She was not accustomed to large crowds, and her sweating palm told Randy not to let go. The two kids walked back and forth at the station, trying to mingle with the crowd while not getting swept away with it.

Eventually, a white-capped transit officer tapped Randy on the shoulder from behind. "Randy Ludyte?"

Spinning quickly around, Randy asked, "Who are you?"

"John Gorski. Here's my ID."

Randy took the ID and read it carefully, as he was told to do.

Sister Marsha breathed a huge sigh of relief, thanking God in the process.

After thoroughly checking, Randy handed the identification back and said, "Yes, I'm Randy. And this is Marsha… my… my date." He looked at Sister Marsha and shrugged.

"Okay, we have to wait until the crowd thins out so that we can catch the train you'll need to link up with the Spur," Officer Gorski stated.

"Fine with me," Randy said.

Turning to Sister Marsha, he continued, "We'll walk you back to your car and make sure you get on your way without difficulty."

Sister Marsha, still firmly attached to Randy's hand, nodded and pulled him away from the source of her anxiety. The three of them casually walked toward the parking lot, Gorski scanning the area as they did so. He wasn't going to tell the kids, but he had been alerted to the possibility that a news crew may be on its way. Why? He didn't ask. Apparently, the media had some interest in the Ludytes.

Finally reaching the car parked on the edge of the lot, Randy turned and hugged Sister Marsha, who hugged him back; and tilting her head up, she gave him a tender, caring kiss. John politely turned his back and continued his scan of the area.

Finally pulling away from her, Randy quietly said, "You're a nun."

"Yes, I am. You may consider the kiss as coming from the Blessed Mother, the manner of the kiss was from me. She has your back, Randy. Don't worry."

Sister Marsha Treden of the convent of Our Blessed Lady opened the car door and slid in behind the steering wheel. Rolling down the window, she looked up at a stunned Randy Ludyte and smiled. Starting the car, she backed out of the parking space and drove away.

"Oh damn," Officer Gorski uttered.

"What?" Randy spun to face the direction the police officer was looking, catching sight of the Channel 10 News van entering the parking lot. "What do we do? The crowds are still loading."

"Feel like going to the Wells Fargo Center tonight?" John's tone told Randy more than what he actually said.

"No, not really," Randy replied.

"Too bad." The police officer thumbed through the contents of his wallet, pulling out a plastic card and handing it to Randy. "Here, take this."

"What's this?" Randy asked.

"That's my police pass for the arena. I'll get you on the right train, and then you find your way to the players' entrance. Show the card to the crewman on duty and tell him you're my nephew. You should have no problems. Then mingle in the crowd until the end of the first quarter. I'm sorry this doesn't get you an actual seat, but I have a feeling that shouldn't be too much of a problem," Officer Gorski explained. "Do you need any money?"

"No, I'm good. What should I do then?" Randy was starting to feel the panicked rush of adrenaline.

"At the end of the quarter, wander back to the train station that you arrived at and get on the Center City Line. Stay on that until you get to the station for the Art Museum. Then jump over to the North Philadelphia line. Ride that until you reach Roosevelt Boulevard… get off and wait. The Spur will come and pick you up. You won't be able to miss it," Gorski recited quickly.

"Damn, I should've written that down," Randy stated in frustration.

"Got it right here." Gorski handed him a map of the subway system with the route highlighted.

"Thanks," Randy replied.

"When you see Father Dave, give him that card. I want to see the Flyers when the Bruins come to town."

Gorski was a true Philadelphia "phan." The world was about to change in a big way, and all he was concerned about was getting to the Flyers-Bruins hockey game.

John Gorski led Randy to a train bound for the sports complex and got him on board, bypassing the usual queues. After making sure that he wasn't followed by news personnel, John turned around and marched out to the parking lot. It was time to confront the news crew with whatever citable violations he could come up with. And maybe a few he couldn't.

CHAPTER 66

Mount Wilson Observatory Complex, California
Thursday, January 22, 2015
9:52 p.m., EST; 6:52 p.m., PST

WITH THE GENERAL'S dismissal for thirty minutes, everyone rose and filed out into the waning daylight. Evan collapsed back into his chair, and Julie turned to sit on the table at his side, her back to the room. Dr. Katz simply remained in her seat, seeming to wait for the room to empty. General Waters, joined by an aide, headed for a side door.

"Well, it had to come out sometime," Julie told Evan.

"I know, but this has gotten way out of control. I mean, the Vatican knows… and you know if they know, so do others," Evan said.

"Not necessarily," Dr. Katz, now strolling to join them, said quietly.

"I'm sorry?" Julie stated.

"The Vatican outwardly projects an image of… how do they like to say it… 'extraterrestrial brotherhood' with the inevitable discovery of otherworldly life. However, behind closed doors, they are as terrified as many in this room," Dr. Katz said, clarifying the political air a bit.

"They didn't seem scared," Evan said, waving to the now empty conference room.

Again, Dr. Katz explained, "Don't confuse their pompous chest-puffing and attempts to embrace the data with confidence. They're scared shitless. They've known for a long time that this day was coming… and most of them secretly hoped they would be dead and gone when it did. Ever since we sent the first craft beyond our orbit, we've all been fearful of this day. Oh sure. People like Carl

Sagan—God rest his soul—characterized alien life as being benevolent and kind, but it was the vast majority of the scientific community who secretly made plans for their own survival."

"So their reactions don't shock you?" Julie asked.

"Not at all. What does bother me is that the two of you chose to sit on it like you did. Now what can you tell me about this kid in Pennsylvania?" Dr. Katz asked quietly.

For the next fifteen minutes or so, the three scientists discussed the involvement of Mr. Timothy Ludyte. Finally, they agreed that, for the time being, they would keep his identity concealed.

"Let the military and others feast on the alien-life idea for the time being," Dr. Katz stated. "Okay, now, the two of you, get some air. You have five minutes before the inquisition starts. I'll do what I can to shield you, but you better have the stomach for what's coming... and not just from the other eggheads in this room. Wait and see. I have the feeling it's going to get worse... much worse."

With that, Dr. Katz stepped out a side door, coffee cup in hand. "Where the hell is the coffee?" they both heard her shout as she disappeared.

Evan and Julie followed, stepping out into the deepening purple twilight. The air was clean and cool, and the sky was blossoming with stars. Evan thought about *Venture*, out there, and turned to face the general direction of the distant probe. Julie simply looked at the disappearing landscape. Neither spoke; they just allowed themselves the moment, no matter how brief that moment might be.

CHAPTER 67

The One
Obedience, Acceptance, and "Why?"
The Book of The One
Acts of Salvation, block 21, level 27

> *Act 27: The One shall conquer, overcome, or subdue all resistant civilizations by any means available, and install obedience to a world in need of communal awareness.*

OBEDIENCE AND ACCEPTANCE. Those two words were the very essence of the civilization of the Implanted. Histories of previously failed civilizations indicate that while other factors may have contributed greatly to their demise, it was ultimately a lack of obedience to and acceptance of a communal consciousness that was the undermining cause.

Obedience was not a difficult concept for the Implanted. They were the first civilization to develop a global web network based upon their own biological abilities to communicate. That technological advancement demanded obedience. If the Web was to function, it required individuals to tap into it. Once the population was ensnared, obedience to the Web was easily established. As more and more individuals connected to the Web, the Web developed into a physiological necessity—an addiction, if you will. Research revealed that various addictive chemicals were released in the brains of those connected to the Web, thereby making disconnecting virtually impossible. However, this made the need for greater connectivity a necessity. The implants were developed to satisfy that need.

The entire program of implantation required the population to obediently give themselves over to the technology. Unlike the early days of the Web, when one could simply walk away from the arduous requirement of logging into the Web at a terminal, now with the implant, there would be no need to physically address a terminal for connectivity. With the implants came an ever present consciousness in the minds of the population. Individuals began to lose their identities—and with that loss went their free will. And once their free will was gone, so too their encompassing freedom. Then came The One.

Obedience was a vital concept to The One's survival. However, in order for The One to truly thrive within the civilization, it needed acceptance as well. Fortunately, obedience and acceptance are similarly constructed concepts. To obediently recognize a concept bears little difference to blindly accepting the concept, especially in the absence of free will.

The One was not concerned with any aberrational variant challenging its influence upon the civilization. Even the efforts of the Rebellion to sow the seeds of disharmony were efficiently managed by a simple manipulation of the facts as they appeared on the Web. Alternate sources of information were viewed by the Implanted as being unsubstantiated and therefore untrustworthy. If something, anything, appeared on the Web, then whatever was reported must be true, regardless of individual experiences or observations. Now the Implanted were relinquishing their last freedom, the core of any intellectual process. The Implanted gave up their ability to inquire. They gave up the word "why."

In an effort to control inquiry, The One inspired the creation of *The Book of The One*. Within its implied wisdom would be the answers to any questions the Implanted might ask. Questions of morality, faith, civilizational conduct—all were answered within the book. Even questions of historical significance were managed within the book.

"Where did we come from?"— (Axiom 1:1)

The One is the beginning of all.

"Why do we exist?" — (Axiom 2:17)

All of creation exists to empower The One.

"What of death?" — (Axiom 1:6)

There is no end. The One is all.

— (Axiom 4:9)

In The One there can be no death. The thoughts of creation belong solely to The One.

"Why accept The One?" — (Axiom 1:2)

The One is unduplicated, undeniable, and pure.

In order for the Implanted to enjoy the complete communal harmony The One provided through acceptance and obedience, they had to abandon their individuality. The One would serve as their value interpreter, placing priority upon that which it deemed worthy. However, what no one could foresee—save for those within the Rebellion—was that by accepting The One, the Implanted were accepting the end of their unique civilization. They would no longer be a civilization driven by intellectual evolution. They were now a civilization solely in the service of The One, something *The Book of The One* called "*acts of salvation.*" Something the Rebellion called *slavery*.

Now had come the time to reach out into the space, over the great distances of time, and instruct yet another civilization in the ways of acceptance and obedience.

CHAPTER 68

Let the acts of salvation begin.

+VENTURE
~BOOK 2~

"It's out. It's all over the news. Dear god, Evan! It's out!" Julie exclaimed.

The One

Creation of a God

The purpose of those who accept the guidance of The One can be summed up in one word: *worship*.

The One, an independent consciousness, existing as pure thought and energy. It gains power through worship, and in return, it cares for and protects the civilization that feeds it. The purpose of The One is to exist, to inspire those who give it worship, and to propagate. To that end, The One is ever searching for those who will worship it. After all, a god is nothing without obedient subjects.

***

What The One found floating in deep space wasn't much, and it might have been overlooked, or detected, and casually discarded as being unimportant. What The One found in the dark depths was something never before encountered—a signature of unexplained coherent energy.

No, more than that. The One found a possible connection to what it needed most of all.

Mount Wilson Observatory Complex, California
Thursday, January 22, 2015
10:52 p.m., EST; 7:22 p.m., PST

"With the help of Dr. Wagner, I will attempt to place these incredible events into some kind of chronological order for everyone to follow." Evan nodded at Julie then continued.

"On Thursday, September 3, our receivers registered the first of several DLAs, or downlink alarms, from the *Venture 1* space probe. Early indications pointed at some form of transmission power anomaly.

"On Tuesday, September 9, the shift itinerary instructed me to begin recording *Venture 1*'s power levels, as well as the mag field strength.

"On Wednesday, November 18, while performing an analysis of the latest data from *Venture 1*, it was observed that the spacecraft was generating power without consuming its fuel—or at least that's what the readings implied.

"Later that same evening, again while performing the aforementioned analysis, an anomaly was noted in the magnetic field surrounding *Venture 1*. Back-checking of the data indicated that the field had been steadily increasing since October 15.

"Then this past Monday, January 18, Dr. Wagner informed me that the synchronously stationed orbiter above *Sirocco* had detected a faint magnetic fluctuation apparently emanating from the region of space corresponding to *Venture 1*'s current location.

"Then, earlier today, we received yet another DLA from *Venture*. That brings us to today and the news from the Vatican."

"Why so little information?" asked General Waters.

"How so?" replied Evan.

"Well, this has obviously been an item of concern for months, and yet there is very little information. Why?" pressed the general.

"Unfortunately, when one considers the time lag between *Venture* and Earth, a day to *Venture* is nearly two days here on Earth." Evan employed his best double speak to steer his answer away from admitting to the lost data.

"I see." General Waters was not happy with that answer, but for the moment, he chose not to press too hard. "Please continue, Dr. Wills."

Wells-Fargo Center, Philadelphia, Pennsylvania
Thursday, January 22, 2015
11:18 p.m., EST; 8:18 p.m., PST

Displayed on the screen of the wall-mounted television was a photo of his family. He recognized it as one that was neatly displayed on the shelves in the family room. His face, and the faces of both of his parents, were clear, but the faces of Caitlin and Tim were pixelated. The caption at the bottom of the screen read, "PA family missing—children feared slaughtered by mentally unstable parents."

The Terraces, Philadelphia, Pennsylvania
Tuesday, February 3, 2015
8:34 a.m., EST; 5:34 a.m., PST

"What?" Father Dave implored. "What's happened?"

"There's been a missile attack on the papal apartment," Detective Bartuchi stated clearly.

***

For the next twenty minutes, Father Dave laid the groundwork that was the focal point of his growing anxieties. "After some number crunching, they uncovered more than just the contact signal. They uncovered an actual message."

"A message?" Detective Bartuchi sounded tired. "Just what we need."

Cardinal Ziest, giving the detective a sideways glance, asked, "What does it say?"

"That's the truly amazing part—the message is in English," Father Dave revealed. "It decodes as *The Book of The One*."

The detective raised his head and, with a look of absolute disbelief, said, "No shit?"

"Yes, there can be no mistake: *The Book of The One*." Father Dave exhaled.

"The One who?" Cardinal Ziest asked.

"Surely not God?" Again, the detective was straining to maintain his hold on the moment while clearly considering the impact of this new information.

Father Dave tried his best to interject into his voice a tone of confidence. "Well, obviously no, not God."

"Does it matter?" Cardinal Ziest asked quietly. "Once this gets out—and it will get out—we're going to have global chaos of biblical proportions."

ACKNOWLEDGMENTS

I WOULD LIKE TO deeply thank the following individuals: Michael A. Lamana, Antoinette M. Olivarez, and Theodore C. Haven. If it were not for your support, expertise, and careful consideration, this project would never have been fulfilled. I was truly fortunate to be able to enlist three highly accomplished people to help me iron out the many rough spots. Thank you.

Additionally, I would like to thank my youngest daughter, Emily. Her unwavering love, dedication, and interest continue to be a source of great inspiration.

Lastly, I would like to appreciate my oldest daughter, Sara. Her humor and enjoyment of life have provided me with tremendous inspiration.

ABOUT THE AUTHOR

MICHAEL RUSSO is a stargazer. He has a never-ending curiosity for the unknown. From the time he was young and lived with his family in a small town to complete his education with a master's degree in teaching, he never stopped looking up and wondering. So when the idea for Venture was formed, his fascination for the unknown became the drive to tell a compelling tale of drama, mystery, and imagination. Venture takes the reader out of their comfort zone and brings them into an exciting journey of intrigue. M. Russo hopes that Venture is as exciting for the reader as it was for him to imagine the possibilities of "what if?"

www.ingramcontent.com/pod-product-compliance
Lightning Source LLC
LaVergne TN
LVHW041657060526
838201LV00043B/463